DETROIT PUBLIC LIBRARY

3 5674 04597034 1

Take It There

KNAPP BRANCH LIBRARY
13330 CONANT
DETROIT, MI 48212
852-4283

D1070106

AUG 0 7

KNAPP BRANCH LIBRARY
13330 CONANT
DETROIT, MI 48212
852-4283

Take It There

Kaira Denee

URBAN BOOKS
http://www.urbanbooks.net

This book is a work of fiction. Any references or similarities to actual events, real people, living or dead, or to real locales are intended to give the novel a sense of reality. Any similarity in other names, characters, places, and incidents is entirely coincidental.

URBAN SOUL is published by

Urban Books
10 Brennan Place
Deer Park, NY 11729

Copyright © 2007 by Kaira Denee

All rights reserved. No part of this book may be reproduced in any form or by any means without the prior written consent of the Publisher, excepting brief quotes used in reviews.

ISBN-13: 978-1-59983-028-5
ISBN-10: 1-59983-028-5

First Printing: September 2007

10 9 8 7 6 5 4 3 2 1

Printed in the United States of America

Brittany

Damn, I really am fine, I reassured myself while focusing on the small diamond stud in my navel, sparkling like freshly fallen snow.

Positioned in front of the full-length mirror on the back of my bathroom door, I dabbed Chanel in all the pertinent places: between my thighs, behind my earlobes, at the small of my back, at the nape of my neck. Sexy spots. Subtle and soft. On the other side of the door was the finest specimen of a man that I'd seen in a while. Finally, I tied my thick mane up in a ponytail so that it fell just below my bra line. Because it reminds me of Momma, I love my hair.

The clearest memory I have of my momma is her ass-length hair. My parents were born in Trinidad. Married at eighteen, they headed straight to America to start their lives together. Two years later, I was born. Every day for work, Momma would style her hair in one arm-width braid and twist it up into a tight, military-style bun. When she'd come home, the first thing she'd do was unravel her cascade of wavy hair, and it would slap her on the ass. I'd always giggle, because it looked like it hurt. Momma was a gorgeous woman; with her darkly tanned skin and long, jet-black, wavy hair, she looked like a Hawaiian empress.

Unfortunately, Momma died when I was thirteen—just coming into womanhood. My little sister, Tangela, was six at the time. Momma's death was sudden and unexpected. At thirty-three, she was taken into glory by a heart attack. As Momma was being lowered into the ground, I stroked my onyx-colored hair, vowing never to cut it off. This way we'd always be connected. Our hair was the only thing we had in common. Otherwise, we were as different as mangoes and tomatoes. She was a sweet, old-fashioned kind of woman—never wore make-up or a dress above her knees. Me . . . no way. Never that. From the moment that I could smell myself, I wanted to be grown. Wanted to shave my legs, wanted to wear my hair down, wanted to wear lipstick, wanted to buy a bra to cover my little breast buds. I prayed every night that my period would come. Oh, I couldn't wait to become a woman. Momma always told me that I was too damn wild, like my daddy.

My daddy. The ladies' man. I look just like him. People used to say that if I hadn't inherited my mother's beautiful hair, they wouldn't be able to tell she had anything to do with me. I have his Cream of Wheat complexion and his striking, big black eyes. Tall and slender. Of course, I have all the curves where it counts for a woman. Well, I guess I got that from my momma, too. Good lookin' out, Momma!

The summer after my senior year in high school, my daddy died in a four-car pileup on I-95. Good thing, too. I picture him and Momma turning over in their graves so many times that they've probably covered half the earth by now. I've become the woman they worked so hard to keep me from becoming.

I stroked my hair while savoring the tidbits of memories my parents left behind. *Damn, I'm fine,* I thought again as I checked myself out one last time. I was standing there in sheer white, looking like a new bride on her honeymoon, but the man waiting in my bed was hardly my husband. He was just some guy I'd met at the club about three hours earlier. I turned around to catch a glimpse of my firm, yet soft, ass and couldn't help but grin. I loved what I saw. The sight of my own body always turns me on. My pear-shaped breasts are still as perky as the day they grew into their full potential. With a wink of self-approval, I turned out the lights and headed out of the bathroom.

Dwayne, the man of the hour, was waiting eagerly for me. He still smelled of the club we'd just left. A mixture of sweat, smoke, and alcohol. I told him that he couldn't touch me until he took a shower. Without any hesitation, he jumped up and raced into the bathroom to handle his business. I decided to throw back another drink while he washed the club residue away. After gulping down two shots of Absolut—my favorite—I instantaneously felt a warm tingle and wantonness down below. The pulsating rhythm of the shower was all I could hear, and it annoyed me that he was taking so long.

Dammit. I couldn't wait, so I pushed my sheer white thong to one side and began massaging my velvety flesh. It never takes much to make me wet. With one hand, I squeezed and teased the tiny erections that protruded from my breasts. My body temperature started rising, and my leg began to twitch. By then, I had four fingers inside of my swollen diamond. *Oh hell, no,* I thought. He had to hurry up. I couldn't wait another minute, so I catapulted from the bed like damn Cleopatra Jones and busted through the bathroom door. He was singing and lathering up like we had all night. I jumped into the shower—lingerie and all—and fell straight to my knees. He was surprised when I took him into my mouth and did the damn thing. When I felt his leg start that ever too familiar twitch, I stopped.

"Why did you stop?" he whined.

I stood up, pulled my hair out of the ponytail, and dipped my head backwards under the water. Then I turned around and firmly placed my palms on the tile in front of me, leaving the streams of water pouring down the small of my back, over the curve of my ass, then between the warm flesh between my legs. He knew the deal. He pushed my thong to the side and went to work, first with his tongue, then with his third arm. Whew! It was getting hot in there. We sounded like hungry coyotes as I screamed and he panted with pleasure.

"Say my name!" he said.

"You say my name!" I replied. The truth was, after

those shots, I had temporarily forgotten his name. I'd met so many men that night. Shit. I couldn't remember them all.

"Brittanyyyyy!!" he squealed as he pulled out of me and desecrated my shower tiles.

We washed in silence, got out, and dried off. It was that simple. There was an unspoken understanding. No strings attached. Drained, I lay down on my bed.

In a tone barely above a whisper, I told him, "You can find your way out." And he did, without even looking back.

The next morning I woke with a splitting headache. I popped three Excedrin and went back to sleep. I was finally awakened—sans headache— by the neighbor's badass kids. Every Saturday morning they terrorize the whole neighborhood with their noise. I live in the small community of Courtland Gardens, where everyone has known me since forever. Tangie and I once shared a bedroom in this condo. After Momma died, my father sold our four-bedroom house, and we downsized to this two-bedroom condo, which he left to me after his death. When I went away to college, I rented it to a nice couple for four years. That money put me through college and then some. Coupled with the insurance money from my parents' untimely deaths, I was set for a while. Since Tangie was only ten when Daddy died, she was sent away to Boston to live with my father's sister, our auntie Niki.

Tangie and I had never really been close; we would call each other on holidays and stuff like that, but not much more, until now.

One morning Tangie called me out the blue, asking me to pick her up from the Greyhound bus station. Auntie Niki had kicked her out and was dead serious about not letting her return. Tangie was twenty but was still sneaking boys in her bedroom window and stealing Auntie Niki's car, like a teenager. So . . . she had to go, and now she lives with me.

After college, I immediately started working. My major was in graphic design, so I took an entry-level position at a local design firm. Four years later, I'm the Creative Director and manage a team of twelve. I make all the decisions, from coloring to lettering, presentation, and orientation. Everything. Your girl has skills. Working for this firm has allowed me to meet interesting people, including my best friends, Shari and Nia. At first, we hated each other. It's a story that anyone who knows us knows has bonded us for life.

Quincy Malone. Two words that sum up why three beautiful and educated black women were clawing at each other like chicken heads at Freaknik. This man was amazing. As the president and CEO of a printing company in New York City that my firm uses quite often, he was even featured in *Essence* for his accomplishments as a young black entrepreneur. Fine, well-dressed, and knew how to treat a woman. He opened doors, gave amazing foot massages, was a great kisser, and was unbeliev-able in bed. I could go on and on, but I won't.

Our story begins with Quincy and Shari. They met at a Starbucks one afternoon and dated for six months before he met Nia. Shari actually intro-duced the two. Nia was having a little trouble with her finance class, and Shari asked Quincy to help her out. It was another six months later when Quincy walked through my office door, looking like he'd just stepped out of *GQ* magazine.

Quincy wasn't as tall as I usually like my men; he stood just under six feet. His deep brown eyes were nestled under a set of solid jet-black eyebrows and were the same hue as his bronzed chocolate skin. Blessed with chiseled cheekbones and a distin-guished nose and chin, Quincy was able to finance the start-up of his business by landing a very lucra-tive modeling contract with both Tommy Hilfiger and FUBU. You know, I wasn't letting him get away without giving him a sample of my treats. Now, I'm not sure how many other women he had tangled in his web of deceit, but it was the three of us that met head-to-head one rainy day.

It was mid-September and I was headed to Man-hattan—affectionately known as "the City" to locals. I was riding the Metro North train because I hated driving into the City. Too hectic. Once I sat down, I relaxed and pulled out the latest Eric Jerome Dickey novel and dove in where I'd left off. Where I live in Stamford, Connecticut, is about a forty-five-minute train ride to the City, if you take the Ex-press. Although the endless banter of countless people talking way too loudly on their cell phones contaminated the air, I was able to concentrate on the sexy scene I was reading. Once in a while, I would shoot a disapproving glare at the man sitting across from me, because he put his stinking-ass bare feet up on the seat next to me.

When I arrived at Grand Central Station, Quincy was already waiting for me, with thirsty eyes. We pecked each other on the cheek and stepped away into the bustling streets of New York City. As always, there was a Lincoln Town Car waiting for us. Inside, we shared a glass of Cristal and slobbed each other down until we reached our destination—his penthouse on Park Avenue. As we passed the concierge desk, the attendant handed Q about ten messages; in return, Q handed him a twenty. I wondered whom they were from but decided not to ask. He was with me now, and that was all that mattered.

At that point, we'd been dating for about seven months and faithfully saw each other twice a week. I'd take a half day off from work every Wednesday, and we would do lunch and rent a room in the Stamford Suites for the night. Saturdays I would take the train out to his territory, and we'd shop, dine at the best restaurants, take romantic walks in the botanical gardens, or just veg out at his place.

That night we decided to stay in, and as the day slipped into night, we loved each other continuously. The next morning I woke with a migraine; mind-blowing sex does it to me every time. As I turned over to bury my head in his chest for comfort, I realized he wasn't there. Figuring he had run out to pick up some breakfast for us, I popped a couple of Excedrin and decided to take a shower so that I'd smell as fresh as the morning when he returned. I took a twenty-minute shower, making sure there were no traces left of the last night's passion, wrapped myself in his royal blue terry-cloth robe, and crawled back in bed to await my omelet, pancakes, or bacon and eggs. Whatever he brought back, it didn't matter, because at that point I was starvin' like Marvin.

After waiting another half an hour, I started to fume. I called the concierge in a rage.

"Park Towers concierge. How may I be of service?" a man's cheery voice answered.

"Hi. I'm calling from apartment P10, Mr. Malone's residence," I began.

"Is this Ms. Mitchell?" he asked abruptly.

"Yes," I answered warily.

"Mr. Malone said that you might be calling. He left an envelope with me. Would you like me to bring it up now?"

"No, I'll come down. Thanks."

An envelope, I thought. Obviously, he wanted me to leave, or else he would've just left it inside his apartment. A note left at the concierge was meant to be picked up on the way *out!*

The phone rang a second later, and I hastily grabbed it.

"Hello?" I almost screamed.

"Ms. Mitchell. It's Andre, the concierge. I thought I also should let you know that Mr. Malone arranged a car service for you. The driver's been waiting for about a half hour . . ."

I hung up on him, dressed quickly, and left in a frenzy. I was pissed!

I approached the concierge desk, where a young-looking brother was standing, holding an envelope with my name on it. I purposely opened it in front of him so that he could see how much money was inside. There were four crisp one-hundred-dollar bills inside. The boy probably thought I was some kind of call girl. To clear the situation up, I fabricated a story about being Quincy's fiancée and how we'd had a big fight, so I needed to find him. I offered half the contents of the envelope in exchange for any info. He gave me the address that Quincy had ordered his car to, and I hopped in my waiting Town Car and was on my way. I was not in the mood to be bullshitted.

We drove for about two hours, until we finally reached Southern Connecticut State University in New Haven, Connecticut. My stomach growled from a combination of anxiety, fear, and hunger as I exited my luxury taxi. The sign out front read SCHWARTZ HALL. Q was at a college dormitory.

Upon entering Schwartz Hall, a handsome thug-scholar, who was monitoring the sign-in sheet, greeted me. His name tag read RONNELL.

"Who you here to see?" he asked.

When did God start making college-aged men look so damn good? In '96, when I started school, they weren't that fine. Ronnell was dayum fine! He had the body of a grown-ass man, but his eyes displayed an innocence that made me throb. After a thirty-second daydream about taking Ronnell into the limo and teaching him a thing or two, I remembered what I was there for.

"Well, I'm looking for a friend. I was wondering if I could take a look at the sign-in sheet to see what room he's in," I slurred, finally snapping out of it.

"I'm sorry. I can't do that for you. You wanna speak to the Dorm Director?" Ronnell covered the sheet so I couldn't get a sneak peek.

"Sure," I said flatly, thinking about how to explain that I was hunting down my man to a pencil-pushing, pompous asshole of an authority figure.

Ronnell pushed a paging button. "Ms. Paine, there's someone out here that needs to see you."

Then a girl, who appeared to be Ronnell's age, emerged from the back office. She had honey blond hair that stopped about shoulder length. Caramel apple complexion. Stood about five-five, wearing black Capri pants, platform sandals, and a tank top the color of her golden tresses. Cute girl.

"Hi. I'm Shari. How may I help you?"

I could tell she was sizing me up the same way I'd just done her. I was on point, though. Although I wasn't at my flyest, I was looking quite cute in my coral velour sweat suit and pink and white Pumas. I felt relieved because I knew a sista would understand why I'd journeyed two hours to find my man.

"Can we speak privately?" I asked, with a sister girl friendliness, feeling at ease.

"Sure. Come into my office." Shari motioned for

me to follow her. "Ronnell, stop looking at her ass," she teased as they exploded in laughter.

Inside her cluttered office, I explained what the deal was, and she seemed more than happy to help me out. She said that she knew Quincy very well and that he came up there twice a week to tutor one of her residents.

"Female?" I asked, leaning my head to one side and narrowing my eyes for emphasis.

"Yes, bright girl. She's on the dean's list and track team, and in the drama club. This is her senior year," Shari bragged like a proud parent.

"What does she look like? Is she a sista?"

She saw where I was going with my line of questioning. A solemn look took over her cheery disposition. Shari grabbed her master key and pulled me out of my chair by the arm.

"Let's go," she barked.

"Why are you so anxious all of a sudden?" I teased as I hustled to keep up with Shari.

She cringed.

We found our way to the fifth floor of the apartment-style dormitory and to the third door on the left. We barged right in on the two of them—buck naked—getting down on the living-room couch. I felt the blood flowing through my veins heating up. My head was about to explode.

"Quincy Malone, what the fuck is going on?" shouted Shari.

I hadn't even found the right words in my vocabulary before Shari blew the fuck up. The professional I was previously introduced to was replaced with the stereotypical neck-rolling, fast-talking, hands-on-the-hips angry black woman, which I'd pictured myself turning into the whole limo ride up there. You would have thought that Shari and I were Aaliyah and Left Eye walking through the door by the expression on Quincy's face as he pushed homegirl off his dick.

"Why the hell are you so concerned?" I asked Shari, with displaced anger.

"Outside now. All of you!" Shari directed, using her authority.

They scurried around, putting on their clothes, while Shari and I headed to the back parking lot. As soon as the two lovebirds caught up to us, the face-off commenced. It was clear that I was the other woman and had no priority in telling Quincy off. Shari was running the show.

"Q, I am tired of this! First, this high yellow heffa comes into my office, talking about how you are her man and she's trying to track you down," Shari yelled, pointing in my face. "Then I come upstairs to check on you, and you're bonin' this young chick. One of my residents!" she added. Shari's tears started to flow just as the rain began pouring down on us.

"Who you calling a heffa? You better watch your damn mouth, 'cause you don't know me like that!" I'd finally found my voice.

In response, Shari gave me the hand.

"You're only five years older than me, so you can chill with that young girl shit," Nia fired at Shari, in a feeble attempt to put her in her place.

"You know he's my man, Nia. I was trying to help *you* out, and this is the thanks I get?" Shari said, stepping up in Nia's face.

The rain was pouring down, and we all looked like wet Raggedy Ann dolls at that point, but no one cared. Quincy was standing with both hands on his head in frustration, looking like he would break down and cry at any moment. He was mumbling his two cents, but no one was paying him no mind; we were concerned with confronting each other.

"Why did you pretend not to have a relationship with him when we were in your office? Why did you let me tell you all my business when you knew the whole time he was two-timing us?" I asked Shari, with one hand on my hip and the other pointing in her face.

"Do you know how many groupies this man has? I can't believe every weave-wearing skank that comes in my face, talking shit," she replied, giving me her best "you better get your fucking hand outta my face" look.

And that's when the shit hit the fan. I slapped Shari so hard that she fell to the wet pavement. I didn't stop, either. I dropped on top of her and commenced beating that ass. Quincy had the nerve to try to get me off of her and pulled me by my hair.

"No, you didn't . . . I'll kill you!" I shouted as I kicked him where I knew it would hurt the most. As he doubled over in pain, I dropped down on him and tried to scratch his damn eyes out. Then Nia came at me from behind, pulled my hair, and started punching me in the face. I guess she called it protecting her man.

From there, it was an all-out brawl. Shari joined in to get some licks on Nia, too. Soon we were all wrestling on the cold, wet concrete—all except Quincy. With all of our energy exerted, we sat on the ground in defeat. Hair tangled and mangled, a bloody lip, make-up streaking down our cheeks, a swollen eye . . . a hot mess! Then we realized that punk Quincy had retreated to his awaiting car service and was long gone.

Seconds later, the campus police arrived, who in turn called the New Haven Police Department. We were arrested for aggravated assault and breach of peace. After the three of us spent a night in jail, followed by numerous court dates, we slowly learned to like one another and eventually became the best of friends.

Our first civilized encounter after the fight was on a lunch recess at our third court appearance. We all happened to be at the same crowded diner and ended up sitting within a couple feet of each other. Soon Nia approached Shari's table, with an apologetic look on her face. By the end of the lunch hour, we ended up sharing a table and some juicy Quincy stories.

Shari lost her job at SCSU. Nia was kicked out of the dorms and had to commute for the remainder of her last semester. I occasionally gave Quincy a piece here and there for another six months after that, but I never told the girls. Who knows, they were probably still seeing him, too. He had that kind of effect on a sista. It's been about a year and a half since the rainy day at Southern, but from our strong bond, it's almost like it never happened.

Shari and I were at this new club called Heat that had a sophisticated crowd going on. The DJ was on this old-school kick, playing Frankie Beverly and Maze's "Before I Let Go." Shari and I couldn't resist throwing our hands over our heads and waving them in the air as we sung along. The club was illuminated like a room full of teenagers with the latest 50 Cent record playing. That's the sign of a mature crowd: they can appreciate real music.

Although Heat was only big enough to hold about three hundred people, close to five hundred young and old squeezed between the sweaty walls.

All of the walls, or at least what I could see of them through the sea of dancers, were painted black and adorned with red neon lights and flame-shaped signs. The see-through ceiling gave the illusion that the club was more spacious than it actually was. The upper level's floor was made of red Plexiglas that was just clear enough to reveal the tops of the people's heads on the first floor.

The best feature of Heat was the bar. Aside from the numerous bottles of alcohol in varying shapes, sizes, and colors, there was a donut-shaped aquarium that housed several vicious, but sleek-looking, black sharks. Red lighting at the top and bottom of the aquarium gave the illusion of bloodred water.

To top off the whole Heat theme, the bartenders were even decked out in all red.

That night we were dressed to the nines. Shari wore a short black skirt that hugged her behind like it was painted on. Her barely-there shirt laced up the back. The front was sheer black, so her nipples were visible since she hadn't worn a bra. She didn't realize that her shirt was so revealing, and I wasn't going to tell her, because she'd just get all embarrassed and want to go home. I was wearing a short skirt as well. Mine was electric blue, with a little bra top to match. I had on delicate electric blue sandals. I loved showing off my washboard stomach and little, round booty. Shit, I deserved it. I worked hard for it to look that way. Oh yeah, I had a little electric blue stud in my belly button to match. You couldn't tell me nothing!

"Electric Boogie" came on, and I exited stage left. Not my style to do that dance in public. Family reunions, maybe, but not in a club, looking as good as I did that night. Shari was out there having a ball, kicking and spinning to that ridiculous song, so I meandered over to the bar where I ordered an Absolut martini with a twist of lemon and lime. I had finished my drink and was about to order another when I felt a tap on my shoulder.

"What's up, beautiful? What's your name?" asked the tall black figure standing before me.

So far, so good. This man was massive and charcoal black, with a contagious smile. He was a cross between Tyson Beckford and Tyrese, but with dark gray eyes. Dressed impeccably from head to toe, he had expensive taste, I noticed.

I breathed in his essence. "Brittany," I finally replied.

"Well, Brittany, are you here with someone?" He paused to press a button on his two-way to make it stop vibrating. "No, you're not. Girls like you never have a man," he answered himself.

"And what, might I ask, do you mean by that?" I was offended.

"I mean people like us, we can't be tied down. We're just too fine."

He laughed. I laughed. We laughed.

"Just joking. I'm just trying to break the ice," he added.

There is nothing worse than an insecure man. They get all jealous and possessive on a sista. This man glowed with confidence. What a turn-on.

"Would you like to dance?" he asked as he gazed directly into my eyes.

Eye contact, another plus. Usually I intimidate men. They think I'm some kind of stuck-up bitch . . . which I can be when I want to.

"Maybe later, sweetheart." I decided to play hard to get.

"No, maybe now."

He pulled me onto the dance floor and worked me like an exotic dancer. I secretly wondered what his stage name was. Probably Chocolate, Lover Boy, or something sexy like that. We danced until I started to sweat. Which, by the way, I never do. Usually, after one song, I politely walk away. That time was different, though. I was actually enjoying the show he was putting on for me. He was really working me, but I couldn't let him show me up, so I was working him right back. I decided to give him a dose of my confidence by grabbing his hand and pulling him off the dance floor.

"What's wrong? You can't hang?" he challenged.

"Oh, I can hang, believe you me, but I just realized that I don't even know your name."

"My name's Warren. Warren Banks." He beamed.

What a conservative name for a man with so much freak in him, I thought. But I liked it. A mature, sexy name.

"So what do they call you at work?"

"Would you like something to drink? A brotha is thirsty!" he said, changing the subject and nodding his head to get the bartender's attention.

"Yes. I'll just have water. Thank you."

Warren ordered my water and a Remy VSOP straight up for himself before turning back to me with his million-dollar smile.

"So why do you think they call me something other than Warren at work?" he wondered.

"Because you must be a dancer, with that body and the way you were moving out there."

"Flavor. They call me Flavor. You're a smart woman, very observant," he remarked, winking his eye at me.

He probably thought I was going to start tripping and asking him all types of questions. Deep down, I wanted to, but I wasn't like other women. I wouldn't try to get all up in his business too soon.

"Well, Warren Banks, it was nice meeting you. I have to go," I said curtly, grabbing my bottle of Evian.

"Will I get to see you again, Brittany . . . ?"

"Mitchell," I answered, extending my hand for him to shake.

"Brittany Mitchell, will I get to see you again?" Warren asked, shaking my hand and then holding it in his.

As soon as possible, I thought. But I said, "If you want my number, then just ask for it." I snatched my hand away. Playing hard to get was getting more fun by the minute.

"Sweetheart, if all I wanted was your number, then I would have asked a long time ago. But for now, I'll take your number." He grabbed my hand again and kissed my palm.

Without any further games, I wrote down the digits and passed them over.

"How are you getting home?" he asked.

I'd just realized that the club was half empty and Shari had left me. I have my own car, but we had decided to take hers because it's sportier. *Wait 'til I see her!* I thought.

"It seems as if my friend has left me. I'll just take a cab," I confessed, a little embarrassed.

"No, you won't. I'll take you. This is no hour for a woman to be riding in a filthy cab with a filthy stranger."

"I don't exactly know *you* too well, either, Mr. Warren," I coyly replied, twisting a lock of hair through my fingers. My good sense told me not to ride home with this stranger, either, but I just couldn't refuse. Plus, Warren had presented the perfect opportunity for me to see what kind of whip he drove. We got our coats, his leather and mine suede, and were on our way.

Pearly white, tan leather interior, sparkling chrome rims, lightly tinted windows. I was looking at his 2003 Lexus ES 330. I decided right then and there that he was a keeper.

Shari

"Honey, are you asleep?" I whispered in my husband's ear.

"No, I was waiting up for you," he said, softly embracing me. "You know I get nervous when you go out with Brittany."

"Well, guess what? I had to leave her tonight. She was all wrapped up in some guy all night and totally ditched me. I wasn't there to get my groove on. I just wanted some girlfriend time with her. I know she's going to be mad, but she ditched me first! If that guy was worth dissin' her friend for, then *he* can drive her black ass home!" I was heated.

"Bay, stop cursing. You know I hate that. Why would you expect anything more from her? You know how she is," he lectured. "She's a gold digger, which is why she always winds up heartbroken. She values the wrong things in a man. Next time, just drive separate cars, because I know you feel guilty about leaving her there."

"No, I don't." I did.

"Yes, you do. Who you think you fooling?" He poked my ribs, tackled me, and started tickling me all over.

"I have a surprise for you," he said, climbing off of me.

"Oh, Dexter, you are so sweet," I crooned.

"For the umpteenth time, don't call me by my full name. It reminds me of my mother. And, with you lying there looking all sexy, the last thing I want to do is think about my mother!" he yelled as he headed out of the room.

"Whatever. Just hurry back here, because I love surprises!" I began taking my jewelry and shoes off and placing them in their respective spots.

Dex returned about five minutes later, with a small metallic gift bag, a chilled bottle of champagne, and two glasses.

"What's the special occasion, Dex?"

"Damn. Just be patient, Bay."

He poured two glasses of bubbly to the rim and passed one to me.

"A toast to us. May our love last forever," he said, then gingerly planted a kiss on my forehead. Then he got up to turn on the CD player. Musiq's song "Don't Change" floated across the room.

"All right. I can't take it anymore. What's going on?" I squealed.

"Okay. Today is October eleventh," Dex said, taking a seat next to me on the bed.

"And?" I interrupted.

"And . . . a year ago today was the day that I realized I loved you and wanted you to be my wife."

"No, it wasn't. You told me that you loved me on my birthday that August," I said matter-of-factly, placing my champagne on the nightstand.

"Yeah, I know that. On your birthday, you looked so beautiful, and I knew at that point that I would never lay eyes on a more beautiful woman than you. So, at that time, I did feel that I loved you, but on October eleventh, I knew for sure." Dex nervously looked into my eyes and put my hand into his.

"What happened on October eleventh? That doesn't ring a bell."

"If you interrupt me again, I'm going to sleep, and you'll never know this piece of me that I'm trying to share with you." He sighed, pushing my hand away.

"I'm sorry Bay. Please continue." I sat up on the bed in a perfectly Indian-style position, interlocked my fingers, and placed my hands in my lap to give Dex my full attention.

"Anyways, on October eleventh, you were sick with the flu. I made you some soup and fed it to you. You looked horrible. You were pale, your eyes were bloodshot, and your hair was all over the place. Afterwards, I undressed you and put you in the tub. I remember you barely had enough strength to walk. As I washed your body, I felt warm inside because for the first time I felt that you needed me. We'd been together for close to a year, and you'd never asked me for anything. You had your own car, paid your own bills, and bought your own clothes. The same places I caressed while we made love were the same places that I was washing with exquisite care. Usually touching these places would make me sexually aroused. I didn't feel that way. I felt like I was doing what I'm here for—to take care of my baby. Then I gave you some medicine and lotioned your body from head to toe. I brushed your hair into the neatest ponytail that I could manage, put your nightgown on, and tucked you in."

Tears flooded my face, and my voice trembled an "I love you."

I'd barely remembered that day. I can't believe he remembered everything in such vivid detail. It's funny how one thing can mean so much to one person and nothing to the next. He evidently had Musiq on repeat, because after what seemed like a twenty-minute story, my song was still on.

He passed the shiny bag my way, and I attacked it like a hungry hippo. Inside, I found a long, black, shiny box. I opened it, and inside was the three-carat tennis bracelet from Zales that I'd been drooling over every day for the last five months.

"Oh my goodness. I love you, Dexter Brown!" I screamed as I tackled him onto the bed and smothered him with kisses.

I didn't always have men like Dexter in my life. I have been through my share of liars, cheaters, users, and abusers. The good Lord knew that I would have a nervous breakdown if He sent another loser my way. Just when I thought I had reached my wit's end,

Dexter popped into my life. I had given up on men completely and had vowed never to love again. After losing my job at the university over a three-timing asshole, I had met and fell for Chris. Now Chris was a trip. It takes all my energy just to tell this story.

Chris and I met at the unemployment office. Okay, okay. I know that should have been a red flag for danger. But you know what we women do. "Girl, I can work with him. He can change."

Big mistake. The relationship lasted for all of eight months, but this man had caused more damage than all of the other screwups before him combined. First off, he remained happily on unemployment until his benefits ended. Then "the Shari Foundation" supported him. He lived in Bridgeport, which is only about twenty minutes north of where I live in Stamford. He borrowed my car every day so that he could "look for work" and managed to collect two speeding tickets and get into a small fender bender, which made my insurance skyrocket. Don't you know the damn insurance company made me put his name on my policy. I guess it was because every time something happened, it was his trifling ass driving.

A month into our relationship, I contracted gonorrhea. Chris blamed it on his previous relationship, explaining that the chick had been cheating on him. I forgave him because it had happened before me, and I couldn't be mad at that—right? From then on, we used protection every time, no exception. Then he moved in with me because he and his roommate were beefing because he couldn't help out with the bills.

During this time, if Chris wasn't out at the damn club, this fool was home on the Internet, running up my electric bill. I fell two months behind on the rent. It's expensive trying to support a grown-ass man! His only saving grace was that the sex was phenomenal. I mean, the brotha had me crying genuine tears on more than one occasion from pure pleasure. Why do we women get hypnotized by the dick? We start tolerating things that we would never take from a weak-dick brotha.

Anyways, while I was still under hypnosis, we opened a couple of joint accounts at clothing stores so that he could dress for success. We also opened a checking account at the bank that I worked for at the time, as the front-end supervisor. To top it off, we started receiving harassing phone calls from his ex-girlfriend at all times of the night. He explained that she was a hater and just didn't want him to be happy.

Enough about all the small things. What ultimately ruined my life again actually began as a good day. Chris had finally found a job in his field, so we had planned to go out and celebrate that night. He even promised to pay me back for everything I'd done for him. But when I reached home, he wasn't there. Finally, he moseyed in around midnight, saying that he'd gone out with his boys instead. He also told me that he would be moving out because one of his friends had extended their extra room to him. I was beyond mad. Happy that he was finally leaving, but mad, nonetheless, because he had stood me up without a phone call. He wasn't even home for five minutes before I heard a knock at the front door.

"Hello?" I asked.

"Open the fucking door!" It was a squeaky female voice. I opened the door. On the other side stood a tiny, but very pregnant, woman with a little boy that appeared to be about three.

"Junior, are you in there?" she squealed, trying to peek around me.

"There's no Junior here!" I yelled.

Then Chris came out of the bedroom, with his tail between his legs.

"What are you doing here, Rhonda?" he barked.

"I'm your wife, Junior. What are *you* doing here?"

"You kicked me out. Where was I supposed to go?" He paced up and down the floor, looking like a crook caught red-handed.

"Junior, we just had such a beautiful time tonight celebrating your new job. We made love for the first time in months. I knew it was too good to be true. That's why I followed you here." She turned and began screaming at me. "We reconciled tonight, and he promised he would change. He is supposed to be moving back home tomorrow!"

"Look, lady," I said, "I am not the one who deceived you. Direct your anger that way." I pointed to Chris.

And she did. She lost it. She charged past me, toward Chris, swinging, kicking, and scratching like her life depended on it. Don't you know this fool

laid her out? Knocked her big, pregnant ass out!
Hit her like she was a man!

The little boy ran into a corner and covered his
eyes. I spazzed out. Grabbing the nearest thing,
which was the cordless phone, I started wailing on
Chris. I didn't care what the situation was; I
couldn't tolerate him hitting another woman in my
presence—and one pregnant at that! I called him
every foul word I could think of. Then he tried to
lay me out, too, but I'm not tiny like her. I can take
a punch like a man. I felt my lip swell as the familiar taste of blood filled my mouth. Just as he tackled me to the ground, the police came busting
through the door. He was arrested, and the ambulance whisked his wife away. I assured them that I
did not need medical attention, but I did want to
press charges, though.

The next morning I still managed to go to work,
swollen lip and all. I was the supervisor, you know?
Around noon, three sistas came marching up to my
desk. Judging from their greased-up faces and wrin-
kled clothing, I could tell they weren't there to
open an account.

"May I help you?" I asked in my most professional
tone.

"Yeah," the tallest one answered. "Can we step
outside?"

"No, whatever you need, we can handle it right
here," I said, professionally and boldly, I might add.
On the outside I was trying to maintain a holier than
thou disposition, but my insides were starting to take

turns twisting around in my body, until my heart felt like it was going to explode out of my mouth.

The tiny, pimple-faced dark one to her left couldn't hold back any longer. "Bitch, do you know that it's your fault that my little niece is dead?" The tears she'd been trying to keep inside began escaping against her will.

"Huh?" I asked, shocked.

"Rhonda lost her baby, you fucking ho. If you weren't trying to steal her man, it would have never happened!" The tall one was holding the dark one back as she was trying her damndest to get to me.

Now the entire bank was frozen and staring in my direction, including my boss. The mouth of the overly flamboyant head teller, Twon, fell open and stayed open. "Oh no, she didn't," he remarked, slamming down the box of deposit slips he was bringing to the front and placing both hands on his hips, anticipating their next move. His high-pitched voice seemed to boom through the entire building. To make matters worse, Jasmin, the college intern I'd just hired, actually responded. "Oh yes, she did," Jasmin said, staring the girls up and down from behind the counter. I suddenly wished we had taken this mess outside. I felt terrible that Rhonda had lost her baby, but I really had nothing to do with that, and I was pissed that these hood rats had brought this drama to my job.

"Can you leave now? You're talking to the wrong woman about this. You should be asking Rhonda why she kicked him out with nowhere to go. She should have been a more caring woman. Then

maybe her man wouldn't have had to run to me."
I stood up. Now I was pissed.

Brittany always says that I was asking for the ass whooping that followed. And I mean they jumped on my ass! Messed me up good, too. They ran off before the police arrived, but I was arrested because witnesses said I'd provoked it.

I was promptly fired as they led me out in handcuffs. How embarrassing. My boss just yelled it to me as they were pushing me through the door.

"You're fired! Don't let me see you around here again!"

I spent a night in jail, and the next morning I was released on a promise to appear in court. Brittany and Nia came to pick me up. I felt so ashamed. All I wanted to do was take a steaming hot shower, crawl up in a comforter, and sleep.

"Look," Brittany lectured during the car ride home, "I told you from day one that the nigga was no good. He wasn't even worthy to kiss your feet, never mind living up in your spot with you. Fucking bum! You keep messing with these bums. Shari, what is wrong with you?"

Nia added, "Karma's a backstabbing bitch, and she always finds a way to come back around when you least expect her to."

What the hell did Nia mean by that? I thought, but I didn't have the mental energy to challenge her. I didn't care about what they were saying; I just wanted to get home.

Brittany stopped at Starbucks to grab us all some

coffee. What I really needed was a little something in mine, though, but I didn't complain.

Brittany parked her silver Infiniti in front of my five-story apartment building. Nia got out and extended her hand to help me out of the car. I was bruised, dirty, stinking, tattered, and every other word to describe looking plain torn up.

In spite of all her fussing, Brittany spoke in a gentle voice. "Shari, girl, don't worry. We'll get everything cleaned up. You just get straight in the shower."

"Yeah, girl, and I'll cook us a nice brunch," Nia said. "Brittany and I can sit around and watch some DVDs all afternoon while you catch some shut-eye."

"Thank you," I managed to say through gulps of steaming hot coffee.

"I hope that Negro doesn't come after you when he gets bailed out. I don't wanna have to go Bobbit on his ass," Brittany teased.

"I'm not thinking about him," I protested. "He's a punk. He'll probably go crawling back home to his wife. And she'll take him back in, because she loves his punk ass. He ain't thinking about me."

When we reached my front door, a fluorescent pink sign was taped over the peephole. EVICTION NOTICE: NONPAYMENT OF RENTAL CHARGES AND EXCESSIVE DISTURBANCE.

Jobless, homeless, moneyless, manless, and prideless . . . again.

Nia

Brittany, Shari, and I decided to have lunch together at Catalina's, an elegant restaurant in downtown Stamford. As I approached my friends, already
seated at the table, they were playfully arguing
about Shari deserting Brittany at Heat last week.
Those two were always bickering over something.

"Leave me again and watch what happens," Brittany threatened.

"Yeah, okay," Shari replied, lightheartedly brush-
ing off Brittany's comment. "We'll see."

"We'll see you get your ass beat," Brittany spat.
"That's all we'll see."

"If you feeling froggy, then leap, bitch! That's all
I gotta say. Leap!"

"Okay, break it up, girls. Damn!" I yelled, holding
Shari back by her shoulders as she was trying to get
out of her chair and advance toward Brittany.

"You lucky she's holding me back," Shari told

Brittany. At that point we all started cracking up at their foolishness.

"I swear, you two deserve an Academy Award for your little dramatic displays sometimes."

"You know it," Brittany agreed as she and Shari high-fived across the table.

It was our first visit to Catalina's, but the atmosphere already impressed us. We chose an outside table to enjoy the crisp air. It was still fairly warm for mid-October. Fresh tulips had been placed delicately in the center of each table. Less than two minutes later, we were approached by our waiter.

"May I start you ladies off with a cocktail?" he asked.

Without looking up, I scanned the drink list. Brittany ordered her usual—Absolut martini with a twist of lemon and lime. She is so predictable. Shari ordered a frozen Kahlua cappuccino. I decided that sounded very appealing, so I shifted my eyes from the menu to say I wanted one as well. But when I went to order, no words came out of my mouth. I couldn't believe who was standing before me. After six years, Mike had matured into a handsome man. He, too, was paralyzed by this unlikely encounter.

"Nia, what do you want? Girl, he's waiting for you to order!" Brittany hissed.

"Uh . . . I'll have what she's having," I stuttered, pointing to Shari.

He backed away from the table, with a look of shame and complete remorse.

"What was that all about?" asked Shari. "He wasn't that fine!"

They didn't know Mike or the story behind him, either. After a constipated pause, I finally replied.

"That was Mike," I admitted.

"Who?" yelped Brittany.

"Who is Mike, and what is he to you?" Shari wanted to know.

I didn't want to relive one the most devastating moments of my life, but I considered Brittany and Shari to be family.

After a long sigh, I searched my memory bank, and that night came clearly back to me.

Then I was startled by our drinks being placed on our table. This time it was a bubbling blond waitress. "Are you ready to order?" she asked. She smiled, taking out her pad to scribble down our order.

"Where's the man that took our drink order?" Brittany wondered.

"He asked me to take this table for him," she answered. "He has too many tables and is too busy to take another one right now."

We ordered our lunches and another round of drinks. Blondie smiled politely and skipped away to start our order.

"Okay. So who is this Mike dude?" Shari urged.

My freshman year in college, I lost my special gift from God—my virginity. My boyfriend at the time was Mike, the DJ. He was the guy that threw all the live parties on campus. The ladies swooned over him constantly. But he was all mine, and everyone knew he was off-limits.

We'd dated for almost a year. Everything was perfect, and I really believed that he respected that I wanted to wait for marriage before giving up the goods. Late one night, we were at his dorm room, watching a movie . . . and he raped me.

I called his room "the Tribute to Hip-Hop Museum." Posters covered every inch of the walls. Everyone from Run DMC, Queen Latifah, and Big Daddy Kane to new schoolers like Snoop Dog, Lil' Kim, and Foxy Brown were on display. This tiny room is where he kept his infinite crates of albums. Alphabetically arranged, nonetheless. Plus, Mike must have owned twenty pairs of sneakers, which he also kept clean and lined against his wall, arranged by year, from oldest to newest.

"Mike, stop. Let's just watch the movie," I protested as I shoved him away.

"I don't feel like watching this stupid movie," he whined as he resumed kissing my neck.

"You're never in the mood to do anything I want to do," I complained.

"Yeah, and you're never in the mood to do anything *I* want to do."

I knew he was referring to sex or some form of physicalness that I was not in the mood for, but I didn't care.

"Mike, what you have in mind is not my idea of having fun," I managed to say in my most serious tone. Then he gave me those sad, puppy-dog eyes.

"Don't look at me like that! You should know by now that I'm serious!" I said.

He huffed over dramatically as he got up to turn off the television; then he popped in one of the rap tapes he'd recorded and turned the volume knob until it wouldn't go anymore. Facing me, he gyrated over to the bed in a manner that would either make Ricky Martin jealous or offended at making such a mockery of his craft. It was hard to decipher which. I couldn't help but start cracking up right in his face.

"Come here, boy. You so stupid!" I chortled. I hugged him tight, appreciating how he always made me laugh.

Minutes later, I was half naked, lying on my back, with my legs spread wide. We had gone there before—plenty of times—but I never let him have all of me. *Never* all of me. Mike slid my panties off with his teeth. He knew that drove me crazy. His tongue journeyed up and down my thigh and calf and stopped at my foot. He paid special attention to each toe, slowly taking them one by one in and out of his warm, moist mouth, while massaging the sole with just the right amount of pressure. The next stop on his escapade was my soft spot. As usual, by this time I was in a full frenzy.

"I love you, Nia," he said between licks. "I love you so much."

Without thinking, I heard myself say, "I love you, too." It was the first time we'd exchanged those words. It felt so natural, so right. I *did* love him.

"Make love to me," Mike said as he stared straight into my eyes.

And then, scrreeeeech! It was just like a moment from the movies. You know, when the romantic music is playing in the background and the mood is sultry and perfect, and then something un-expected happens—like the man says another woman's name. The music abruptly stops playing, and you hear this loud noise, like tires skidding to a halt. Yeah, that's the noise that I heard so clearly in my mind.

"Excuse me?" I asked him, sitting straight up.

"Nia, I love you, and you know I respect you. I can't wait any longer," he pleaded.

"Look, I'm sorry if I led you on, but you know better than to ask me that. I'm not ready."

"Well, can I just feel your warm softness against me? I promise I won't put it in."

I stupidly agreed with the compromise. He rubbed his manhood around in my wetness. I felt how hard it was, and it made me nervous, although I have to admit, it felt damned good. I writhed and groaned in ecstasy, and my juices started to pro-duce at a quicker pace.

"Relax, baby," he bent down to whisper.

"Okay," I murmured.

And then it happened. Mike proceeded to thrust himself into me with what felt like all his might.

"Nooooo . . . What are you doing? Take it ouu-uttt! Mike, stop. It huuurrrts!" I got no response, except that he continued on the mission he'd begun.

"Mike," I screamed again. Then he grabbed my wrists and pinned them back on the bed.

"Stop acting like a baby!" he yelled. "You said you loved me. Now prove it."

I couldn't believe this was the same man that had just professed his love for me! His *respect* for me! I felt my soft flesh swelling and burning from the friction. He continued. In and out. In and out. After a while I was numb. No more burning, no more feeling, no more love.

"Would you please just stop!" By this time I was crying like a newborn baby with colic. I squirmed around, but his overpowering strength left me helpless. And there I lay, digesting what was happening to me, crying tears so hard and filled with so much hurt and fear that I thought I'd never be able to see again. I felt blinded by betrayal.

When he reached his peak, he squeezed my wrists even tighter. I screamed so loud. I wanted the whole world to hear me, but no one could over the music.

"What is your problem, Nia?" he scolded, like I was a child.

"Just leave, before I call the campus police." I didn't know what else to expect from him.

"Leave my own room? You know what? I will leave. I don't want to look at your face another second. I'm out. Don't be here when I get back!" he fired.

I guess I was having a Wonder Woman moment because I sprang up butt naked and attacked him like a wild dog attacks an alley cat. I was swinging, kicking, and screaming like I'd lost my mind. I really had. I was doing some serious damage to this

Negro, too, because I saw blood running down his nose. Finally, he picked me up and threw me like a rag doll against his wall. His crates of records fell on top of me. And so I lay there, defeated and defiled. My heart continued to beat to the rhythm of the hip-hop beats. Then he left.

Moments later I collected my thoughts, and I bolted. My dorm was right across the green, so I sprinted all the way to my door. Once inside, I showered like never before. A long, slow shower. I felt scarred for life. I didn't make it to any classes the next day. I cried. I didn't eat a thing. I cried. I waited for his call. I really thought he would call. He didn't. I cried. Conflicting thoughts of whether or not to report him haunted my every moment. Would they believe me? How would I prove it? Most importantly, I prayed that I wasn't pregnant. It turned out that I wasn't, and I never ended up reporting him.

I gave the girls the abbreviated version of what happened that night, not wanting to get too mushy in public.

"You should have. I would've," said Shari, referring to me never reporting him. "How often did you see him after that night?"

"I would run into him at parties on campus and stuff. He wouldn't even look my way. I would see him with other girls, and it made my heart hurt. I'd see him in the cafeteria with his boys, and it seemed like they were all laughing at me. Mike didn't return to school the next semester. Deep down, I was looking forward to seeing him. I'm not sure why."

"Damn, Nia. I'm so sorry you had to lose it that way," Shari sympathized.

"Thanks, Shari. I love you."

"Fuck that. When I see his sorry ass again, I'm gonna curse him out," Brittany yelled, interrupting my peace of mind.

"No, it's not even worth it, Brittany. That won't erase the pain. I'm over it, anyway," I pleaded.

We all agreed to just leave it alone and eat our lunches in peace. Revealing what happened that night brought back a very difficult memory that I was trying to erase, so we also agreed never to bring it up again. Instead, we discussed Brittany's new man friend. She told us that he looks exactly like Tyson Beckford. That wasn't hard to believe, because all her men are superfine.

"I'll be back. I'm going to the little girl's room," I said as I grabbed my purse and headed inside.

The bathroom was immaculate. Sensors controlled the toilets and sinks. The tiles were gold and white to match the gold faucets and handles. The sweet aroma of potpourri filled each stall. Fresh flowers added an unexpected ambience to the room. I stared at myself in the mirror, thinking about the secret I'd finally revealed. My blank stare turned into a bright smile. I was happy. Nothing more to hide. No more feelings to suppress. I left the bathroom, feeling like an enormous weight had been lifted off my shoulders.

"Nia Lopez, I thought I'd never see you again."

The voice was coming from behind me, but I would know that voice anywhere. What could he possibly have to say to me? My first instinct was to keep walking and ignore him. Instead of running from my demons, I faced him.

"Mike Johnson," I replied flatly.

"Nia, I'm. . . ." He paused and sighed. "Look, I'd love to get together with you. We have a lot to talk about. Believe it or not, I've thought about you every day for the last six years."

"Well, Mike," I spat, "I don't believe it. It's hard to believe that after all these years, you're still so full of shit."

"Please, Nia, I know you're not a coldhearted person. Can you give me your number so that we can talk? Just five minutes. Please?" he begged, adding, "I've changed."

It was so hard for me to be mean to him. Mike has these unbelievably forgivable eyes. I never could resist those eyes. He seemed to be taller now, too. His face hadn't changed a bit, and his honey brown complexion still had its after summer glow. A neatly trimmed caeser that flaunted his wavy hair had replaced those awful cornrows. He'd even grown a goatee. I had to admit, he'd really been taking care of himself. I gave him my cell phone number and walked away without any further conversation.

I didn't tell Shari and Brittany. The weight that had been lifted was back on my shoulders. Yet another secret among friends. This made me wonder what kinds of skeletons were haunting them. I figured that he might not even call, so I'd tell them everything on a need-to-know basis. Was I desperate? No. He was a child when he did that to me. He hadn't known any better. He's a man now. Right?

I returned to the table to see Brittany's eyes bulging out of their sockets. Shari was telling the story behind her new tennis bracelet. It was dazzling. I was so happy that she'd found such a wonderful man. One day I hoped to marry a man just like Dex. There was a time when I thought Mike would be that man.

Nia

Brittany and Shari are like the kind of sisters I always wanted. My two sisters and I never got along. Krystal and Angel's father died of a sudden heart attack, and in less than two years, Mommy remarried and I was born. That really tore the house apart. My sisters resented Mommy for falling in love again, and they hated Papi for taking their father's place. But, mostly, their hatred toward Papi was because he's Cuban. Because of Papi's Hershey bar complexion, most people couldn't even tell he was Cuban until they heard his thickly accented Spanglish.

The reason my sisters treated me so badly was because I'm of mixed heritage. They'd always say that I thought I was all that because I had good hair. I just don't understand why society is programmed to think there is such a thing as "good hair." If my hair was the same texture as theirs, I would be just as happy with it. That type of thing never mattered to me.

By the time I turned six, my hair was down to my ass. Mommy always gave me two long braids, one on each side of my head. Papi called me Pocahontas, and so did all my friends, until I was about sixteen.

It was the beginning of summer. I was awakened by my Strawberry Shortcake alarm clock at seven o'clock for camp. I rose from my bed, and when I turned around to make it up, there lay my two braids. I grabbed one in each hand and bolted downstairs, screaming bloody murder.

Mommy was flipping pancakes in her new kitchen. Papi had just remodeled the kitchen for Mommy in shades of pale yellow and royal blue. He'd built an island in the center, with yellow cabinets trimmed in dark blue all around it. The linoleum was a pattern of white, yellow, and blue squares. With her new kitchen, Mommy was always cooking up something.

"Mommy, Mommy . . . loooook!" I screamed.

"Stop hopping around my damn kitchen, girl. What do you want?" she asked as she turned around. She didn't even have to think twice about what had happened, who had done it, or why.

"Krystal . . . Angel . . . Get down these stairs now! You have five seconds, and if I have to come upstairs to get you, believe me, you will regret it!" she belted out. "Honey, come here." Mommy motioned for me to come into her arms, swooped me up, and hugged me tight.

Krystal and Angel made it downstairs in record time. Mommy wasn't big on corporal punishment, but that day, she really let them have it. She gave it to them right there in her beautiful kitchen, with the spatula she was flipping pancakes with. Moments later, Papi appeared and had to peel her off of those two. All the while I was bawling about my hair.

"That's enough, Miriam. Leave these two alone now. I have an idea that will fix them even more than the beating they just got," Papi said, remaining collected.

Half an hour later, I'd finally stopped crying and finished eating my breakfast. Mommy and I were sitting at the table, reviewing the do's and don'ts of appropriate camp behavior, when Papi returned with Krystal and Angel on each side. Papi had made it so that we'd all have short hair that summer, all less than three inches. Their eyes were bloodshot, and dried tears streaked their cheeks. Mommy laughed right in their faces; I guess we all looked pretty funny-looking. The laughter sent them bolting up the stairs in tears.

My sisters ended up getting the short end of the stick that time. By the end of the summer, my hair had grown down to my shoulders, while theirs was only about double the length from when Papi first chopped it off. They have never forgiven me for that day, as if it were my fault.

There was one other major event, that I can recall, anyway, that really pushed us further apart. Another summer, six years later, Papi and Mommy organized a graduation party for Krystal and me. She was graduating high school, and I had just finished junior high. Angel was entering her junior year that fall.

In our household we weren't allowed to date until we were sixteen. I was fourteen at the time. Angel had always been a bit like Brittany when it comes to men. Not quite as bad, though.

Two weeks prior to graduation, I was searching for my satin slip to wear under the dress Mommy had made for me. Upon opening the door to the laundry room, in the basement, all I could see was the black, hairy booty of some guy and Angel stuck up underneath him. I screamed in disgust.

"What are you doing, Angel? You are so nasty!" I hollered.

"Get outta here, you stupid Spanish nigger. If you tell Mommy or your stupid Papi, I'm gonna kick your ugly spic ass."

That was all she had to say. I had had my share of ass kickings from those two, and I had learned that reporting them just earned me another ass whooping. I walked out, defeated. The last time we had had a falling-out, they'd jumped me and locked me in the closet until they saw Papi's truck pulling up from work. I knew better than to tell him what they'd done to me. So I didn't.

On graduation day, I looked radiant in my home-made white dress. It had an empire waist with a satin sash that gathered in the back. Mommy had paid special attention to ensure the open back was just closed enough to cover the big tan birthmark on my back, which I absolutely hated and still do. It just drew way too much attention, and everyone thought I had been burned in a fire. Krystal had opted to purchase a dress. I guess she felt she was too good to wear a homemade dress, but for me, it was an honor.

My crush at the time had just finished his freshman year. His name was Walter, and he was my best friend's older brother. So you know I was at her house all the time, right? She and I always visited his basketball practices to root for him. Walter Cummings. I will never forget that name or that day.

After my ceremony was over, we all were whisked away to Krystal's. I told Papi that I had to visit the girl's room before we left, and he agreed to wait out front for me. I ran into Walter on the way out.

"You look kinda pretty with your hair up like that, Nia," he commented.

"Thank you," I answered sheepishly, suppressing the urge to scream.

"Can I get a hug?" he asked, spreading his arms wide.

"Sure."

As I reached out to hug him, he pulled me in for my first kiss ever—tongue and everything. It was actually pretty gross, now that I think about it, with his tongue everywhere but in my mouth, where it belonged. But at the time, you couldn't tell me nothing; he was the best kisser in the world. After it ended, I stood there frozen, and he just walked away, with his cool limp.

"Nia, come on, *bonita*. We are about to leave you. What are you doing anyway? Waiting for a personal invitation? *Si tengo que decirlo de nuevo* . . ." Papi began as he threw his hands in the air in frustration.

"Coming, Papi," I yelled, thankful that he hadn't come thirty seconds earlier. Then he really would have broken me down in Spanish. I couldn't concentrate after that. I was in ecstasy for the remainder of the day, until after dinner.

Of course, Mommy invited everyone Krystal and I had ever met to the house afterward. My best friend, Katrina, and Walter were included. Dinner was an exotic array of foods. Mommy had prepared everything from *arroz con pollo* to curry goat, collard greens, cornbread, red beans and rice, and potato salad, to name just a few. For dessert, Mommy sent me to the store for some Cool Whip to top the homemade apple pie, sweet potato pie, ice cream, and peach cobbler.

On the way back home, I felt a trickling down my leg. When I looked down, blood was running down my shin, ever so slowly. At fourteen, I wasn't startled by my period. I was expecting it any day. But in my perfect white dress on the most perfect day of my life?

I sprinted the rest of the way home, dropped the bag at the door, and darted upstairs. I literally kicked the bathroom door open, because I was so damn mad. The door flung open, and I saw Walter standing there and Angel kneeling before him, with his dick in her hand. She'd probably just taken it out of her mouth.

"You bitch!" I yelled. As angry as I was, there was no way in hell Angel could have beaten me that day.

I jumped on her ass like she was a trampoline. Walter jetted. Guess he feared he might be next.

I whooped her tail like there was no tomorrow. The best part about it was that no one could hear me throwing her around, because Papi had his merengue blasting and everyone was laughing and having a great time. I had learned not to leave any facial scarring, so Mommy and Papi wouldn't find out. Krystal and Angel had inflicted upon me plenty of leg, stomach, and back bruises in my day, so I knew the technique.

My dress was ruined, and Angel didn't dare tell on me. That was the day the tables turned. She never messed with me again. And, with Krystal gone off to college, she wasn't so damn tough anymore.

The next day, I saw Walter at the Yerwood Center, playing basketball with his friends. The place was packed since everyone had just gotten out of school for the summer break. I was with Katrina and a few other chicks, who I can't really remember. When the game was over, everyone crowded around the court to socialize. Walter walked over to my group and started teasing me about the previous day. He was calling me Carrie, exposing my little bloody secret to the whole gym. He jumped in the air, with a karate kick, to mimic my moves.

"What? You never saw a dick before?" Walter asked.

"Shut up, Walter, and leave her alone," Katrina said, sticking up for me.

You know black folks . . . when they see a little

drama brewing, things get a little quieter. Everyone started crowding around us.

"You wasn't saying all that when you told me I was pretty yesterday and was kissing me all up in the hallway," I said, standing up for myself.

"Oooh . . . damn . . . Ha-ha-ha-ha . . . You sprung, nigga!" sounded from the spectators.

Walter's face mutated from embarrassment to indignation in a matter of seconds. Then he replied, "I would never kiss a Spanish fly . . . and, yeah, I said you were pretty . . . pretty ugly!"

Brittany

The transition from summer to autumn had finished. Autumn's cool breath had crept up on us, with a promise to get even cooler. I was sitting on my queen-sized bed in T-shirt and panties, with my hands arched over my head, trying in vain to wrap my hair. Frustrated, I threw my big black brush to the foot of my bed and gave up, with half of my hair slicked perfectly behind my ear and the other half strewn over my face.

All set for bed, I tuned into *The Cosby Show* on Nick at Nite and turned off the overhead light. A second later, Tangie switched the light back on and stood in my doorway.

I was hoping for a pleasant exchange, because we'd been arguing over the smallest things that entire week. This week wasn't too much different than the previous six weeks since she'd moved in with me. It was just that lately, I was running out of patience, and she was running out of chances.

Her laziness drove me insane. She'd lie around

all day, doing nothing but eating, sleeping, and leaving dishes around for me to bitch about when I got home from work. Tangie even took it upon herself to use my perfume, scented lotions, tampons, and whatever else she felt she needed whenever she liked.

As soon as my eyes adjusted from the darkness to light, I realized the little bitch was wearing my chain-link Guess belt around her narrow hips.

"Take my damn belt off now," I yelled, almost springing out of the bed.

"Damn, what's the point of having a big sister if you can't even wear her shit?" she snidely replied, unclasping the belt and throwing it on my mahogany dresser. Then Tangie turned to leave.

"What did you want, anyway?" I asked, realizing that I had jumped down her throat before she could say what she'd come to my room to say.

"Nothing now," she replied, with a wave of her hand. "Fuck it."

"Oh, well," I said, shrugging my shoulders and pulling the sheets back over my body. "And come turn my fucking light back off!" I screamed.

Tangie stormed back into my room and shut the light off, with a loud slap to my switch. It took all my strength not to say something to her.

"Oh, well," she agreed, walking back down the hall.

I was annoyed to the highest point of annoyance. "Why the fuck you always gotta have the last word?" I yelled to her.

Tangie was in the kitchen by then. "Why *you* always gotta have the last word?" she mimicked as I heard the refrigerator door slam.

"Bitch," I whispered, figuring she was probably saying the same thing about me at that same moment.

Our relationship had reached an all-time low for childish and immature behavior. And every little issue was intensified by our inherited explosive island tempers. At that point, I was so pissed that I couldn't force myself to sleep. Propping my pillows against the headboard and sitting up, I began channel surfing to find something more interesting to watch. I could hear Tangie's muffled voice. She was talking shit and slamming pots around as she made herself something to eat.

After a hilarious episode of *Everybody Loves Raymond,* I couldn't believe Tangie had the nerve to be standing in my doorway again. I gave her a "don't start nothing, won't be nothing" look.

"Brittany, why didn't you send for me?" Tangie said out of nowhere. She'd caught me off guard, and I wasn't even sure what she was talking about. She suddenly looked eerily innocent and youthful, unlike the fiery superbitch she'd been only moments before. "I mean," she continued, "I know you wanted to finish school and everything. But I just figured once you got out and got a good job, you'd want me to move in with you." Tangie's eyes shifted around the room and didn't reach my face once.

"I . . . I never knew you wanted to live with me—," I began, but she cut me off.

"You would've known if you'd ever called me," she said, with a little bit of attitude seeping back into her voice.

"Don't even act like that, Tangie. I called you," I

said, trying to defend myself when I knew damn well she was right.

"Yeah, only when I left you messages on your machine. You never once picked up the phone unless I'd called you first!" The bitch was back.

"Does it matter who called who? We spoke, didn't we?"

"It *does* matter. You're my big sister. You were supposed to show me that you cared about me."

"I sent you half the rent money I got for the condo every month when I was in school." We were both yelling again by then.

"I could've gone without your fucking money, Brittany. Auntie Niki had plenty of that. But obviously neither one of you bitches knows how to show love with anything but your money or your pussy!"

"You ungrateful little tramp! Auntie Niki took you in when no one else cared enough to. And, I took you in after she didn't even care anymore." At that point I was talking to myself, because Tangie had stormed down the hall.

I sprang out of bed and followed her to the spare bedroom, where I found her packing up her stuff.

"Oh, so you're leaving? You don't have anyone else!" I yelled. "Where you think you're going at this time of night?"

"As if you care," she cried. "Just leave me alone. Why don't you just go back to your room and wait by the phone for one of your men to call you for a booty call. That's all you're good for, anyway!"

My phone began ringing, just in time to prevent Tangie from catching a beat down. I was torn between finishing up the fight with my sister and knowing who was calling.

"Hello," I answered, out of breath after sprinting to the cordless in the spare room.

"Did I catch you at a bad time?" Shari asked.

"Actually, yes. This little girl has lost her damn mind, disrespecting me in my own house. I'm about to kick her ass up in here!" I screamed, losing control.

"You ain't gonna do shit," Tangie said, rolling her neck and looking as if she was daring me to step to her.

"What happened?" Shari asked, panicking.

I was strolling around the room, heated, trying my best not to bust Tangie in the head with the phone I was holding. She wouldn't shut her mouth. At that point, as she was throwing all her stuff into suitcases, she was calling me every name in the book.

"Remember, Brittany, that's your sister!" Shari screamed. "Do you want me to come over?"

"Hell, no! She's getting outta my house tonight. Actually, in the next five minutes, 'cause that's all she has until I go apeshit in here!"

"Where is she going?" Shari asked, more concerned than I was.

"I don't know and I don't care! The little bitch can sleep on the front porch for all I care," I told Shari. "What you say?" I asked Tangie, who was still going off at the mouth.

"Ignore her, Brittany!" Shari instructed me. "Put her on the phone."

"Why?" I asked, stopping in my tracks and giving Tangie the serious ice grill.

"Just put her on the phone!" Shari yelled.

"Somebody wants to talk to you," I yelled, throwing the phone at Tangie's chest. It bounced off her chest and onto the bed.

"Hello," Tangie fumed, with her raspy voice. I could hear a series of "no," "hell no," "nope," "never," "I don't know," then finally an "ask her."

"Here," Tangie said, throwing the phone back at me, but I was prepared, so I caught it.

"Brittany," Shari said, "let her sleep there one more night. I told her that she can stay with me and Dex for a few weeks. She moves into the dorms in January, right?"

"Yeah," I answered, eyeing Tangie, who was now standing against the wall, with her arms folded across her chest. "All I know is that she has to get up out of here. I guess I shouldn't let her sleep outside tonight. Okay, you're right. Thank you, Shari. You know you really don't have to . . . all right . . . yes, I'll try . . . I promise . . . I'm going straight to my room . . . okay, love you, too."

Finally calm, I hung up the phone. Tangie was sitting on the bed, with mascara tears on her cheeks.

"Be ready by nine thirty tomorrow morning, and I'll give you a ride to Shari's house," I whispered, not looking at her.

She didn't reply, and I wasn't looking for one, either. I left her room, slamming the door behind me.

Shari

Tangie arrived at about ten thirty the next morning. Brittany waved to me from her car as I greeted Tangie at my doorstep. That damn Brittany didn't even have the decency to get out of the car to introduce us.

Even though I knew neither hide nor hair of this girl I was letting in my house, I knew Brittany. And girlfriend is a trip. My heart always went out to children of broken homes. Obviously, Tangie had experienced rejection from the only family she knew, and she still persevered and was on the path to college. I didn't want a little squabble between siblings to jeopardize her plans for the future. Dex wondered why I got in the middle of it all, too, but in the end, he stood behind my decision. My big heart was one of the reasons he loved me so much.

"Hey, Tangie. Finally we get to meet. I'm Shari." I extended my hand.

She pulled me in for a huge sister friend hug.

"I really appreciate this, Shari," she said as she patted me on the back.

"Mi casa es su casa," I replied as I pulled her inside. "Come on in here, girl, and get out of this rain."

Tangie stood at about five-seven. This girl was beautiful; she reminded me of myself in my younger days. Remember when Jada Pinkett Smith used to wear her hair short? That is who she favored, with that short, curly fro look going on. Surprisingly, she was dressed pretty casual. I guess I had expected some kinda ghetto hoochie mamma with a pierced eyebrow, four-inch red nails, and a blond wig to be on the other side of the door. That's what I get for assuming. Actually, what she was wearing looked like something right out of my own closet. Tangie wore low-rise, boot-cut jeans, with a ribbed black turtleneck and a pair of stiletto-heeled boots. I wanted to ask her where she'd bought the damn things. Sista's boots were bad.

"Dexter, come down here and meet Tangie," I screamed up to the attic.

Dex writes poetry in his spare time, which is usually every Saturday morning. He refurbished the attic to look like a jazz club. Hanging on the walls, which were painted black, are framed pictures of Ella Fitzgerald, Miles Davis, and B.B. King, and a poster of Denzel from *Mo' Better Blues*.

Several minutes later Dex decided to bless us with his presence. Tangie and I were gabbing over toast and herbal tea. She was explaining to me how half of the things I had heard about her were not true. Tangie said her aunt Niki never had kids of her own, so she didn't know how to handle the smallest amount of stress.

"Good morning, ladies. You must be Tangerine." He exploded in laughter.

"You're so corny, Dex," I said, laughing a bit. "Sorry, honey, but my husband thinks he is the next Chris Rock." I gave Tangie a "you'll have to excuse this fool" look. "Bay, this is Tangela, but she likes to be called Tangie."

He grinned. "Nice to meet you. I'm Dex, and I *am* the next Chris Rock. I don't care what y'all say. Do you guys want some real breakfast? I'm in a cooking mood. How about some country omelets, sausage, grits, homemade biscuits, and fresh-squeezed orange juice?"

"Uh-oh. He's trying to show off now, Tangie. Sure, Bay, hook us up."

"Oh stop, Shari," he explained. "You know I love cooking for you."

"You love to, but how often do you actually do it?" I laughed.

Over our smorgasbord of breakfast, we went over the rules of the household.

"Although you will only be here a short time, there are a couple of rules that we need to discuss with you," I said.

"Okay, I understand," Tangie replied.

"Anything and everything you see here, you are welcome to as long as you do so with respect. We bought you three calling cards to use for your long-distance phone calls. We don't mind you having company, male or female, but we would appreciate that they stayed in your room and not in the common areas of the house. No overnight visitors. No drinking. What you do outside of this house, of course, we cannot control, but we don't want to be held responsible for allowing underage drinking."

"I don't drink," Tangie assured me.

"Just a couple more things. Dex and I both have very early workdays and usually go to sleep before eleven. If you need to get calls any later than ten at night, have them page you and then you call them back, because the ringing of the phone can be very disturbing if we are trying to sleep. No smoking in the house."

"I don't smoke."

"Okay, I think that is about it . . . Oh yeah, please have your callers address both Dex and me with respect. None of that 'Yo is Tangie there?' And clean up after yourself. Dex and I don't want to clean up after you."

"Agreed," Tangie said as she stood up and shook my hand all businesslike.

"One more thing. I need you to sign this, just to make sure everything is understood," I said as I handed her a contract outlining everything I'd just said.

"Shari, you are being ridiculous," Dex complained.

"It's no problem, Dex." said Tangie. "I understand that if I have to live here, there are certain things that I will have to respect. I don't mind. I am so grateful that I am willing to do anything Shari wants."

Tangie took the pen and signed on the dotted line.

"Whew, I think I caught niggeritis up in here.

Can you show me to my room so I can get my nap on?" asked Tangie.

"Sure. I'll grab your bags. Just follow me," Dex offered.

Our guest room is located on the main level. That is one of the things that attracted me to this house. Guests can have privacy, and more importantly, Dex and I can have our privacy. About five minutes later, Dex joined me in the kitchen to clean up the disaster area he'd created cooking breakfast.

"Hey, Bay, let me help you," he offered. "You wash. I'll dry."

"Thanks," I said, handing him the dish towel.

"You know you were a little harsh on Tangie, don't you?"

"I know, but I am not used to sharing my space with anyone else," I defended myself. "I want her to know up front that I am not her aunt. I don't love her, so I am not going to tolerate any foolishness in my home. Point blank."

"I understand. I just felt bad for the girl is all. But you are absolutely right." He kissed my forehead, and I handed him another plate to dry.

"I remember when I was her age. Twenty is such an awkward age. It's like you still have the mind of a teenager, but you are stuck in a grown woman's body, and you have a grown woman's responsibilities. It's a big adjustment. You couldn't pay me to start the twenties over again."

Brittany

"I don't have any ugly friends," I boasted. "So you're wrong. Believe me, your friend would love Nia. She's about five-three. Beautiful body. She's the color of brown sugar over candied yams. Her hair is long, like mine, but it's naturally curly. Remember Chili, from the group TLC? They could pass as sisters."

"Well, the other one must be ugly, because you never meet a group of sistas that are all pretty. Never." That was Warren, with another one of his ignorant-ass statements.

"First of all, her name is Shari, and she is beautiful, too. She's also very married."

"Married!" he asked, with astonishment. "How old is she?"

"She's only a year older than me. She's twenty-eight."

"Well, being married doesn't mean anything

these days. I've been with plenty of married women. What does she look like?"

Yet another ignorant blunder that I ignored. "She's about five-five. I always call her caramel apple, because of her complexion and round face. Her hair is dyed a golden blond and cut into a bob that hugs each side of her chin. Her best feature is her almond-shaped light hazel eyes. Is that good enough for you?"

"Well, I'll believe it when I see it. My boy needs to date someone, and soon. He's been in this slump ever since his girl left him."

"I'll run it by Nia. Then I'll get back to you," I lied. "I'm sure she'll be down."

I knew full well that I'd have to do some heavy convincing to get Nia to go on a double date with Warren and me. Especially a blind date.

Warren was dressed in mostly black, which is my favorite color. That bald head of his was covered with a black derby. His muscular chest and arms were accented by a tight Lycra shirt. He wore beige slacks that were perfectly starched and pleated, with a small cuff at the bottom. Last, but not least, Warren had donned black suede shoes that complemented his black suede coat. Damn. He looked good enough to serve on a platter.

After our plans to go on a double date next weekend were made, it was time to eat the dinner I'd prepared. Four-cheese lasagna. I'd have him wrapped around my little finger after he experienced my skills in the kitchen.

He devoured three plates full and asked for the recipe.

"A chef never tells her secrets," I said.

"I thought it was magicians that never tell their secrets," he challenged.

"Well, when I cook, it's like magic," I fired back.

We laughed and finished the bottle of wine he'd brought over. After about a half an hour more of joking around, it was time for dessert. I cleared the table and brought out a bowl full of fresh strawberries and a smaller bowl with whipped cream.

"Nice, very nice," he said and smiled mischievously.

"Are you referring to me or the berries?" I flirted, placing my hands on my slim hips.

"I'm talking about you and what I'm going to do with those strawberries and whipped cream." Warren started walking backwards toward my living room while giving me the "come here" motion with his fudge index finger. I floated to him like a person lost in the desert to a mirage.

Once in the living room, I walked over to the radio and tuned in to *The Quiet Storm* on WBLS. The fireplace illuminated the room just enough for us to see each other up close. Very close. We popped open a bottle of chilled Veuve Cliquot and poured two glasses. With the blanket positioned in front of the fireplace, and us lounging squarely in the center of it, Warren started to feed me the whipped cream–covered strawberries. I enjoyed watching him watch me slowly consume the fruit. I could tell by the way his eyes followed my every move that he wanted me. When he could no longer resist, he started kissing me with the strawberry still in my mouth. It slid back and forth between our tongues. Then he pulled away and ate my strawberry.

Now, without the strawberry, he kissed me again. Slow, deliberate movements. He dipped back into the bowl, but this time he rubbed the cream from my neck to the top of my cleavage. By the way, I purposely made sure I displayed my 36Ds whenever possible. His tongue, soft like silk, caressed my senses as well as my skin. Soon the bowls were empty, and there we sat, sipping the last of the champagne. The warmth of the fire bounced off our faces as we stared into each other's eyes.

"I'll be back," I said, feeling all tingly from the champagne. "I'm going to freshen up a little."

We both knew what that meant. Truthfully, my intentions weren't to make love to him that night, but I just couldn't help myself. Also, I knew that it was what he wanted. Sometimes it doesn't hurt to give a man what he wants.

Women are always trying to hold out on men to gain some kind of respect. The truth is, a man knows what kind of relationship he wants to pursue with a woman after their first meeting. He can sense if she's wife material, a ho, a gold digger, or whatever falls in between. Also, by no action of your own can you change their mind. So you might as well just go with what you feel. If you feel like fucking him on the first date, fuck him. That's my philosophy.

I decided on the newest addition to my Frederick's of Hollywood collection. A short, sheer baby-doll nightie. Gold to match my skin. Underneath, a matching gold thong. I untied my hair so that it hung wildly down my back. After performing my Chanel routine, squirting the fragrance very strategically, I returned to the fireplace.

Warren tried not to show his excitement, but I could feel the air get thicker when I appeared before him. No sooner had I sat back down than he was all over me. I lifted his shirt over his head to expose his sculpted chest. The glow hit every chisel mark of his six-pack.

"Girl, you look so sexy."

"Yeah, I know," I whispered as I straddled him.

I finished undressing him until he lay there with nothing but an impressive erection. I started at his already-hardened nipples, flicking my tongue wildly over them. He grabbed two handfuls of my full ass with his strong hands. Then he released the grip of his right hand and slapped me. The vibration that follows a good slap on a healthy ass always turns men on.

I massaged his erection with my hands and then with my tongue and lips. That is my specialty. As I performed, he twisted my nipples, slapped my ass, and squeezed my breasts in ecstasy. When I thought he couldn't handle it anymore, I climbed on top of him and pushed him inside of me. I rotated my hips up and down, back and forth. Fast and furious, then slow and deep.

By the time we both climaxed, I was still on top. I climbed down from his tower of pleasure, we wiped off our privates, and Warren fell fast asleep.

After cleaning our mess and doing the dishes, I took a long, hot shower. While in the steaming shower, I pretended he was watching me as I slowly lathered my body. He gazed at my every move, loving every curve. My fantasy shower ended when the water turned cold. I threw on my short peach silk robe and headed back to the fireplace.

He hadn't moved an inch. I chuckled at the sight of what was once big and throbbing. It was now a limp, little noodle.

"Warren, wake up," I whispered in his ear as I climbed back on top of him. "Come get in my bed."

"Oh shit!" he spat. "What time is it? I gotta go. Gotta get up early in the morning." He pushed me off of him and onto the floor.

In one smooth motion, he was fully dressed and on his way.

"Thanks, baby," he murmured as he raced out the door. "See you later."

Nia

I had a blind date with Brittany and her new man friend. I could've strangled her when she told me that she'd already told Warren I'd obliged. Since I hadn't been out in a long time, I was a little excited. After rummaging through my wardrobe, I decided on basic black. I wore my skintight stretch bootlegs with a black shirt that hung off one shoulder to match. Sounds boring, but I spiced it up with my red and black leopard-print belt, my new red boots, and a red handbag to match. It's all about accessorizing!

I was looking in the mirror, wondering what to do with my hair. Couldn't decide, so I gave Brittany a ring.

"Brittany, what are you doing with your hair? I can't think of anything."

"Bitch, you should be ready by now," she reprimanded me. "We're on our way out the door to come get you."

"I'm dressed," I assured her while tossing my

damp hair around in the mirror. "I just need to do my hair."

"What are you wearing?" Brittany asked impatiently.

"Black pants."

"Why can't you try to look sexy? Damn, Nia. You're going on a date, not to the office!"

"I know how to dress myself, Brittany. I don't have to let it all hang out like you."

"Fuck you, girl. Anyways, you should wear it down and just keep it curly. We're not going anywhere special. We'll be there in ten minutes. Bye!"

CLICK!

That worked out great. I was glad I didn't have to blow-dry my mop out. With the extra time, I decided to make myself a cosmopolitan to calm my escalating nervous energy.

Fifteen minutes later, Brittany and friends showed up at my door. The two Olympic figures behind her could have passed for brothers. I was duly impressed. Dressed impeccably from head to toe, these guys had class. Or at least they knew how to look like they did. As they stepped in, Brittany introduced me to the slimmer of the two.

"Nia, this is Kori. Kori, this is Nia. Fine, ain't she?" She nudged him.

"Nice to meet you, Kori." I said and blushed.

As I attempted to shake his hand, he reached out and pulled me in to his chest. He proceeded to planting an innocent kiss on my cheek. His Egyptian musk aroma made me feel like a mermaid drifting on a smooth wave. I love it when a man smells good. As I backed away, he donned a confident smile. He stood there looking like Morris Chestnut's stunt double, with that beautiful smile.

"Well, Nia, get your coat, girl," Brittany instructed. "Let's go!"

I headed down my hallway, and I heard Brittany shuffling after me.

"Bring a bathing suit, a sexy one. We are going to this after-hours place with private Jacuzzi rooms," she said once she reached my room and closed the door behind her.

"Brittany, I know you didn't tell those brothas that I was going to no Jacuzzi!" I whined, stomping my feet like a toddler throwing a tantrum.

"Would you loosen up? Your body is tight. What's the problem?" She was serious.

"The problem is that I don't know either one of these men. They don't need to be seeing me half naked!" I was serious, and I was pissed, ready to call the whole thing off. Brittany tends to forget that not everyone is as nasty as she is. She does have a magic way with words, though, so after about five minutes of our bickering and her promising to treat me to a manicure and pedicure, I grudgingly agreed. Good thing I'd just shaved my bikini line, because if not, Kori would have been scared to get in the water with me. Also, I wouldn't have heard the end of it from Brittany. Finally, I grabbed my red coat, and we all headed out the door.

We rode in Warren's Lexus to the restaurant. Conversation was flowing lovely. The guys were so damn charming. And funny. We were all having a ball. Over dinner, I learned that Kori was a real estate broker. Apparently, a very successful one. He'd sold Warren his condo about a year ago, and ever since, they'd been road dogs. Warren and Brittany couldn't keep their hands off each other from the moment we walked in the door.

"Y'all need to get a room or something," Kori joked. Warren and Brittany had just shared their third tongue kiss in less than ten minutes.

"Don't hate the playa. Hate the game," Warren said, with a sexy wink to Brittany.

"I don't know what kind of playa you supposed to be, with all that PDA," Kori started. "You look more like a pussy-whipped fool."

Brittany choked with laughter on her martini, and I laughed so hard that I had to cover my mouth with the white linen napkin on my lap to prevent any food from escaping.

"Nigga, you just wish you could be doin' the same with Nia right now," Warren retorted, throwing a tiny piece of biscuit at Kori's chest.

"You got me on that one, dog," Kori admitted, sounding only half joking. "You right. I'm hatin'."

I could tell he was only half joking, because as he said it, his hand found its way to my knee. Not the type of girl to make a scene, I smiled politely at his gesture, just hoping he didn't push his luck by moving any farther up.

"Nia," Kori said, facing me and rubbing my knee. My stomach began to flutter. I didn't feel comfortable with him feeling me up, but I played it cool. "Do *you* believe in public displays of affection?"

Oh, that's what PDA means, I thought, feeling totally out of the loop. I exhaled my nervous energy before answering.

"I think there's a time and place for everything," I began.

"See, even Nia thinks y'all are being tacky!" Kori yelled, thinking he'd proved his point.

Brittany's drunk ass started cracking up. Warren's mouth was too full with stuffed shrimp to utter his rebuttal.

"But," I continued, "sometimes when you're head over heels for someone, you don't care who's watching. All you know is that you're feeling that person, and that's all that matters."

Kori obviously took my comment literally, 'cause he moved his hand up to my inner thigh.

"Oh yeah," Kori said, slightly squeezing my leg.

"I just don't give a fuck," Brittany quipped.

I was grateful for her sudden outburst; it broke the dense cloud of air that had just formed between Kori and me. I turned my glare from him to my tipsy friend, who had her thin index finger pointed in the air like she had an important message for us to hear.

"That's why I do it," she continued, taking another swig of alcohol. She swallowed a deep gulp. "If people have a problem with it, then don't look. Right, baby?" Her voice was slurred, as she leered at Warren, then leaned over to stick her tongue back in his mouth.

There were four people at the table, but Brittany and Warren were definitely in their own world. After another cosmopolitan, Kori's groping didn't seem to bother me much. Thanks to the alcohol, I was finally at ease.

After cocktails, appetizers, entrees, after-dinner drinks, dessert, and coffee, our three-hour dinner ended. I was worn out from all the conversation and flirting. We boarded the Lexus again and were on our way. The Jacuzzi sounded really relaxing at that point. I was actually looking forward to it. As we waited in the line for this Jacuzzi club, throbbing hip-hop beats filled the streets. I nudged Brittany.

"I pictured this place to be a lot less crowded and a little more peaceful." I whispered to her.

"Girl, this is where all the celebrities come," she sang as she did this little booty dance. "Last week I saw Jermaine Dupri up in here," she added.

This must be illegal, I thought as we entered the club. On every speaker, there were women wearing nothing but glitter, shaking all over the place. The middle of the club is where the bar and dance floor were. A great majority of the girls were dancing in bikinis, with strings up their asses. Definitely not my crowd! The perimeter was lined with what they called "private Jacuzzi rooms." Private? Glass walls guarded each room.

Inside, activities ranged from kissing and lesbian licking to all-out sex. Women's wet breasts were pressed against the glass as men took them from behind. They were on display and didn't even care. I couldn't hide my astonishment. Kori's pearly whites were stretched across his face when my eyes finally met his.

"You guys wanna share a room with us, or do you want your privacy?" he asked Warren.

"Privacy? You can't have any privacy in this place even if you wanted to," I yelled over the music.

"Well, we can go back to your place and get it on there," Kori said as he grabbed me around the waist.

"Are you fucking serious?" I replied. "I'm not having sex with you here, at my place, in a hotel, or in a goddamn palace. How dare you think I'm some kind of ho. I just met—"

Brittany grabbed my arm and started dragging me toward the bathroom, all the while apologizing to Kori for my actions and promising to be right back.

"What is wrong with you?" she asked. "Why do you always have to act like your shit don't stink? You don't have to have sex with him. Just have a little fun. You're embarrassing me."

"I don't give a damn about embarrassing you, or myself, at this point. I'm leaving. I don't believe you brought me here." I was still screaming on my way out the door.

The entire cab ride home, I was fuming. Times like that make me wonder why I am friends with Brittany. Once I reached home, I made a cup of tea and popped two Advil because my head was pounding. After a steamy shower, I felt relaxed again and decided to call Shari. When she answered in a raspy tone, I realized that it was 3:00 a.m. and she was definitely sleeping.

"Sorry, girl. I'll call you tomorrow," I said.

We hung up, and I drifted to sleep.

Shari

We hadn't seen that Mike guy since the first time we'd visited Catalina's, so we figured it was safe to make this place our regular spot. Nia said that she wasn't feeling well and couldn't meet with us. Let the truth be told, I think she was still mad at Brittany about the Jacuzzi club incident. When she told me about what happened, all I could do was laugh. Nia should've known better than to hook up with someone Brittany had suggested.

Of course, I arrived first, so I ordered a frozen Kahlua cappuccino. Catalina's was the only place in town that I could find this drink. It's made with vanilla ice cream, chocolate syrup, Kahlua, and cappuccino mix. I know because I asked the waitress for the recipe and began making them at home for me and Dex.

Brittany made a very dramatic—Marilyn Monroe type—entrance. She's such a drama queen. You would have thought she was auditioning for a Pantene commercial the way she was slinging her bouncy mane off her shoulders.

"I am so sorry I'm late," she managed between heavy pants.

"It's okay. My drink hasn't even arrived yet." It was lunchtime, so Catalina's was more packed than usual, and service was a little slow.

"What did you get? That milk shake thing again?"

"Yes, as a matter of fact, I did." I chuckled.

Just then, the waitress returned with my tall frozen delight covered with whipped cream and a cherry. My eyes lit up like a child blowing out birthday candles.

"I'll have a club soda with a lemon and lime," Brittany ordered.

"Something must be wrong with you," I teased. "No martini today?"

"No, not today. Warren stood me up last night. I called him every ten minutes for an hour, and then I just gave up. He finally called after midnight and promised to treat me to breakfast this morning. I'm embarrassed to say, but he stood me up again!" Brittany pouted.

"Mmmm, mmm, mmm," was all I could say as I shook my head from side to side and sipped my drink. Brittany wasn't used to getting stood up. Usually, men were hounding her. Warren was turning the tables on her, and she couldn't handle it.

"You're not interested in knowing how Tangie's doing?" I asked, knowing I was pushing it.

"Not even a little bit," Brittany answered through tight lips. I decided to leave it alone. Being that

I'm an only child, I didn't feel right lecturing her on sisterhood.

Our food arrived, and everything looked scrumptious. To lighten up the mood, I decided to ask her about that double date she and Nia went on. I needed another good laugh. Her version was about the same as the one Nia told me, so I asked her what happened after Nia left.

"Do you know what DP stands for?" she asked, with a devilish smirk.

"DP? No."

"Double penetration," she said matter-of-factly.

"No, you didn't!" I squealed, putting my hand over my mouth.

She put her hand in the air, expecting a high five. I left her hanging. My mouth was wide open in disgust. I knew she was wild, but damn! I was full of questions.

"So you had both of them inside of you at once?" I asked. I was genuinely curious.

"One in the front entrance, and one in the back exit. I always see those white girls on the Playboy channel doing it, so I wanted to try it. Kori looked so pitiful after Nia left, I couldn't leave his fine ass hanging."

Brittany started picking the tomatoes out of her salad and placing them on her napkin. "Didn't I ask for *no* tomatoes?" she vented. "Damn!"

"So you had a threesome . . . in a hot tub . . . in front of the entire club?" I was shocked.

"Yes, I did," she bragged. "With all the wild stuff going on in there, people actually stopped at our room to watch us. We stole the show! No one else was as freaky as us that night. I am a celebrity there now. They gave me free passes for the whole year." The way she beamed indicated she was actually proud of herself.

"Didn't that hurt? Dex tries to stick his dick back there every once and a while, and I can't take it. That shit is too painful."

"Yes, it hurt. Like hell. But after I relaxed, I enjoyed it. Especially after the small crowd of spectators gathered. I loved it. Don't knock it until you try it."

"Would you ladies like another drink?" It was our waitress. She was wearing all black and had a pen sticking behind both ears and one in her hand.

"Yes, please," I whispered.

"I'll have an Absolut martini with a twist of lemon and lime," said Brittany.

Brittany had snapped back to her regular self.

"You're disgusting. I hope you know that," I said as I popped the cherry from my drink, which I'd saved for last, into my mouth.

Our meal finished on a light note. After that DP story, though, I was a little wary of the decision I'd made to let Tangie stay with us. Did these sisters fight so much because they were a little too much alike?

Later that evening, I cooked Dex's favorite dinner, tuna casserole. I poured two glasses of chardonnay and lit candles all around.

"This is a setup," Dexter said as he entered the

dining room and noted the atmosphere. "What do you want, Shari? Whatever it is, you can have it. You don't have to wine and dine me." He lowered his head to kiss my cheek, which was our greeting ritual.

"Dang. I can't just be a good wife and cook my wonderful husband his favorite meal just because I love him?" I whined, pretending to be offended.

"If you say so," he replied sarcastically. "Where's Tangie?"

"She's back in her room, talking on the phone as usual," I said, pointing in the direction of our guest room.

"Don't you think she might want to eat, too?" Dex asked as he put his briefcase at the bottom of the stairs. Then he returned to the dining room.

"She's a big girl. She'll come eat if she's hungry."

"Yes, boss." Dex imitated the stereotypical slave voice. "How was your day at work?" he asked, talking normally again and taking the seat parallel to mine. "I got your message saying you were leaving early to meet Brittany for a late lunch."

"Yeah, I was just a little overwhelmed."

Since losing the best two jobs I'd ever had on less than honorable terms, it had been hard to find a decent-paying job with no references. I ended up taking a job as an administrative assistant, getting paid a fraction of what I had gotten at the bank and university.

Recently, my independently wealthy boss had decided he had nothing better to do with his money than to hire a girl fresh out of college to assist me.

Who ever heard of an administrative assistant with an assistant?

"Yeah, Becky was tap-dancing on my last good nerve," I complained, angrily slapping Dex's tuna casserole onto his plate. "She thinks she knows every damn thing."

"You know you're training your replacement, right?" Dex said.

"Yeah, I already figured as much," I sighed, fishing around in my dish with my fork.

"Or maybe even your future boss," Dex said, pointing his fork at me. "Pretty soon you'll be answering to her."

"Over my dead body. If that happens, I'll be out of there in a heartbeat."

"Why don't you just quit now, Bay?" Dex said, with a mouthful of food. "I make enough to cover us for a couple years. And, if not, I'll get a second job."

"Dexter, please." I waved him off. "I want to pull my weight around here."

"Okay. I offered." Dex put his hands in the air in defeat.

Dex had been telling me for the longest time to go back to school while I was still relatively young. Although I wanted to contribute financially, the prospect of going back to school was starting to sound very tempting.

After dinner, I poured two cups of coffee, his with a shot of whiskey and mine with a shot of Bailey's. Tangie emerged from the room, fully dressed.

"Want some tuna casserole?" Dex offered.

"I'm good, Dex," she answered politely as she

walked out the front door. "I have a dinner date, but thanks, anyway."

After Tangie left, Dex locked the door, and we headed upstairs to bed.

"Bay, I got a weird question for you," I said, with my best Clair Huxtable smile, as we lay in the bed watching TV and sipping our coffee.

"Shoot," he replied.

"You ever heard of DP?" I asked.

My question was followed by a barrel of laughter.

"You've had too much to drink, Bay," he snorted.

"Answer my question." I was a little tilted, but I still wanted to know.

"Of course, I have. You haven't?"

"No. Not until this afternoon."

He laughed like I'd just told him the funniest joke ever.

"I hope you don't want to try it, because I don't need another man that close to my Johnson."

"No, no. Someone I know did it and—"

"Brittany," he interrupted, knowing her reputation all too well.

"Who else?" I replied.

"Now does she really think any man would respect her after that? That's a little too freaky."

"Don't talk about my friend," I yelled as I playfully punched him in the shoulder.

He grabbed me and started tickling me softly all over.

"Let's go to sleep, Bay. I don't want to talk about Brittany anymore."

"Me, neither," I whispered, reaching over to turn off the lamp on my nightstand.

"C'mere, girl," Dex demanded, pulling me on top of him.

Brittany

As I stood in the long line at the bank, I observed everyday interactions. One of the people ahead of me was a mother chastising her son for picking his nose in public and wiping snot on his shirt. Yuck! I think my facial expression offended the mother, because when our eyes met, she was as red as a strawberry Jolly Rancher. She rolled her ice blue eyes at me and shot a killer glance my way. I laughed.

The man directly in front of me had Jherri Curl juice dripping down his neck, ever so slowly. I can't believe that people still sport those. His stone-washed jeans were about as tight as mine. Jherri had on some white snakeskin cowboy boots. He looked a hot mess. I chuckled aloud at the pitiful sight before me. Again, I wasn't as discreet as I thought. When our eyes made four, he smiled at me with his big, ashy lips. Of course! You can't have a Jherri curl and skintight jeans without two gold caps covering your two front teeth. Just as it looked like he was about to utter something ignorant, the teller yelled for the next customer to approach.

"Next!" yelled another teller. So I sashayed on over.

"Hello, beautiful," said the teller.

"Excuse me?" I said, with much attitude.

The man behind the counter was kinda cute, if anything at all. Only about five inches taller than me. Beige complexion. Medium build. Clean-cut. Very blah. Not my type.

"I said you're beautiful."

"Thank you. I'd like to deposit $150 into my checking account please," I stated professionally.

"You're not very friendly." He paused. "Are you having a bad day or something?" he asked, taking the money and beginning the transaction.

"That's none of your business. Please deposit my money and give me a receipt. Thank you," I replied, pausing to squint at his name tag. "Vaughn."

I was only that rude because I was in a rush: I only had twenty minutes left on my lunch break and still hadn't picked up any food.

He didn't say another word as he handed my receipt over and yelled, "NEXT!"

When I reached my car, I checked the receipt to make sure the idiot had put the money in the right account. There, in bold red letters, were his seven digits, followed by his name and a smiley face.

"How corny," I said aloud.

Back at work, it was hard to concentrate on anything but Warren.

I made a couple calls, got a temp to cover one of

my graphic artists for a week, made some minor changes to a PowerPoint presentation, ordered art supplies, drafted a memo to my creative team, and sent some files to the printer, but when I looked up, it was only three.

"Dammit!" I yelled. The day was dragging. My office door was open, so nosy Suzanne heard my outburst.

"Brittany, what's wrong, sweetie?"

I wanted to tell her that I was horny as all get out, and since she didn't have the tools for the job, she need not be concerned.

Suzanne danced her hundred-pound self into my office and took a seat in front of me. "Man problems?" she asked.

Suzanne was lucky she wasn't part of my team, because I would have told her ass to get back to work. But she was on Devon's team, and since I couldn't stand his uppity ass, I let Suzanne stay.

I always tried to remain as professional as possible in my dealings at work, never letting the two Brittanys collide.

"No, not man problems," I lied. "Not at all. This day is just dragging."

"You must have big plans for tonight, huh?" She shrugged her shoulders suggestively and winked her eye.

"Not really. Probably just a Blockbuster night for me. I'm just tired is all." I yawned to drive my point home.

No matter how much she pried into my business, I wouldn't relent. I don't let anything mess with my money, so the real me was checked at the office door every morning and picked up each night on the way out.

Devon walked by and lingered at my door, noticing Suzanne chatting it up with me.

"All right. Let me go," Suzanne said as she tossed her head in his direction. "He keeps swimming around here like a damn shark looking for prey. Damn! Can't even talk for five minutes," she complained, getting up to leave.

"All right, Suzanne. I'll talk to you later," I replied.

I text-messaged Warren and decided to do some filing while I awaited his return phone call.

It was four thirty when I finished filing and approving time sheets. And there was still no call from Mr. Warren Banks. I was so outta there. After e-mailing my approved time sheets to the payroll department, I grabbed my coat and left for the day.

When I reached home, I decided to call Warren. After one ring, his voice mail picked up.

"Hey, it's me. I was wondering if you wanted to come over tonight and have a little . . . I mean, a lot of fun. Be here by eight thirty. You know I have to go to work in the morning. Call me."

I soaked in my best Victoria's Secret bath oil. To set the mood, I lit candles all around, poured a glass of wine, and popped my Jaheim CD in the stereo in my bedroom. As I submerged my body in the water, I visualized Warren coming through the door, wearing nothing but a smile. His titanic presence made my heart beat and my softness throb. I reached down to feel my creamy juices in contrast to the thin water. That made me even hotter. My hands were his as I caressed my breasts and teased my nipples. I rubbed myself until my body jerked and I squealed with pleasure. So fresh and so clean and waiting on the man of my dreams.

By nine thirty, I realized that Warren had stood me up. I reached into my purse to get my vibrator. Yes, I carry it in my purse. You never know when you'll need to use it. But when I peered into the purse, right next to my "buddy" was my bank receipt, with Vaughn's name and number blinking like a red-light special.

Not Warren, but he'll do in a jam, I reassured myself, so I dialed.

"Hello," said a male voice.

"Hi, Vaughn. This is Brittany, the woman from . . ."

"I know who you are."

"Well, I was wondering if you wanted to come over tonight. I'm wearing a short silk bathrobe and a matching silk thong underneath. I've been thinking about how your tongue would feel exploring my body."

"Whoa. Slow down! We don't even know each other like that."

"You've been on my mind since the moment our eyes met," I lied. "Look. I'm horny, and I need you. I want you, so either you'll be here in less than thirty minutes, or you will have missed the opportunity of a lifetime." I hate that I had to proposition him.

Enough said. I gave my address, and he was on his way. Men. So weak.

Twenty minutes later Vaughn was standing at my front door. Surprisingly, he looked better than he had earlier that day. He even smelled better. I peeked around him to see what kind of car he drove, but I didn't see anything.

"Come on in," I sang.

By this time I'd consumed two more glasses of wine and was feeling very warm all over. With his average body and average looks, I was going to need at least one more glass to see past his mediocrity. I gave him a lap dance to turn myself on, since he couldn't arouse me. I pulled it out and climbed on top of it. I rode him like I'd done Warren just a week before. Ha! It was his loss!

Ten minutes later, he was done. I was done. I was contented for the moment, and he was on cloud nine.

"Call me," he said on his way out. "I had so much fun tonight."

"Okay," I replied. *Yeah, right!* I thought. *Don't hold your breath, sugar.*

Nia

Monday morning. Need I say more? Whoever plans meetings for eight thirty on a Monday morning must be stupid. I have the attention span of a two-year-old that early. To prevent nodding off, I doodled in my notebook and gulped down two cups of coffee.

I work as an account executive at Glow, the fourth best-selling hip-hop publication in the New York, New Jersey, and Connecticut area. Basically, what I do is find stores or venues that would like to sell the magazine and then make sure they remain happy with our business. My job entails making sure they pay us on time, visiting the stores to make sure we are displayed properly on their shelves, and kissing as much ass as possible to acquire new clients. So far this year, I head my department in sales and customer satisfaction.

Glow is a small company that consists of about thirty employees. Our goal is to expand our market by first targeting the major cities, like Chicago, Los Angeles, Houston, and D.C. That was what the meeting was about. They were planning to send one of the four top-selling account executives to each city to start marketing and, hopefully, secure some accounts. Right before Christmas, I was being shipped off on an all-expense-paid trip to Houston, Texas, for two weeks. Of course, I got the most challenging area, right? I was up for the challenge, though, especially since we'd get a tax-free thousand-dollar bonus for each customer we sign.

"Are there any questions or suggestions before we adjourn?" asked the president, Capri Ingram. She's a very fashionable young woman. I think she is in her early thirties. Girlfriend has it going on. Designer this, name brand that. It must be nice to have it like that. She's a young sista doing her thing, but what really bothers me about her is that she is easily threatened by other intelligent, fashionable young sistas. More specifically, me. Last month I suggested that we start including subscription cards in every issue to broaden our market and expand revenue.

Girlfriend said, "Nia, that is a very cute idea, but financially, we really aren't at a place where we can gamble on subscribers that decide they may or may not want to pay their bills on time. Right now we need to stick with more sound investments, such as bookstores, coffee shops, and convenience stores. But thanks anyway."

You're welcome, bitch.

"Nia, any new ideas this month?" Capri asked.

She smirked. I, and everyone else at the meeting, knew she was trying to be an asshole.

Yes, I have an idea. Why don't you stop being such a bitch and leave me the hell alone, tramp, I thought.

I said, "Oh no, Capri. Looks like you have it all under control."

"Well, then, meeting adjourned," Capri added, with a clap of her pale hands.

Instead of heading into my office, I decided to go check out my ten accounts and make sure everything was A-OK.

"Daynel, I'm going on spot checks. I should be back around three," I said to the receptionist on my way out the door.

"Okay, Nia. I'll two-way you if anything comes up."

"Thanks, Daynel. See you later."

I stepped out into the brisk New England autumn air, with my new brown pea coat, a tan scarf around my neck, tan gloves on my hands, and a tan hat on my head. You got to "co-or-din-ate," like the father from Boomerang said. The trees are all bare in preparation for the harsh winter ahead. Once the beautiful hues of autumn fade, the world looks so solemn. Lifeless, you know? I decide that my first stop will not be at my first client, located only a block from the office, but at Dunkin' Donuts, to buy a bagel and an Earl Grey tea, light and sweet.

I copped a squat at the narrow table located in the rear of the tiny shop and pulled out my planner to pencil in my trip to Houston. While flipping past

November to get to December, I realized that Thanksgiving was quickly approaching.

Mommy and Papi had invited me to come over for dinner. They live in the Bronx, which is only about a half an hour away, but I never go to visit. Krystal and Angel are always over there with their barrage of rug rats and hugely successful husbands. Isn't that just great for them? I'm hatin' big time. If I at least had a fiancé, I wouldn't feel so insignificant around them. Papi is always saying, "Nia, when are you going to give me some *nietos*?" Mommy is always saying how she introduced Angel to her husband and how I should let her play matchmaker for me. No thanks. It is so damn embarrassing, and I don't speak to either one of my sisters, except to say hello or good-bye. I'm sure Shari and Dex are gonna cook something, anyway, so I'll just feast over there.

My cell phone rang. I can never find that damn thing. After fumbling around in the bottomless pit I like to call my purse, I found it, with a message blinking 1 MISSED CALL. I hoped it wasn't a client. After dialing back the missed number, I gathered my stuff and decided to begin heading to my first customer.

"Hello," an energetic male voice answered.

"Hi. This is Nia," I said as I opened the door and stepped out into the gray, cloudless day. "Did someone just call me?"

"Yes, hold on please. Hello?"

"Hi. This is Nia Lopez. Sorry I missed your call. Whom am I speaking with, please?" I rushed to button my coat.

"Hi, Nia. This is Mike. How ya doing?"

"Oh, Mike," I stated in a professional tone. "I'm doing well. Thank you."

"Is this a bad time?"

"Well, actually, I'm on my way to a client's right now, but I have a minute."

"Client's, huh? Where do you work?"

"I work for Glow. I'm an account exec."

"Oh, I love that magazine. But, anyways, I want to meet up with you. Think you can squeeze me in?"

"Mike, I don't know about all that. We really have nothing to talk about."

"I understand where you're coming from, but I really want to see you."

"When?" I asked.

"Is today all right?"

"I'm making rounds all day. If you can be at the Dunkin' Donuts on Main Street in ten minutes, I'll wait. And then we can talk for ten minutes, and then I'll have to get going."

"That's perfect. I'm right downtown, so I'll be there in a minute."

I made a U-turn and went back to the table I'd just left. Before I could take off my coat, Mike was coming through the door. I started shuffling nervously around in my seat. I had thought I would have enough time to get myself together before he got there.

"Hey, girl," he said as he kissed my cheek and took a seat across from me.

"That was fast." I was half-joking. "What? Were you following me?"

"It's a weird coincidence, but I was just across the street, buying a magazine, when I spotted you come in, so I called your cell."

"Okay. It makes more sense to me now."

Mike was looking great that day in his black leather bomber and gray skullcap.

"I'm gonna cut through all the bullshit, small talk," he said. "I'm sorry. I was young. I was stupid. I really did love you. And, it will never, ever happen again."

Not the apology that I'd always dreamed of, but sometimes you gotta take what you can get. It actually was a great icebreaker, because I thought it was funny as hell that he was so nonchalant about the whole thing, but in a sincere, cute kind of way.

"I must admit," I assured him, "It hurt for a really long time, but I think I'm over it now."

"Now that I finally got that off my chest, what's up?" Mike put his hands on the table, obviously feeling relieved that he'd apologized. "Let's go out sometime. When are you free?"

"You think I'm going to let you back in my life that easily?" I said, with a smirk.

"We can just start with a date and see where it goes. If you never give me a chance, you'll regret it." He gave me a wink and a smile. "So when are you free?"

"Same Mike. Can't take no for an answer, huh?"

"Very funny, Nia."

"I'm free next Wednesday night." I gave in.

"Okay then. It's a date. I'll call you later in the week to confirm."

"All right. See you then."

As quickly as he had appeared, he was gone. It had been a quick, uncomfortable exchange, but the message had been conveyed: he was sorry.

After making my rounds, I arrived back at the office at three-thirty, and Daynel handed me a bouquet of purple, red, and yellow tulips. They were absolutely stunning.

"Who are these from?" I questioned.

"I dunno," she replied, with her deep, raspy voice. "Read the card."

"Thank you, Daynel," I said, cautiously walking away with my gargantuan bundle of flowers.

"No problem."

They were from Papi.

My little angel, sending love in hopes to brighten your day. Please come for dinner on Thanksgiving. It would make Mommy very happy.
  Te amo,
  Papi

I knew I'd have to call him with a great excuse or else he'd be upset. *Maybe I'll tell him I'm sick,* I thought. I couldn't be around the kids if I was sick, right?

Shari

"Is she flirting with you right in front of my face, Dex?"

He laughed. "Bay, calm down. She's a kid, and she's just being friendly."

"You think this is funny. I'm getting angry." I crossed my arms across my chest.

"She's a waitress," Dex assured me while buttering his roll and taking a large bite out of it. "It's part of her job to smile and be friendly."

"It's not her job to turn her back to me while you two have a pleasant little conversation."

"Don't act insecure. It's not very attractive." He laughed even harder, now holding his belly.

"I'm not acting insecure," I complained. "But she's disrespecting me, and you're laughing right along with her like nothing's wrong."

I couldn't take it anymore. From the moment we walked in the door, this little girl had been smiling all up in Dex's face. And there he was, smiling right back in hers. If the tables were turned, Dex would be on the ground, rumbling with homeboy by now. Miss Thang had one more time to come over to our table and smile in my husband's face before I would put my foot in her ass.

"Shari, if you want me to ignore her, then I will, okay?" he said, trying to hold in the laughter. "Don't ruin our evening over this."

"Okay." I pouted, still fuming.

"I won't lie. She's a cute girl, but, Bay, you're gorgeous. You know that. Sometimes I think you just act up so you can hear me tell you how beautiful you are and how much I love you."

He stood up on top of his chair and lifted his wineglass. While tapping it with his fork, he called for everyone's attention in the restaurant.

"May I have everyone's attention please?" he yelled. "I have something very important to say!"

If it were possible for a sister to turn red, I surely would have at that moment. I grabbed for my glass of water and hastily gulped it down.

"You better sit down, Dexter. Don't embarrass me," I whispered, tugging at his hand and slamming my glass back down.

"Shari, we've known each other for a long time now," he recited as he climbed down from the chair and got on one knee. "I've grown to love you more and more with every passing minute, hour, day, month and year. I can't picture my life without you. Shari, I guess what I'm trying to say is . . . Will you marry me?"

The restaurant exploded in applause.

"We're already married, stupid," I whispered in his ear.

"She said yes!" he yelled as he picked me up and started spinning me around.

The crowd continued to applaud his foolish little performance, including Miss Thang.

"Okay, okay, Dex." I was elated, though. "That's enough. Thank you, Bay. I appreciate that."

"That'll teach you not to challenge my love for you, girl," he sang.

I tried my best to finish my Cobb salad but couldn't resist studying Dex's handsome face. As he chewed, I appreciated his strong, high cheekbones and angular jawline. He was in need of a shave, but the ebony stubble forming on his chin gave him a rugged appeal.

Dex seized his pint-sized glass in his large brown hands and took a long swallow of iced tea. My eyes followed his movement as he wiped his thick, perfectly arched lips with a crisp white napkin.

Dexter was one of those rare fine men who either didn't know they were fine or just could care less. He was never cocky, nor did he put much effort into looking good. He just did.

"Bay, why are you staring at me?" he asked.

I thought I was being slick, but he'd obviously noticed me drooling over him.

"Hey, Bay?" I said, biting my bottom lip with anxiety, ignoring his question.

"S'up?" Dex asked.

I leaned over to whisper in his ear. "Let's go to the bathroom together."

He gave me a "girl, you trippin'" look.

"I'm serious. Let's go. I promise I'll make it worth your while." I sealed the invitation, licking my lips in a slow, circular motion.

"You don't have to ask me twice." Dex wiped his face and placed his napkin on the table.

Sneaking to the ladies' room made me feel like a teenager again. We were carefully watching to make sure no one was watching. Following closely behind and watching every move that my skirt made, Dex eagerly pushed me into the dark bathroom. Thank goodness it was the kind that only allows one person in at a time.

After locking the door, I fell to my knees, unzipped his pants, and pulled my husband's dick through the easy-access hole in his boxers to give him some serious knowledge. It was so dark that Dex had to feel around a little before landing on my breast with a tight grip.

"Damn, Bay," he moaned. Then he put both hands behind my head to guide me into a rhythm he was feeling. With the new rhythm, he began to moan a little too loudly. With my right hand, I stroked his dick, and with the left, I pulled my watermelon thong off and flung it behind me.

"Hush," I whispered as I placed my index finger over his thick lips and stuck my tongue in his ear. We began to kiss as he undressed me completely. The second Dex touched my pussy, he froze.

"Damn, Bay, you're so wet already."

The small public space and the darkness were such

a turn-on for me. In response, I let out a slightly embarrassed chuckle.

Dex firmly grabbed my arm and turned me around so my ass engulfed his hard rock. He was leaning against the sink as my body pressed against him. Dex's hands were traveling from my nipples, to my pussy, and in and out my mouth, like he couldn't decide which spot he liked the most.

"Bend over, Bay," he instructed. But before I could obey, he gently pushed me over by my shoulders.

With my ass still against him, he gave it two quick slaps.

"I wanna see this shit," he said.

Without moving out of position, he searched for the light switch with his left hand, found it, and flicked it on.

In my half-bent-over stance, I turned my head halfway around and asked if he liked what he saw.

"Hell, yeah," he said, inserting himself. A mutual gasp filled the taut air.

It was our first experience in public, and we were loving it. Dex was digging me out so feverishly that I had to put my palms against the tiled wall in front of me so I wouldn't fall over. Trying my best not to blow our cover, I stifled my moans by biting my bottom lip.

It took Dex about five minutes to cum. With his still-hard dick inside me, he lifted me up so that my back pressed against his chest. He kept one hand grasped on the front of my pussy to make sure I didn't make the wrong move and let him slip out. With his free hand, he turned my head around and forcefully stuck his tongue in my mouth. Then I began to slightly rotate my hips.

"You want more?" I whispered.

"I love you, girl," he answered

I hated to lose our connection, but I had to in order to switch positions. Dex was still leaning against the sink, fully clothed. I held on to the back of his neck while I pulled my body up and wrapped my legs around his waist. I reached down to insert him again and began rocking back and forth. He held my ass and guided me up and down as he thrust in and out. I forced my right breast into his mouth to mask his intensifying moans. Two minutes later he climaxed again and finally lost his erection.

For something that only lasted about ten minutes, we were worn out, like we'd made love for hours. I dismounted, and as soon as our eyes met, we busted out laughing.

"My wife is crazy!" he teased. "You nasty girl."

"Yeah, but you love it, though." I winked.

"You know I do."

Dex did a quick rinse off in the sink and grabbed a paper towel to dry off with.

"All right, you go out first," I said. "I'm gonna freshen up and get dressed. I'll be out in a couple minutes. And don't be going out there looking all guilty!"

"Okay, Bay," he agreed as he pecked me on the lips.

I met him back at the table about five minutes later. And Miss Thang was standing over him, shamelessly poking out her huge breasts and flirting with my husband again. As I approached the table, her cocky grin widened.

"There's my baby," Dex remarked, interrupting Miss Thang mid-sentence as he took my hand and we began walking toward the door.

Instead of giving her a dirty look, I gave her a wink and a smile. I don't know how I had let her make me feel threatened before. There's no way she could compete with me for my husband's attention.

Brittany

"Message received Monday, November seven-teenth, at three fifteen p.m," said my voice mail.

"Hey, girl. It's Warren. I've been out of town for a minute. What's up with you? I want to see you as soon as I get back, okay? I miss you so damn much. My plane comes in on Friday. I'll call you as soon as I touch the ground. I can't wait to see you."

So that's why he hadn't called. I missed him, too, I realized. I wondered what took him out of town so suddenly, though. I hoped everything was all right.

I'd just gotten in from work and had to beeline to the gym, or else I'd end up getting lazy. After taking a quick shower, I threw on a pair of sneaks, leggings with a matching sports bra, and my leather coat, and I was out the door. I am a member of the Stamford Athletics Club, which is the most comfortable gym I've joined thus far. Each treadmill has its own tele-vision set with all the cable channels included.

Monday nights, I do my running at nine, just in time to watch *Girlfriends*.

After the show ended, I stepped off the treadmill to do some cool-down stretches. Sitting on the floor, with my legs spread far apart, I bent down until my nose touched my knee and repeated that on the other leg. When I stood up, I noticed that the bank teller whom I'd met the week before had been cycling behind me the entire time. I tried my darndest to look the other way, but he spotted me.

As he got off the bike, he greeted me with this corny-ass line. "Hey, Brittany. Fancy meeting you here."

"I'm sorry. What was your name again?" I continued stretching my arms over my head. I actually did remember his name, but I just wanted to make sure he knew that I was not impressed by him.

"Vaughn. You remember me, so stop fronting. What you been up to?"

"Nothing much. Just trying to stay in shape, you know?" I bent over to do a couple toe touches.

"Yeah, I know. I come here three times a week."

I made a mental note to switch gyms as soon as my contract was up.

"Oh, okay. I come only twice a week." I began gathering all my gym paraphernalia. "Well, it was nice talking to you. I'll see you later."

"Hey, you wanna grab a bite to eat with me? I know this great Japanese place. My treat." Vaughn extended his arms out like a car salesman offering a great deal.

"No, thanks. I'll have to pass on that one," I

answered, although my stomach was grumbling and I was craving some California rolls. I tried to walk around him, but he stepped to the side to prevent me from doing so.

"Why don't you stop playing hard to get, girl? You're passing up free eats?" Then he nudged me on the shoulder like I was one of his boys. "Look. It's just a friendly gesture. That's all. I'm not trying to get in your panties. I already did that, remember?"

"Ha ha ha. Very funny. Fine. I'll go with you. Just give me about fifteen minutes to take a shower."

"I don't care if you're funky. Now I heard your stomach growling, so let's just go. If it makes you feel any better, I'm funky, too." Vaughn put his right arm up and sniffed his armpit.

"Whatever. Look. I'm parked in the garage. I'll meet you out by the entrance and follow you to the restaurant, okay? Now move out of my way."

"Cool. See you in about five," he said, finally letting me pass.

I was riding behind his Ford Taurus for about a mile and a half before we reached Kotubiku, the best Japanese restaurant in town. How could I go in there looking like I did? I contemplated making a U-turn and taking my black ass home, but, damn, I was hungry. Vaughn pulled into the first slot, and I pulled in directly to his left. He met me at the driver's side door and extended his hand to help me out.

"I don't need your damn help," I snapped as I yanked my hand back.

"You know something, Brittany? You would be

even more beautiful if your attitude wasn't so nasty. I'm just trying to be a gentleman. Lighten up."

I guess I was being a little abrasive with the guy. It was just that I was so stressed out. Warren was out of town, and I was starting to get sexually frustrated waiting on him to come back. And Vaughn wasn't even an option, not that night. I needed filet mignon, not a Philly cheesesteak.

"I'm sorry, Vaughn. Truce?"

"Truce." I finally took his hand and he helped me out of my car.

As we entered the restaurant, the pale-faced hostess with the red kimono looked at us like we were straight out of the Merrell Avenue projects and didn't deserve to eat there.

"Good evening," said Vaughn, sounding all sophisticated. "Can we have a seat at the hibachi?"

"No, hibachi," was all she had to say.

"Do you mind sitting at a regular table, Brittany?" he asked.

"I don't even know what a hibachi is, so it really doesn't matter," I replied.

"Fine. We'll take a regular seat," said Vaughn.

Without even looking in our faces, the hostess escorted us to our table, placed our menus down, and turned around in one smooth motion. Vaughn pulled out a chair for me, and then he took the seat facing the kitchen.

"Worse seat in the house, huh?" he said and smiled.

"I hate to sound ignorant, but what is a hibachi, anyway?" I asked.

"That's a hibachi," Vaughn said as he pointed to the grill on which a tiny Japanese man was flipping grilled shrimp and veggies in the air. Then he made a mountain out of sliced onions and set a fire that blazed up way above his little head.

"It would have been nice to sit over there. Wow, that looks like fun," I said. I really was impressed; I'd never seen a hibachi before.

"You'll enjoy the food, nonetheless. It's phenomenal. Can I order for you?"

"Sure. The only thing I know about Japanese food is California rolls. I love those damn things." I folded my menu back up and placed it in front of me.

"Me, too. I'll make sure to order enough for both of us."

After surveying the drink menu, I decided on an apple martini. For some reason, I was in the mood to try something different. When the waiter approached, I ordered one, made with Absolut, of course. Vaughn decided to have one as well. Then he really floored me when he ordered our entire meal in Japanese.

"You know how to speak Japanese? Well, of course, you do. I just saw it with my own eyes. That's impressive," I said and nodded, feeling like the Brittany at work, talking to a colleague.

The waiter returned in less than a minute with our drinks. I gulped down half the glass in one swallow.

"Slow down, girl. There's more where that came from." Vaughn chuckled.

"Vaughn, you wouldn't believe how stressed I am

right now. I need this drink," I confessed. "So how did you learn Japanese?"

"I double-majored in international business and finance, with a minor in Japanese. You don't even want to know how long it took me to finish school." He laughed.

"Hold up. You have all this education, and you work as a bank teller? That's such a waste."

He laughed some more. "I really haven't decided which way to go with my degree, but in the meanwhile, I have to pay the bills, right?" He cocked his head to the side and shrugged his shoulders.

"I guess," I replied, slightly repulsed by the lack of motivation that holds our educated brothas back from attaining their goals.

"So what do you do for a living? That's an awfully nice car you drive."

"Thanks. I'm a creative director at Reiny Design. I've been there for four years, and I run a department of twelve."

"Now I'm impressed. You go, girl!"

"I'm trying," I said, this time slowly savoring the delightfully sour martini.

The food arrived, and it looked like a feast fit for a queen. There was boiled lobster, grilled scallops and shrimp, thinly sliced steak, sautéed vegetables, fried rice, some type of thin noodles, and about three dozen California rolls. *How the hell can he afford this?* I thought. I'd probably be reaching down in my purse at the end of the meal to help him out. I'll be damned if I do. I'll leave him sitting there by himself before I pay for all this.

"Bon appetite," He said, gleaming.

"Thank you. You, too." I dove in.

We hadn't uttered a word to each other since we'd started grubbing. Then the waitress returned to check on everything, and Vaughn ordered two more martinis for us.

"How is everything?" he asked me.

"Sorry, I'm so quiet, but this food is too delicious."

"Now aren't you glad you came?" He smiled.

"Am I? I can't wait to tell my friends about this place. They'd love it, too."

"So what do you do for fun?" he asked. Vaughn really seemed interested in learning about me. Warren had never asked me any of these questions before. Actually, I don't think any guy I've dated cared enough to ask.

"You're not going to believe me, so just forget it," I said, waving my hand dismissively.

"No, tell me," he insisted before loading his fork with butter-dipped lobster.

"You're going to laugh."

"I won't. I cross my heart and hope to die. Stick a needle in my eye." Then he actually crossed his heart and raised his right hand.

"I like to write poems. I have this journal I keep, with hundreds of poems in it. Every so often, I pick it up and just write away. There are times when I am sad, and I just sit there and write through my tears. If I flip the pages back, the tearstains are still there from previous entries." I gazed toward one of the hibachis, trying not to recollect some of those painful memories.

"I'd love to read one of your poems one day."

I'd never let anyone, not even my girls, read my poetry. They don't even know anything about my journal.

"They aren't all sad, though. I have some that are incredibly happy." I was glad that someone had shown interest in my talent.

"That's cool." He nodded his head approvingly.

"What do you like to do for fun?" I asked him.

"Me and some of my boys have a band. We play down at Violet's every Thursday. You should stop by sometime."

"How about this Thursday?"

"Since Thanksgiving is on Thursday, we're actually going to play on Wednesday instead."

"Okay then. How 'bout Wednesday then?" I placed my now-emptied martini glass on the table.

"That's fine. I'll put you on the guest list."

"Plus two?" I bargained.

"Anything for you, Brittany. Anything for you."

"I'm there," I said, loading another California roll with wasabi and dipping it into soy sauce.

He smiled, and for the first time, I felt that tingle of attraction for him that I get down under. With our buffet only half eaten, we were both stuffed. I felt a bit lightheaded and tired after an intense workout, three martinis, and the huge meal.

"Are you seeing anyone?" he asked, wiping the corners of his thin-lipped mouth.

"I'm dating someone. His name is Warren." I beamed.

"You guys serious?"

"Not really, but we like each other a lot, though."

"I hope he's good to you."

"He's all right. We have busy schedules, though, so I don't see him as much as I'd like to." I avoided eye contact because I was lying through my teeth. I could never be too busy for a man.

"What does he do?"

I started to lie and say he was an entrepreneur or something, but I decided to go with the truth. Vaughn seemed cool, and I didn't think he'd be judgmental.

"He's an exotic dancer," I finally replied.

"O-okay. Well, Brittany, I think I should get you home. You look a little beat."

"I am." I yawned. "Do you know where the ladies' room is?"

He pointed, and I was on my way. He had chosen to keep his comments to himself about Warren's profession, and I respected that. Otherwise, the date would have ended on a very sour note.

I was glad that I'd agreed to have dinner with Vaughn. Although he wasn't the best fuck, I loved talking to him.

When I returned, he was signing the credit card receipt and handing it back to the waitress.

"Shall we?" he asked as he grabbed me by the waist and guided me out the door.

"Yes, we shall. Thanks for the meal and the wonderful conversation."

"Anytime, girl, anytime. Just call me. You have the number."

He walked me to my car and insisted on following me to make sure I made it home safely. I made it in one piece, and as I approached my front porch, he beeped the horn.

"See you Wednesday!" he yelled.

"See you Wednesday!"

Shari

I arrived at Brittany's door and decided to just use my key to enter. She had called me at work at eight thirty, crying like the baby she is and demanding I take a half day. I made a couple of phone calls and told my boss that I had to leave. I left by nine thirty. When I found Brittany, she was balled up under a blanket, and she looked like shit.

"What did the Negro do this time, Brittany?" I asked.

"Nothing. It's not about Warren. I'm sick," she whined. "I think I have food poisoning."

"What did you eat?"

"Girl, I think I got food poisoning from this Japanese food I ate last night. I've been throwing up all morning. Or maybe it was those cheap-ass martinis I had. I knew they didn't use Absolut like I told them to."

Just then she leaped up and tried to make it to

the bathroom, but ended up regurgitating all over her bed.

"Take me to the emergency room," she whimpered, barely able to find her voice. "I think I'm dying, girl."

"Calm down. I'm not taking you anywhere. You go in the bathroom, take a shower, and wash the throw up out of your hair, and I will make your bed and get you some soup. You need something in your stomach. You didn't get food poisoning. It doesn't take affect that quickly. You're probably just hung over." I laughed.

"See y'all think I be bugging, but I can't drink any vodka other than Absolut. Look. Now I'm all bent over." She managed to laugh.

With fresh linen, hearty homemade soup, two Excedrin, and a strong cup of coffee, my friend was starting to feel a little better.

"You saved my life," she sang. "I knew I could depend on you. So how are things with Tangie? And please don't tell me no drama, 'cause I'm feeling weak right now." She waved her hand through the air.

"Actually, things have been just fine. She even went down to the campus and got a little part-time job to support herself. I barely even notice she's there. She's been the ideal roommate."

"I'm glad to hear that, girl. I thought I was going to have to go over there and jack her up for you."

"Oh, don't worry. If I feel she needs to get jacked up, I won't hesitate to do so," I laughed. "Just kidding, girl. The last thing I need is to be scrapping with a girl almost ten years younger than me."

"I feel you. We are getting up there now."

"You know . . ." I hesitated, contemplating speaking my mind or not.

"What, chick? Spit it out."

I wrung my hands together because I really hated telling people how to live their lives.

"Brittany, you need to call your sister. This is ridiculous."

"Fuck that bitch." Brittany laughed, thinking she'd made a joke.

"Not funny," I scolded. "I mean she has no one here. You two need to make up."

"I know, Sha-Sha. I was just fucking with you. I do miss the little chick sometimes. I'll call her. Promise."

"Sure. Well, look, Brittany. You need to take a nap. I'll be here when you wake up, okay? I think I'll call Dex's office and see if he wants to do lunch with me, since I have a free afternoon." I tucked Brittany under the fresh linen.

When I got sick as a kid, my nana would sprinkle baby powder on my mattress before she put the sheets on. That scent would help me relax and sleep better. I'd done the same for Brittany.

"Okay, Shari. Thanks. Just use your key to let yourself back in."

"I was planning on it."

I left my ailing friend to drift into a healing slumber. After checking my watch, I realized that it was five minutes to noon, so I'd better catch Dex before he left for lunch. I sprinted across the living room and snatched the cordless phone from the wall in the kitchen.

"Hi, Laurie. This is Shari. Is Dexter in, please?"

"Oh, I'm sorry, Mrs. Brown, but Dexter left early today."

"Are you sure?" Dex hadn't told me anything about leaving early. That was unlike him.

"Positive. He only came in for about an hour this morning. Then he left, I don't think he's feeling very well."

"Well, thanks, anyway, Laurie. You have a good day."

"You, too."

After hanging up the phone, I decided to call the house to see if my boy was okay. He picked up after four rings.

"Dex, it's me. What's wrong? I just called the office, and Laurie said you'd left early."

"Yeah, I tried calling you at your job, but they said you had left early, too. What happened?"

"Brittany was really torn up from a hard night of drinking. She just needed a little babying, is all. What's wrong with you?" I asked my husband as I opened the refrigerator door to look around for something to eat.

"Aw, girl, don't worry about me. Just a little stomach upset. You know I can't take a decent dump unless I am butt naked in the comfort of my own home. You just take care of Brittany, and I'll see you when you get home. Bay, hold on a sec."

"Sure." In the background, I could hear a muffled conversation. One voice surely belonged to Dex.

"Hello," said Dex.

"Who were you talking to, Bay?" I quizzed, holding a pack of hot dogs, then putting them right back.

"That was Tangie. She has the day off from work. She was wondering if she could borrow my car to run and get some groceries. I told her as long as she brings some Maalox back, it's cool with me."

"You sure you can trust her with your car?" I asked, now peeking into one of the white Styrofoam containers marked Kotubiku.

"Shari, cut her some slack. I'm sure she'll be just fine."

Although Dex was the sweetest man ever, I knew when he called me Shari, he was laying down the law. And, I never questioned him when he used that tone with me, which wasn't very often.

There was chicken lo mein in one container. I decided to give up my food search, so I closed the container and the refrigerator.

"Agreed. I guess I'll just run to the deli around the corner and pick up a sandwich. I'll probably leave here around three or so. Since I didn't take anything out for dinner, how about I pick up some pizza on my way in?"

"Don't worry about it. Tangie's on top of it. She's making lasagna tonight."

"Fine with me. I'll see you later, alligator."

"After a while, crocodile."

After hanging up, I decided against going out into that brisk weather. Instead, I munched on the leftovers from Brittany's dinner the night before.

After all, I was sure she wouldn't mind. I filled my stomach with so much lobster and steak, I thought I would bust if I didn't sit my ass down somewhere.

I waddled over to her sofa and sunk perfectly down into the soft cushions. After a decent episode of *Ricki Lake*, *The Jenny Jones Show* came on at one. I hate her show; she repeats the same topic over and over again. It's always paternity tests; or I was a geek then, and now look at me; or those fast-ass young girls that get sentenced to a day in boot camp and miraculously turn their lives around. Today the topic was paternity tests. It was the topic I hated the most because, first of all, I hate to see these young girls being so promiscuous. But if I watch enough of the show, it hooks me, and then I can't wait to see the results. Then you know what Jenny does? She makes the damn show a two-part series, so you have to tune in the next day just to see the results. Ain't that some shit?

I figured that I might as well catch up on some sleep while the drama queen was still napping. Have you ever had what I call the "Pee-Pee Dream"? It's when in the middle of your dream, somehow a trip to the bathroom is incorporated. It happened to me for the first time when I was eighteen. At that point I wasn't aware of the "Pee-Pee Dream" phenomenon. I was dreaming that I'd just finished up an intense sex session with my senior math teacher. I visited the bathroom and peed both in my dream and in real life, right in my bed. I woke up from this dream feeling like a fool. Almost a grown woman peeing in the bed.

I was there on Brittany's sofa when the dream hit again. This time, and every time since the first, I was prepared. Now I have this instinct that whenever I find myself going into a bathroom in the midst of a dream, I spring awake before it is too late. And so I sprang. I noticed that Brittany was now situated in the living room, on the love seat, sucking down a smoothie. I couldn't even stop to exchange pleasantries with her. Straight to the bathroom. Do not pass go: do not collect two hundred dollars.

When I returned to the living room, Brittany was still curled up with her blanket, sucking on her smoothie.

"Sha-Sha, go look in the freezer, girl. I made you one, too." She was obviously feeling a lot better. "It is mango, peach, and papaya. Mm-mm-mm. It is divine."

"Thank you." I felt so damn groggy after that nap. That smoothie would be just the thing to refresh me. Then I noticed that the sun had set outside.

"Brittany, what time is it?" I yelled, with my head still poked in the freezer. I thought I heard her say, "Six o'clock," but I wasn't sure.

"What did you say?" I asked nonchalantly as I returned once again to the living room.

"Six o'clock," she replied.

"Oh, my goodness. Dex must think I've lost my mind." I couldn't believe that I had slept for five hours. "I'm going to have to take this smoothie to go. Tangie cooked dinner tonight, and I know they are probably waiting on me to get started."

"Tangie cooked dinner?" Brittany asked.

"That's what Dex said."

"What is she doing home, anyway? I thought you said she worked?"

"She does, usually from four to eight, but today she had the day off," I replied.

"Let me get this straight. Tangie and your husband have been home together all day long. She cooked dinner for him. And you have been over here the whole time like Sleeping fucking Beauty. Are you really that naïve?"

"Brittany, you watch too many damn movies, girl. Wake up. This is real life, and this is your sister we're talking about. And, if you don't trust your sister, then guess what? I trust my man." I took the first sip of my tropical smoothie.

"Ooh, girl. You really believe that shit, don't you? You really are a sad case."

"Go to hell, Brittany," I said as I playfully put her in a headlock. "When you find that one, you just know. That's all I can say. You just know. Dex is so completely infatuated with me, no one could ever fill my shoes, okay? Now, say I'm the woman, and I'll let you go."

"You're the woman," she admitted as I freed her from my grip. Then she pinned me to the ground and pulled my arms behind my back as if she were going to handcuff me. "Now, who's the woman? Look, Sha-Sha. I love you, girl. Just don't be blind, okay? You know I got your back, but I'm trying to have your front, too. That's all. Don't let Tangie have too much free time with your man."

"Okay. Now get your big ass off me. I love you, too. Damn."

"My ass is big, huh?" she said, turning around to look at her ass. "Don't be jealous."

"Jealous of what? You know mine is at least double the size of yours."

"Whatever. That's not what Dex said."

"Now, I'ma have to cut ya!" Then I lunged at her with the Swiss knife I kept on my key ring. She dodged it Matrix style. We were acting a damn fool. I was having fun, but I needed to get home.

"All right," I called to her as I headed through the door. "You're wearing me out. Good to see that you're feeling better, though. I'll call you later."

"Thanks again, but be prepared for the worst when you walk through that door," I heard as the door slammed behind me.

The drive home was a long one. Although I remained confident in front of Brittany, her words would not escape my head. I trusted Dex fully, but the thought of him cheating on me with Tangie had never even crossed my mind. That damn Brittany. Now my mind was wandering wildly with possibilities. As quickly as the thoughts entered my mind, I dismissed them. I had made the decision to let this woman into my house, and I was confident that it was a good decision. I thought.

Nia

Wednesday already? Any other time I would have been ecstatic that hump day had come, but since I had the date with Mike that night, I was dreading every passing moment. I was trying to muster up the courage to call him to confirm the night's plans. He'd left me a voice mail letting me know that he'd made dinner reservations for us at Eclise, but said if I had any better ideas, I should just let him know, and he'd cancel the reservations. Earlier that week, Brittany had invited me to Violet's to see a friend perform. I thought this would be a much better environment for Mike and me. Since we'd be in a public place and among friends, our conversation wouldn't get too deep.

Just as I was reaching for the phone for the tenth time in ten minutes, Daynel buzzed me.

"Yes, Daynel?"

"Nia, there is another delivery here for you," she crooned.

"Oh, great. I'll be right out."

Papi was so persistent. Being that it was the day before Thanksgiving and I hadn't called him yet, I guess he felt the need to butter me up some more.

"Somebody's got it bad," Daynel teased.

"I wish. These are probably just from Papi again."

Sitting on Daynel's desk were at least two dozen pink and white roses. Attached to the vase was a little white bear with a pink bow tie. A card was attached to the bear's hand. When I opened the card, it read:

> *My Beautiful Nia,*
>   *To what do I owe this pleasure? Thank you for giving me a second chance to be the perfect man for you. If you trust in me, I assure you that you will not regret it.*
>   *Love,*
>   *Mike*

Love, Mike? I thought that was a really strong word to use with someone you hadn't seen in over five years. I felt all giddy like a teenager after reading that card. The flowers were just the push I needed to pick up the phone and call him. I skipped back into my office and placed the roses next to Papi's tulips. After one ring, he answered.

"Hello."

"Hey, Mike. It's Nia. Thank you so much for the beautiful flowers. I love them." I rushed my words and picked up a yellow pencil and began twiddling it around in my fingers.

"I used to send you flowers all the time, don't you remember?"

"I remember. You were always a sweetheart. But, anyways, the reason for this call is to ask if it is all right to change the plans. One of my best friends invited me to Violet's to check out this band. What do you think?"

"Whatever you want, baby. That sounds great."

"Well, meet me there at eight." I began doodling on my desktop calendar.

"I can't pick you up?"

"Not yet. I'm not totally comfortable with this situation yet, so for now please just understand that." I wrote, "Just be patient," on my calendar as I spoke.

"Like I said, whatever you want. The ball is in your court, there are ten seconds left, and you're up by thirty points."

That made me laugh.

"All right. See you then," I said.

I was suddenly very excited for the night to begin. By the time the clock switched from 4:59 to five o'clock, I was halfway to my car. Before I could head home, I had to stop by the mall to pick up another tube of Sheer Freesia body lotion from Bath & Body Works. I also decided on using the gift certificate to Hollywood Nails that Brittany had gotten me after that Jacuzzi club mishap to get a mani and a pedi real quick. I ended up leaving the mall a little after seven. Now, I'd be late, but Mike would be just fine. I'd get there when I got there.

I arrived home, showered, and decided to wear my black strapless dress, accessorized with a silver chain belt, huge silver hoops in my ears, a diamond tennis bracelet, and the platinum chain Papi bought me for my birthday, one with a two-carat princess-cut diamond on the end. I threw on a little silver eye shadow and a neutral-colored lipstick. I wanted to look my best for Mike. It was too damn cold for sandals, so I wore a pair of ultrasheer black stockings and dug out my knee-high boots to wear. Since I was trying to make a good impression, I decided to take an extra half hour to blow-dry my hair straight. I grabbed my leather coat and a pack of Altoids, and checked the clock before running through the door. It was already 8:45, so I called Mike on his cell and left a message letting him know that I was running late, but I'd be there in less than ten minutes.

I got to the club and assumed he'd be waiting outside for me, but I guess he hadn't gotten the message I left for him. As soon as I stepped in the door, Brittany greeted me.

"Niiiiaaa!" she screeched. "You got on the diamonds tonight. Who are you trying to impress?"

"Shut up, Brittany. Look at you. Who are you trying to impress?"

Brittany always looked nice, though. Although I did put in a lot of extra effort, I was just trying to get the attention off of myself. She was dazzling that night. Brittany wore skintight black leather Capri pants, a tan knit halter top, and tan boots. Her hair was lifted up in an *I Dream of Jeannie* fashion. She'd got a bang cut in her hair and everything. There was no doubt in my mind that she had worn her tan leather coat tonight, too. No matter how hard I tried, I could never outdo Brittany. Not that I wanted to, but tonight I just wanted to feel like the hottest thing at Violet's. I wasn't far from it, though. I can honestly say that Brittany and I held the top spots for fashion and beauty that night. So I was happy.

"Please. You know I always dress to impress," she said. We high-fived. "You'll never guess who is up in here tonight."

"Who?"

"That guy Mike from Catalina's," she said as she pointed toward the dance floor.

He was bumping and grinding and having a good ole time without me. The sista he was dancing with wasn't bad looking, either. I felt a tinge of jealousy start to erupt but quickly suppressed it. He was nowhere near being my man, so I really didn't have any right to say something to him.

"I know, Brittany. That's who I'm supposed to be meeting here tonight," I confessed.

"What? Are you serious? You're giving him another chance?"

"I just agreed to meet with him so we could talk. That's all."

"Just be careful, and let me go peel Tangie away from him."

"Oh, that's Tangie?" I said as I weaved through the

crowd to grab a seat at the bar. "You'll have to introduce me then. Let her dance with him. There's no harm in dancing. Let them have fun. I'll just go order a drink. When he notices me, he'll come to me."

Brittany and Tangie had made up, so Brittany had invited her to Violet's as well. Their reconciliation was bittersweet for me because although I was elated for them, I couldn't help but yearn for the same with my sisters.

"I don't know what's wrong with you and Sha-Sha, but y'all are too trusting with your men."

"He's not my man, Brittany," I reminded her.

"Man or not, I'm going to get her off of him."

Brittany was on a mission. I didn't want them dancing together, either, but I didn't want to look immature, you know? My eyes followed Brittany to the dance floor, where she tapped Tangie on the shoulder and pointed in my direction. *That damn girl,* I thought. Tangie and Mike were looking my way, and I felt so stupid. It would have been asking too much for Brittany to have been discreet about the situation. They all started heading my way, so I turned around and tried to get the bartender's attention to order a drink. I decided on amaretto sours for the night. When my drink was ready, Mike's hand reached over my shoulder to pay for it.

"Hi, baby," he said as he bent over to kiss me right on the lips. "You look good enough to eat." He was being fresh, so I figured he'd had a couple drinks already.

"Thank you," I replied.

"Nia, this is my sister, Tangie. Tangie, this is Nia. Tangie, I see you are already well acquainted with Mike." Brittany introduced us, and then shot Tangie a disapproving glare.

"Get over it, Brittany, we were only dancing," Tangie replied, then stuck her hand out toward me. "Nice to finally meet you, Nia." Tangie and I shook hands. "Mike, thanks for the dance."

He nodded and smiled in response.

"I gotta go find me another dance partner now that you stole mine," said Tangie. She gazed at me in a playful manner. We all laughed as Tangie boogied back toward the dance floor.

"Let's go to the VIP area near the band," Brittany suggested. "I have a table reserved for us down there."

Mike and I followed, hand in hand. It felt so natural. "See the beige one playing the drums?" Brittany pointed. "That's my friend, Vaughn."

"He's cute, Brittany," I assured her. She had told me that he wasn't the greatest in bed, had a crappy job, and wasn't very good-looking. In my opinion, Vaughn was a very attractive man. She could be so ridiculous.

"Yeah, but cute doesn't quite cut it in my book," Brittany sang, bopping her head to the music.

"Brittany, looks aren't everything," Mike added. "If the man has a good heart, you should give him a chance."

"Yeah," I agreed.

"Easy for you to say with D'Angelo sitting on your

arm," she whispered in my ear, referring to Mike. "I'm going to kick it with Vaughn for a little while. See you lovebirds later." She climbed up on the stage and pulled a stool right up next to Vaughn while he played. He looked like he'd just won the lottery, with Brittany on his side while he tapped those drums.

"I really wanted to talk privately with you, Nia. Can we sneak out a little early?" Mike asked.

"Maybe," I teased. "But for now, I'm really enjoying the band."

"Okay. Well, I'll go get us some more drinks. What are you drinking?"

"Amaretto sour," I answered, passing him my empty glass.

"I'll be right back."

Good thing I had decided not to leave, because as soon as I saw Warren walk into the club, I knew all hell was going to break loose. Brittany had said that Warren was getting back in town on Friday. She had planned this wonderful homecoming for him that included massage oil, fresh rose petals, scented bath oils, and plenty of freaking. I think my heart skipped a beat when I noticed a woman step out from behind him and grab his hand. I knew the second Brittany spotted him, it was on. And, you know, Brittany don't know how to act.

"Here you are, honey," Mike said upon his return. "Amaretto sour and a glass of champagne to celebrate us." Noting my horror-filled stare, he asked, "What's wrong?"

"Brittany's man just walked in here with another woman, after telling her that he was out of town," I blurted out. "If she sees him, she's going to make a scene. I have to get her out of here without her seeing him."

"I think you should just mind your business, Nia. It's obvious that he isn't her man, because she is up there in Vaughn's face, and he just walked in with another woman." Mike passed me the drinks.

"You don't know Brittany. Once she gives you the business, if she likes it, you're her man. Whether you know it or not." I gulped down the contents of the champagne flute in two swallows. "Here. Hold these for me please," I demanded as I handed him my necklace, bracelet, and earrings.

"What are you doing?" he asked.

"Like I said, you don't know Brittany like I do. There's about to be a scuffle up in here, and I'm gonna have to be all up in it trying to get Brittany to calm down. I'd just die if I lost this necklace Papi bought me or this bracelet I saved an entire year for."

"All right, if you insist, but, first, I think you should try Plan A and just try to peacefully escort her out without her seeing him."

"I'll be right back, hopefully." He gave me the thumbs-up.

I approached the stage and motioned for Brittany to come down and talk to me. She did, after whispering something in Vaughn's ear that made his smile stretch a mile.

"What's up?" she asked.

"Brittany, I need for you to take me home now!" I pleaded.

"Why can't Mike take you, or why don't you drive yourself? Didn't you drive here?" she yelled over the music.

"Yes, I did drive, but I'm too drunk to drive home," I said as I thought on my feet.

"So let Mike drive you home," Brittany said, dancing to the music. "I'm having a good time."

Shit. Shit. Shit. Shit. Shit. Just then I noticed her glaring past me and stretching her neck to look around me. It was too late. Her radar sensed Warren a mile away.

"Girl, is that Warren over there?" she asked me, squinting and stretching her neck.

Before I could answer, she was knocking me out of the way to go investigate. I scurried behind her and grabbed her arm.

"That ain't him, Brittany," I yelled, trying to look sincere.

"Shut up, Nia. I'm not dumb," she yelled and charged ahead at an even quicker pace. "I know my man. And, who the fuck is that sitting next to him, with her hand on his leg? Oh, hell, no."

"Shit. Shit. Shit. Shit. Shit," I said aloud that time. I had to have my girl's back, though, so I followed her the whole way.

"Warren, what the fuck is going on?" she screamed when she reached the table that he was sitting at with his date. Warren was a brick house.

He displayed no emotion, was cold, and was unmoved by her apparent agitation.

"Brittany, can you get out of my space," he casually replied, pointing to the woman beside him. "I'm on a date here."

"You're on a date? *I* am your woman. What do you mean you're on a date?" Brittany said as she placed both her hands on the table and leaned forward to get all up in Warren's face.

It was obvious that the other woman knew she came before Brittany, because she just sat there looking all smug.

"Brittany, I'm not your man. I never was and never will be," Warren said, shooing Brittany away with his hand. "Now get the fuck out of my face, and stop clucking."

"Chicken head." The other woman laughed as she whispered it to Warren, but Brittany and I both read her lips.

The next thing I knew, my dear friend had straight up tackled the girl to the ground. I knew it was coming. Brittany was swinging her arms so fast and hard, I was scared to get involved. But I had to. As I headed toward the mayhem, Warren threw me out of the way. He threw me so hard, I landed on my ass about ten feet away from the commotion. I don't think he meant to throw me with so much force, but I guess it didn't matter to Mike, who had been no more than a couple of feet away from us the whole time. Although Mike was the smaller of the two men, he grabbed Warren by his collar and slammed him down on the table. The table broke down the middle in two pieces, and drinks splattered everywhere.

"Nigga, if you ever touch my woman again, I'll kill you," Mike yelled as he pulled his arm back to punch Warren in the face. Just then, a bouncer arrived and pulled Mike away.

Brittany was still over there whooping ass. I guess the bouncers figured they should handle the men first. After regaining my composure, I ran over to Brittany and pulled her off of that poor girl.

"Get off me. I'm not done with her yet," yelled Brittany. "Gonna come in here with my man and then call me the chicken head. Who's the chicken head now, bitch? If I ever see you again, you're gonna get it again. Fuck you, you ho ass. . . ."

I had to cup Brittany's mouth with my hand to shut her up.

"Come on, Brittany. You're embarrassing yourself. Just shut up and come on," I said. I dragged her out of the club and locked her inside my car. Mike had made it outside and was standing there fuming.

"Watch her, Mike. Don't let her get out of that car," I demanded. I bolted back inside to get our coats from the coat check, jetted back to my car, and tried to flee the scene before the cops arrived.

"Mike, you follow me. I'm taking her home," I said. I was finally in control. I slammed the door to my little Honda Civic, revved up, and pulled off with lightning speed. I checked the rearview to make sure Mike had followed my orders. He had.

"Can you believe this shit?" cried Brittany. "He had the nerve to embarrass me like that in front of another bitch. I hate his ass. Why did he treat me like he doesn't even know me? Thought his ass was out of town. I am so stupid for believing him. He has a lot of kissing up to do for me to take his sorry ass back."

Was she really talking about still being with that two-timing asshole who'd just disrespected her to the fullest? I decided to keep my mouth shut, because sometimes people just need to vent. If I said what was on my mind, she'd be cursing me out, too, so I just let her ramble.

Brittany went on. "He is lucky I didn't have my knife on me. Wait till I see him. He said he missed me. How could he lie to me like that? Girl, you know he told me he was out of town?" I figured it was a rhetorical question, because I knew that she knew damn well she had told me, but I just let her keep talking. She was pitiful, crying her eyes out, slamming her fists against my dashboard, and just rambling.

When I pulled in front of her door, she reached over and hugged me tight. "Thanks for listening, girl. I really made a fool out of myself tonight, didn't I?"

"Na. I would have done the same thing. Don't worry about it," I said, rubbing her back.

"Thank you, Nia, even though I know you're lying." She was still crying.

"Just go inside, take a hot shower, and get your behind to sleep, Roy Jones."

"Shut up!" She gave me a weak smile. "I'll call you tomorrow, okay?" She exited the Honda; then she stopped in her tracks, doubled back, and tapped on my window. I rolled it down.

"You better not fuck Mike tonight, Nia. Make him wait, okay?" Her voice was suddenly nurturing and sincere.

"Okay, Brittany. Good night." Damn that girl had a one-track mind, I thought.

Brittany

Thank goodness Thanksgiving was the next day, and I didn't have to take another day off from work, because I sure was in a bad way the next morning. The combination of liquor, fighting, and crying all night long had left me nauseous, sore, and with a splitting headache on Thanksgiving morning. It was four in the morning, and I could barely manage to lift my head off the pillow. Thankfully, the sun hadn't risen yet, so I could easily drift back to sleep after my hourly trips to the toilet to throw up. Times like those are when I yearn for a man in my life to take care of me.

"Honey, can you please make me some tea and pass me three Excedrin," I actually said aloud, although I knew damn well there was no one for me to lean on when I was weak.

After I fell back to sleep, my damn bell rang. I peeled my eyes open, squinted to see the clock. It was six thirty. *Who in the hell could be at my door at this ungodly hour?* I thought. "Who is it?" I screamed at the top of my lungs, refusing to get out of bed unless it was someone I really wanted to see.

"It's me, Brittany. Come open this door." It was Shari. I rolled out of the bed and limped toward the door, with my comforter wrapped around my body like a tortilla on a burrito.

"I'm so glad to see you," I grumbled, opening the door.

"That's the last thing I expected to hear from you at six thirty in the morning." She laughed.

"I had a rough time last night. I can't even begin to tell you about it right now. It'll just make my head pound even harder."

"Go lie down. I'll fix you some oatmeal and bring you some tea, okay? Give me ten minutes." I loved Shari.

"Some Excedrin, too?" I whined from my bedroom.

"Some Excedrin, too," she agreed.

"Why didn't you just use your key instead of making me get up?" I questioned.

"Sorry. I can't seem to focus today," she said, shaking her head.

Ten minutes later, after returning from another visit to the toilet—face down, I might add—I found Shari setting up a tray next to my bed, with everything she'd promised, plus a couple of slices of toast. There was a worried look on her face, and I knew something was eating at her. I popped the Excedrin first, took a couple sips of tea, and then motioned for her to lie next to me.

"So why are you out so early?" I asked her.

"It's Thanksgiving. I have some last-minute shopping to do, and then I have to hurry home and do a little cleaning and get that turkey in the oven," she replied as she settled in beside me.

"So what brought you this way?" I asked, nibbling on the toast.

"I just need to talk." She exhaled loudly.

"About?"

After a distant stare, she began. "You know I hate you, right? Ever since Monday, when you put that bug in my ear about Tangie and Dex, I just haven't been right. Everything is starting to look suspicious. I have never felt this way before, and I don't know how to handle it."

"What makes you think something is up?"

"On Monday, when I got home, they'd already eaten without me. Can you believe that? Dex always waits for me. As I walked through the door, Tangie was just clearing his plate for him. I overheard him telling her how delicious the food was and just raving and raving."

"So what?" I said, stirring the sticky oatmeal. "There's nothing wrong with that. The man was hungry, and you were really late getting home."

"I know, but it just seems like at one time, I was all he needed. Now that Tangie is around, things are starting to change. The other night, after I got in from the gym, she and Dex were playing Scrabble together. That's *our* game. Until you said something, I just was really happy that Tangie felt comfortable in our home. Now I think she's getting a little too comfortable. The other day, I woke up in the middle of the night to get a glass of water, and she was in the living room, lying on the couch, with this tiny little housedress on. The way she was positioned, I could see half of her ass. What if that had been Dex instead of me?"

"Did you say something to her about it?" I asked, shoving a spoonful of oatmeal in my mouth.

"No, there was nothing to say. It was only me, after all."

"I'm really sorry I said something. You know Dex loves you, He would never do anything to hurt you. I think you know that, too. All I was saying is, don't trust anyone completely. We're all human and everyone has room for error, but Dex is different. If he does mess up, I doubt he'd cheat on you."

"If you say so. I just know I'm going to start keeping a closer eye on those two." She smirked. "Let me get out of here, though. Gotta get started. Dinner should be ready around five. We're starting without you if you're not there on time."

"I'll be there. I'll be there," I assured her. "I'm about to sleep this headache off; then I'll be as good as new."

Shari left, and all I could do was think about how I'd just lied to my best friend. The whole situation smelled fishy to me, but I would never tell her that. It would hurt her too much. I should have never been so selfish and imposed on her and Dex's perfect little life. I hoped Tangie had more sense in her little peanut head than to push up on Dex. Family or not, if Tangie messed with Dex, I'd beat her ass down and send her packing. *That's if Shari doesn't get to her first,* I thought to myself.

By ten, I felt like a new woman. Before I got in the shower, I tuned into HOT 97 and blasted the radio so that I could jam while I was in the shower. They were playing my song, too. "Monica, girl, I feel so gone, too," I crooned all the way to the shower. When I got out, 50 Cent's "In Da Club" was on. Now I was really grooving. You couldn't tell me nothing, although I was still a little sore. I thought I'd heard the doorbell ring but really wasn't sure, because the music was so loud, so I decided to check, anyway.

I opened the door. My peach silk robe was clinging to me because I was still soaking wet. There stood Warren, looking fine as hell in gray jogging pants and a plain white T-shirt. He pushed me into the apartment by my waist and let himself in. For once I was speechless.

"Look, Brittany. I didn't appreciate you rolling up on me like that, girl," he remarked as he lifted me in his arms like a child and started toward my bedroom. "You were a very bad girl. I think I'm gonna have to spank that ass."

I felt the moisture growing between my legs with his every word. He smelled like Curve, and that alone was enough to get me going. I really was at a loss for words. I was prepared to curse his ass out, I thought. Until he showed up at my door, all cocky like. I wanted to demand an apology for the way he'd embarrassed me the night before, but I suddenly felt weak. The best I could do was try to look mad, but it wasn't working.

"Get on all fours," he demanded once we'd reached my bed and he'd placed me down. I started to take my robe off. "No, leave it on," he instructed, so I obliged. "Bend over and stick that ass in the air." This little game of Simon Says was really turning me on. He lifted the back of my robe up to expose my freshly cleansed bottom. They started out as taps that just made my booty jiggle a little, but soon his taps turned into rough slapping. He was seriously spanking me and was having a ball doing so. When his ten-minute torturous pleasure was over, I was so wet that it was dripping down both my legs and onto my bed. It was a new sensation for me, and I was loving it more than anything else I'd ever done.

"You're done?" I whined. I could have sat there and got spanked all damn day.

"Yup, and I'm out," Warren said, turning to leave.

"Huh? You can't leave me like this, Warren. Please don't leave," I begged, still on all fours. "I want you so damn bad."

"That'll teach you not to embarrass me in public again." He was teasing me, because he knew how bad I wanted him.

"Okay, I'm sorry. I'm so sorry, Warren. I'll never do it again. Just don't leave me like this." I continued pleading as I turned around and attempted to pull him to me. He wasn't having it. Warren enjoyed watching me beg.

"I really do have to run, though. My mom is cooking a big dinner tonight, so I have to get my workout on, 'cause I'm grubbing tonight."

"Warren?" my voice creaked. "Who was that woman you were with last night?" I was damn near ready to cry.

"My date," he said plainly and simply. "Brittany, I never told you we were exclusive. I didn't say nothing to you when I walked in and saw you all up in that drummer's face, did I? You're not my woman, and that's not my place. I really enjoy spending time with you, but I'm not trying to be held down. I wanna keep my options open for a while. Either you take it or leave it." He shrugged his shoulders and walked away.

Half of me wanted to throw my alarm clock at the back of his big, bald-ass head; the other half of me wanted to beg him to stay a little longer. I was so horny. *Damn. At least he keeps it real,* I rationalized.

Not even two minutes later, there was another knock at my door. I was in the middle of taking care of myself, since Warren hadn't. Although I hated to stop stroking my kitty, I just knew it was Warren returning to finish what he'd started. I sprinted toward the door, but when I opened it, there was no one there. On the ground lay a big brown teddy bear. *Warren is a sweetie,* I thought. Underneath the bear was a card. It simply read:

> *You deserve better.*
> *Your friend,*
> *Vaughn*

Shari

My paranoia was getting the best of me on Thanksgiving Day. I couldn't seem to do anything right. After leaving Brittany's, I headed to the cleaners to drop off my and Dex's clothes. After driving all the way across town to our favorite family-owned dry cleaners, I realized that it was Thanksgiving Day and almost every small business would be closed.

Then I went to the grocery store and dropped a dozen eggs in the dairy aisle. I reached the checkout counter and realized that I'd absentmindedly left my purse in the car. I had to hold up the entire line while I ran to retrieve my purse. Everyone had an attitude when I returned, but as far as I was concerned, they could kiss my ass. Eventually, I reached home, and Dex came out to help me with the bags.

"What's wrong, Bay? You don't look too hot," he said.

"Why thank you very fucking much, Dex," I spat, insulted. My day was going bad enough already. The last thing I needed was my cheating husband to be insulting me. Although I had no proof, with each passing day, I was starting to hate Tangie and Dex more and more. All within a week's time, I went from a trusting wife to feeling like a crazed lunatic. I really wished Brittany had just let me live in my little fantasy world, because I was starting to feel seriously threatened for the first time in my marriage.

"She's in a bad mood," he joked with Tangie, who was sitting at my kitchen table, wearing her robe. "Watch out."

I thought her attire was completely inappropriate, but the way I was feeling at that moment, I decided to keep my mouth shut before I had to hurt the girl.

"I'm not in a bad mood, Tangie. I just have a lot on my mind," I said. I shot her a look to hopefully let her know to get out of my damn kitchen since she was half-naked. "And a lot on my agenda today." I forced a smile.

"Mmm," was all she said as she got up from the table. When Tangie stood up, the tie on her robe got caught in a snag on the wicker chair, and the left side of her naked body was exposed. She gasped and quickly pulled her robe back together. Then she walked back to her room.

I spun around to see Dex's expression, but his back was turned, and he was starting the dishes.

She'd better be happy he hadn't seen anything. Or was he just playing things off for my benefit? Did she do that shit on purpose? My head was spinning.

"Dex, I know today is a big day, but I feel like crap. I've been up since the crack of dawn. I just need to catch an hour of sleep, okay?" I tried my best to sound tired and not venom-spitting mad, like I felt.

"Bay, everything will be fine. Is there anything I can start while you sleep?" He walked over and hugged me tight. Basking in his embrace, I realized how ridiculous I was being. Dex was a good man. The best man I'd ever had. I decided to try my best to dismiss any thoughts concerning him and Tangie. *He is good to me. He loves me to death,* I repeated in my mind. *I just need to stop tripping. That's all.* I felt so silly for allowing Brittany to corrupt my thoughts.

"Actually, you can help me out. I'll season the turkey real quick and throw it in the oven. Just keep an eye on it." I turned to Dex. "Can you peel about ten potatoes for the potato salad?"

"Is that it? How 'bout I boil the eggs and dice the onions, too. You know how those onions make your eyes burn for hours."

"Thanks, sweetie. Sorry I snapped at you earlier." I stroked his cheek, once again realizing how much he loved me and I loved him.

I seasoned the twenty-pound bird and put it in the oven, then headed straight upstairs and conked out on my king-sized canopy bed, fully dressed.

Two hours later I woke up and decided to take another shower, just to restart the whole day. It was a quickie: I only stayed in about five minutes. Wrapped in a towel, I plopped on my bed again and decided to call Brittany to see if she was feeling better and was able to come to dinner. When I picked up the receiver, I realized Tangie was already on the phone. My instinct was to hang it right back up, but something told me to listen in for a minute.

"Hell, yeah," Tangie said in her raspy little voice. "We used protection. I'm not trying to get pregnant by the man."

"You know you're dead wrong, right?" her friend asked.

"It's not wrong. He came on to me. Was I supposed to resist? He is too fine to turn down, and I haven't had none in a while, too. Please."

"All I'm saying is that if she finds out, she'll probably murder you both."

"I don't care. It's not my fault he wants me."

"You're just a piece of booty to that man. You know that, right?"

"So what. I used him just like he used me. It was a one-time thing, anyway. She can have him. I'm leaving in a couple weeks, anyway."

That was all I had to hear before I carefully placed the receiver down. My body became so numb that I couldn't even move. My first thought was to charge downstairs and stab the little whore.

Then go after Dex. I needed to clear my head, though, before I did something really stupid.

I threw on some sweats, ran past Dex in the living room, and headed straight out the door. I saw Dex in my rearview as I sped down our street. I'm sure he was wondering why the hell I left the house like a madwoman. "Yeah, I found out, nigga!" I screamed at his reflection in the rearview mirror as I accelerated. That's when the tears began to fall. I reached into my purse to call Nia. I would have called Brittany, but I didn't want to hear her say, "I told you so."

I pressed the number two on the phone pad for three seconds to speed-dial Nia's house. I put the phone to my ear, and Nia picked up on the second ring.

"Happy Thanksgiving," she sang.

"Nia, I'm . . . on . . . my way over," I said between gasps for air.

"What's wrong, Sha-Sha?" she demanded, sounding very concerned. "What happened?"

"D . . . D . . . Dex," I whimpered. That's when I saw the barricades. Police were blocking off streets to prepare for the Thanksgiving Day Parade downtown. I swerved to avoid crashing directly into them. "Nia, hold on," I screamed as I threw the cell down to grab the wheel with both hands. I swerved out of control, bounced off a barricade, and started heading toward a huge oak tree. Slamming on my brakes only made me swerve even harder. It was too late to do anything but throw my hands over my face and prepare for the impact.

"Shari, Shari, are you there? Hello?" I heard Nia screaming into the phone. I tried to reach for it and realized that I couldn't move. I tried to call her name, but she didn't respond. *Why can I hear her, but she can't hear me?* I wondered.

"Nia?" I cried. "Nia?"

Nia

I frantically called 911. Then I called Dex and Brittany and told them to meet me at the Stamford Hospital emergency room. We all made it in less than ten minutes. Dex headed straight to the check-in, with Brittany and me right on his heels.

"I'm looking for Shari Brown," he yelled, leaning over the clerk's desk.

After surveying her log, the clerk looked a little worried. "I'm sorry, sir. There is no one here by that name."

"I called 911 over ten minutes ago. Where the hell are they?" I demanded to know.

"Ma'am, please calm down," said the clerk. Sometimes the EMTs perform necessary aid at the location of the accident. If you all would take a seat, I'll radio them and see where they are."

We all gathered in the waiting area, but no one could take a seat like she'd instructed. The clerk entered the waiting area less than five minutes later, with her update.

"I'm sorry, but I never caught your names," she said. It was hardly the time for introductions and formalities, but we all recited our first names in unison. "Okay. Nia, you said you were the one that placed the call to 911, correct?"

"Yes, I did. It was me," I said. Was I speaking in tongues the first time I'd said it?

"What exactly did you tell them?" asked the clerk.

"Wait a minute. What the hell is going on here? Where is my wife?" Dex interrupted, with misty eyes. Brittany grabbed him by the arm and pulled him outside for some fresh air.

"Our dispatchers are saying that they have yet to find Mrs. Brown. What information did you provide?" the clerk continued once Dex was escorted away.

"I don't know much," I said. "I couldn't give them a location, because I don't know where she was. All I know is that she said she was on her way to my house. I assumed she was leaving her house. I gave the dispatcher my address and her address." I tried to recollect the mysterious phone call from Shari. "I told them she was driving a white Mitsubishi Eclipse. I told them I heard loud screeching and all types of crashing and banging." I broke into tears. "That's all I know. That's it," I yelled as I began pacing in front of her.

"I'm sorry to say that without a location, the EMTs are on a wild goose hunt. Furthermore, with so many blocked-off streets and the Thanksgiving

Day Parade, it could be at least another hour before we can find her."

"Fine. Then we'll find her ourselves," I said. "I jumped up and bolted for the door. Once outside I found Brittany and Dex in a comforting embrace.

"Dex, I need you to listen to me and try to keep a clear head," I said. "They haven't found Shari yet. Brittany and I are going to start looking ourselves. I need you to stay here in case the EMTs find her before we do."

"No way, no fucking way, Nia. I'm coming, too. I'm going to find my wife," he yelled, stabbing his chest with his index finger.

"Dex, please. You're too emotional right now, and the last thing we need right now is for both of you to be laid up on the side of the road somewhere," I reasoned, trying my hardest to fight back the tears welling up in my own eyes. "Call my cell if she reaches here first, okay?"

"Nia, I have to go. Please?" he cried and grabbed my arm and stared deep into my eyes. "Shari is my heart and soul, my world, my breath. I cannot sit here pacing until someone finds her. I'm going and that's final. I'm going to find my wife." Dex had tears streaming down his face, and now so did Brittany and I. We were all falling apart.

"I'll stay behind," Brittany offered. "Dex, let Nia drive, please." Her face was the color of boiled shrimp, and she could barely talk through her tears. "I'll call you guys if I hear something."

Just then the clerk busted noisily through the

automatic sliding doors. Startled, we all turned around, eager to hear her news.

"She's here. She's here, guys. They just wheeled her in a couple of seconds ago." She seemed just as relieved as we were.

"Can I see her?" Dex pleaded, with red, swollen eyes.

"I'm sorry, but she's been rushed to intensive care," replied the clerk. "There's no telling how long they'll be working on her. I'll update you as soon as possible."

"Intensive care?" Dex repeated as he sunk down to his knees and put his face in his hands.

"Why don't you guys go get something to eat in the cafeteria?" said the clerk. "I'll page you on the intercom as soon as she can have visitors. How does that sound?" She sounded like a kindergarten teacher talking to a bunch of six-year-olds.

"I can't eat right now," Dex whispered.

Brittany and I would have normally been a complete mess, but we knew we had to stay strong for Dex.

"You have to eat something, or you'll pass out on us," Brittany instructed. "Come on," she said as she lifted him up by his arm.

I ordered turkey sandwiches for all of us since no one really had a preference, or an appetite for that matter. Surprisingly, Dex managed to finish his entire sandwich. Brittany and I ate one half and picked at the remainder of the sandwiches. My stomach was in knots just thinking about what Dex was going through. It made me think of Mommy and Papi. They'd been together for close to thirty years. What would happen to the other if one suddenly died? I couldn't imagine spending every day of my life with someone and then, poof, they're gone. Thinking of my parents made a rush of guilt flow through me, so I decided to give them a call.

"Guys, I'm going to call my parents," I whispered, getting out of my chair. "Be right back."

Looking up with swollen eyes, Dex said he'd call Shari's mom and fill her in.

I stepped out onto the patio to make my call, and Dex took out his cell right there at the table.

"Papi, hi," I said flatly. "Happy Thanksgiving."

"Would be happier if you were here," Papi replied.

"I know, but right now I'm in the emergency room at Stamford Hospital. Shari got into a really bad car accident this morning, and she's in intensive care." There is something about telling your parents about a tragedy that just makes you feel like a child again. I broke into uncontrollable wailing. "Papi, she's gonna die! My best friend is gonna die. Dexter is going to go crazy. Papi, I love her like a sister."

"Nia, don't worry. Everything is in God's hands. He will do what's best for her. God won't take her before her time."

"What if it is her time?" I pleaded.

"I have a strong feeling it's not. Look, *mija*. Shari will be just fine. I promise. You just help her husband get through this, okay? He needs the strength that only you and Brittany can provide. I'll tell Mom you won't be making it to dinner. Don't worry. Everything will be all right."

I was quiet and really had nothing more to say, but just knowing Papi was on the other end made me feel so secure. I didn't want to hang up.

Papi made the first move. "*Te amo,* honey."

"I love you, too, Papi. Bye," I whimpered.

How I longed to be there with Mommy and Papi at that very moment.

Suddenly, I felt a lot better. Papi never reneged on his promises. Although I placed the fate of Shari in the Lord, if Papi made a promise, then that meant she was going to be just fine.

An hour had passed by the time we'd eaten and I'd talked to Papi. After hanging up, I decided to go back inside to see how Dex was doing. Plus, I was freezing my ass off. When I returned to our table, they were gone. I figured we must have gotten paged, and since I'd been outside, I hadn't heard it, so I ran back to the emergency room, but they weren't there, either.

"Excuse me, Miss. Do you know where my friends went?" I asked the same clerk that had been so helpful before.

"Yes, I paged them about five minutes ago to the intensive care unit. I'm sure you'll find them there. Just take the elevator up one floor and ask the nurse on duty what room they're in."

"Thanks," I yelled to her as I ran to the elevator and impatiently pressed the button several times. When I got upstairs, I joined Brittany in the small waiting room.

"Have you seen her? Is she okay?" I asked.

"No. Dex wanted some time alone with her first."

"Oh, okay. What did the doctor say?"

"She said that Shari will be just fine. She suffered a mild concussion. There are no broken bones, but there's a lot of bruising and swelling." Brittany sighed.

"That's a lot of damage. Was another car involved?" I quaked in fear.

"No, just her and a tree."

"Oh God, as long as she's alive." I grabbed Brittany, and we hugged more intensely than we'd ever hugged before.

"Yeah, but you know she's going to die as soon as she sees her face right?" We laughed, finally relieved to know Shari was alive.

Brittany

After a marathon of sex, Warren and I were finally worn out. He was trying to outdo me, and I, for sure, was trying to outdo him. Four rounds later, we were both spent. His cell phone, which was on vibrate, rang about ten times during our session. I guess he thought I didn't notice, but I did. I knew better than to say anything, though. I really didn't feel up to hearing his "I never said we were exclusive" speech again. I knew he would soon make a weak-ass excuse as to why he had to leave, so I beat him to the punch.

"Warren, I have to leave soon, so I think you should go," I told him. "I'm going to visit Shari in the hospital." I had to keep him guessing because I wasn't about to let him make a fool of me.

"Cool. I have to run some errands, anyway," he replied, looking relieved that he didn't have to make up a colorful excuse. *Yeah, right*, I thought.

He showered, dressed, and was on his way. With

Warren, there was never any conversation after sex, no sharing of dreams. Before Warren, that had always been the norm for me. I preferred it that way, actually. But no one could ever hold my attention like he did. I was really starting to fall for him, which scared me. At least he was always up front, so if I got hurt, it would be my own dumb-ass fault.

I pondered taking a nap before visiting the hospital but decided to go grocery shopping first. I needed to stock up since I'd be home for a while. As always, I'd saved the bulk of my vacation time for the end of the year. The next time I walked into the office, it would be a new year. At the grocery store, I ended up spending way more than I'd expected to. Lotion, deodorant, soap, detergent, tissue, and shaving gel all seem to run out within the same week. I made sure I bought Shari some Ho Hos to try and cheer her up.

"Hey, girl," I whispered as I walked through the door. She looked awful. I mean frightening. I hadn't been able to see Shari all that weekend. On Thanksgiving Day, Dex had stayed in the room with her for so long that visiting hours were over by the time he emerged. Saturday and Sunday the nurses said she was taking no visitors, not even her husband. I knew it must've looked bad. And it did. The bruising on Shari's face was worse than I'd imagined. She had two black eyes, with a huge raised bump in the middle of her forehead. Most of the other swelling seemed to have subsided.

She managed to lift one of her bandaged hands

and waved. A sad look dwelled in her eyes. A hurt that reached further than skin-deep.

"What's wrong?" It looked like she'd been crying all day.

"I don't want to talk about it yet," she replied.

"That's fine. We can talk about something else then," I offered. "Wanna Ho Ho?" I placed the package on the table next to her.

"No, thank you," she replied solemnly. Then she cracked a small smile, and I could see swelling on her bottom lip where fresh blood was gathered. Damn, I felt bad for her. "How's Warren?" she mumbled.

"Warren is wonderful. After that little scrape in the club, we've been spending more and more time together. I think he's starting to realize I'm a really interesting person."

"Really?" she replied sarcastically. "What exactly does he like about you?"

"He likes how I look, the way I lick, suck, and ride," I joked, pulling the navy chair close to her bed and taking a seat.

"Not funny, Brittany." She was so serious. "I bet this man knows no more about you than the butcher at Stop & Shop."

"No, he doesn't, but we are still in the 'getting to know each other' phase of our relationship. Plus, I'm not trying to make him feel all trapped. We have an understanding."

"As long as you're happy," she replied, with no emotion.

"Sha-Sha, why were you avoiding Dex this weekend?" I asked. "You know that tore him up, right?"

"Next question."

"Okay. Sorry." I halted the interrogation, careful not to upset her.

"What ever happened to Vaughn?" Shari asked me.

"Oh, nothing. I haven't spoken to him since the fight at Violet's. I'm sure he thinks I'm some kind of hood rat." I actually chuckled.

"You are," she teased, seeming to be feeling better by the minute.

"Yo' momma."

"Least I got one," she bragged.

"He wasn't that great in bed, anyway, so I'll see him when I see him."

"I just hope you keep your drawer full of condoms, with all the sexing that you do." Shari giggled, adjusting her body a little to the left to face me better.

"Girl, I don't use condoms. They irritate me, and plus, it's like taking a shower with clothes on. Ain't no point to that." I thought Shari was going to drop dead. She sat up as much as possible, eyes bulging out of her head.

"Brittany, I know you're kidding me, right? If I could get up from here and smack some sense into you, I would. What's wrong with you? Are you crazy?" The pitch in Shari's voice went up an octave.

"Chill out, Sha-Sha. I always make them pull out. Always."

"You sound like a fucking teenager, Brittany. The pull-out method is not dependable. First of all, you can get pregnant from pre-cum. Secondly, you can contract certain STDs from just coming in contact with an infected person's genitals. They don't only stem from fluid exchange. I don't believe you just sat there and told me that." She was heated. I felt bad because the last thing I wanted to do was upset my best friend while she was sitting there looking like the Bride of Frankenstein.

"Shari, I can take care of myself. I know my body. I would know if something was wrong."

"Yeah, but what if when you notice something is wrong, it's too late to do something about it? There are some STDs that you can never get rid of, and God forbid, you turn up pregnant." Then I could see her brain working overtime. Stress lines appeared on her face in an instant. "Brittany!" she screamed as loud as her swollen lips would allow. "When is the last time you had your period?"

That was a good question. After thinking about it, I hadn't seen Aunt Flow since the first week in October, and it was the first week in December.

"Oh shit, Sha-Sha!" I stood up beside her bed and then slumped back down in the oversized chair next to her.

"I knew it. Dammit, Brittany. That's why you've been having morning sickness. Those weren't hangovers. You're pregnant."

"I'm not. I told you, I know my body." I sat up.

"Yeah, well, if you know your body so well, tell me why you suddenly can't hold your liquor? Tell me why I had to come over and take care of you twice in the past two weeks?" She was really screaming at me.

I knew deep in my heart that there was a possibility, but I refused to believe it.

"I have a pregnancy test at home," said Shari. "It's upstairs in the medicine cabinet. Bring it back here, and we'll do this together."

"Sha-Sha?" I whined, stomping my feet like a baby and crossing my arms across my chest.

"Just go. It's only five minutes away."

"Fine." I was defeated. "You need something from home?"

"Nope. Just hurry back here before I have a heart attack."

I reached Shari's house in record time. She'd really scared me. I pulled up right beside Dex's car. *What the hell was he doing here in the middle of the day?* I thought. I knocked, then rang the bell, to no avail. Then I decided, against my better judgment, to enter using my key. I figured that with all the stress Dex had been through with Shari being in the hospital, he was catching up on some much-needed rest. The house was completely quiet, except for the sound of music coming from Tangie's room, way in the back.

"Dex!" I yelled out but got no answer. I ran up the stairs two by two, hoping Tangie wouldn't hear me, because I just wanted to get back to the hospital. I located the test fairly quickly. Mission accomplished. On my way back down the stairs, I realized that I hadn't seen Dex in the living room when I first walked in or in the bedroom I just had to walk through to get to the bathroom.

My body froze as I wondered. Is this why Shari

didn't want to see Dex? *I should murder him*, I thought. I tiptoed to the rear of the house. The music became louder, and so did the squeaking of the bed. I put my ear to the door and heard the muffled sounds of passion.

I knew if I busted through that door, I'd catch a case, but I tried, anyway. In a heartbeat, I would have beaten my sister down to the ground and stomped her face in. And Dex? I would've slit his throat. I started banging and kicking on the door and heard the squeaking stop, but the music continued to play.

"Tangie, it's Brittany. You'd better open this door. . . ." Bang. Bang. Bang.

Tangie didn't open the door. She knew better. I ran back to my car, much too vexed to walk.

My hands were shaking on the steering wheel, and it took all my self-control not to barge back into that house. My best friend was laid up, half dead, while these two were having a fuckfest. How could Dex be such a phony? Sitting up in the hospital, crying and shit. He didn't give a damn about Shari. There was no way in hell I'd be the bearer of bad news. Shari was beginning to put two and two together, but I'd just solved the equation.

I zoomed back to the hospital, where Shari was eagerly awaiting my return. I tried my best to hide the emotional turmoil that was brewing inside me, but it didn't work.

"What's wrong, Brittany?" she asked, seeming woozy from medication.

"Nothing," I lied. "Just nervous about this test."

How could I think about myself when my best friend's world was crumbling?

"March into that bathroom, pee on the stick, and bring it right back to me," she directed as she opened the foil package and handed it to me.

"Yes, ma'am." I lowered my head and slunk into the bathroom, located about five feet from her bed. Less than a minute later, I emerged, holding the stick arm's length away from my body. Shari took the stick with care and placed it flat on the bed next to her.

"I'll be right back. Gotta wash my hands," I said.

While in the bathroom, I couldn't help but cry tears of anger and betrayal. I felt for Shari; my mind was occupied with what I'd heard back at the house. I felt like I was just as bad as them for not telling, but at that point, with Shari lying in that bed, looking the way she did, I just couldn't.

I exited the bathroom, trying my best to look collected, but as soon as our eyes met, my heart skipped a beat and I knew.

"You're kidding me?" I asked.

"No. Hon. You're pregnant."

"Shit!" I screamed. The combination of the horrible news and what I'd heard less than fifteen minutes ago was too overwhelming. I plopped down on the chair beside her and rested my head on her lap as I began to sob. She rubbed my hair, and it made me surprisingly stable, if only for a moment.

"Sha-Sha?" I whimpered.

"Yes?"

"You think I'm a fool, don't you?" I cried. "You

think I'm nothing but a ho." What Shari thought of me really meant a lot. I didn't give a fuck what everyone else thought of me, but my friends' opinions count.

"If I thought those things about you, I wouldn't be your best friend. I think you just make some poor decisions, but we all do from time to time." Shari's eyes widened, and a solemn look suddenly came over her face. "Look. God has given you the blessing of life. That's a great thing. Don't look at it negatively. Having a baby is the most beautiful thing a woman can do. Brittany, you should be proud of yourself." She didn't stop rubbing my hair, not even for a moment.

"How can I be proud of myself when I have no idea who I made this baby with?"

Nia

My schedule for that week was so hectic. I had to spend as much time as possible with Mike, Brittany, and Shari before leaving for two weeks. Capri tried to give me a hard time about taking a vacation right before leaving for Houston, but I wasn't having it. I still had seven vacation days left, and I was sure gonna use them. Brittany sounded very ominous when I spoke to her earlier that morning, so we decided to meet at Catalina's to talk. We'd both been a little out of sorts since Shari's accident, but she seemed to be a lot more upset about the whole thing. I was just happy the girl was alive and well. Nothing that a little of Dex's lovin' couldn't fix.

Catalina's was a little more crowded than usual since they'd closed off the outdoor seating for the season. As soon as I spotted Brittany through the crowd of suits and ties, I knew I was in for some drama. She was dressed in a baggy light gray sweat suit and tan Timberlands. Definitely not the diva deluxe I was used to. She wore her hair up in a tight bun that gathered at the nape of her neck. A strand of hair fell over her eye, and she didn't even bother to sweep it away as she strolled over to the table and took her seat, with a loud thump.

"You sick?" I asked the obvious.

"I feel a little better now, but, girl, I've been feeling terrible lately." Her lips were ashy as she spoke, and her eyes were surrounded by gray circles.

"What's wrong?"

"What isn't?"

"Enough beating around the bush. Tell me what's up." I demanded to know why my diva-licious friend was sitting there looking like the Grim Reaper.

"Dex is cheating on Sha-Sha with Tangie," she replied, like she was telling me the weather.

"There's no way. Where did you get that idea from?"

"Nia, I walked into their house and heard them getting it on in Tangie's bedroom."

"How do you know it was Dex in there with her?"

"His car was parked in the driveway."

"Oh shit." A black cloud covered the sunshine in my heart. I had always thought Dex was that one man. That one good man. He was the role model for all men to follow, I'd thought. "What did you do?" I asked Brittany, who was looking around for the waiter.

"Nothing. I tried to bang the door down, 'cause you know damn well Tangie didn't answer it. I was in shock, so I just ran out of the house. I feel like I've betrayed Sha-Sha by not telling her." Moistness started forming in her eyes, but I think she was all cried out, because nothing fell.

"Of course not. That would kill her right now." I felt like skipping lunch and running straight to the hospital to be with my friend. "Plus, nothing should be said until we have hard-core evidence. A simple misunderstanding could ruin Shari and Dex's life."

"How are we going to get this evidence?"

"I don't know. We'll figure something out."

My heart was racing with fear and resentment. Although everything was adding up, I was silently rooting for Dex. I didn't want to think of him on the same level as most men. I wanted this to be a big mistake.

The waiter finally made it to our table after we'd been sitting there for ten minutes. Brittany ordered pink lemonade and I ordered an iced tea with our grilled salmon lunch specials. I didn't want to talk about the whole Dex thing anymore. It truly made my stomach turn just to think about how distraught he was in the hospital. That was no act. That man loved Shari too much to ever hurt her like that. Brittany was no liar, though. I'd just have to wait until we uncovered the truth to deal with it. In an attempt to lighten the conversation and mood, I asked Brittany, "What's new with you?"

"Psst, you don't even want to know."

"More drama, Brittany?" I asked, ripping open three packets of sugar to put in my iced tea.

"Of course, there's more drama. Does the drama ever stop with me?" Her voice sounded matter-of-fact as she took a sip of her lemonade.

"I guess not. What's up?" I tried to sound optimistic.

"I'm pregnant." Brittany gave a deep sigh.

I didn't think anything could upset me more than Dex cheating on Shari, but when Brittany told me she was pregnant and unsure of the paternity, I thought my head was going to explode. Especially since I've been telling her for years to use condoms. I didn't want to risk her getting upset with me, so I kept my real feelings to myself. "Well, which man are you going to tell?"

"Warren, of course. I am about seventy percent sure it is his. I mean, everyone else was only a one-night stand. Warren and I have done it so many times that I can't even count."

"Oh God, Brittany. Are you going to tell him you don't know if it's his or not?"

"Hell, no. As far as I'm concerned, it's his. Period."

"All right then. I just hope he takes this well." I began feverishly stirring my spoon around in my glass to dissolve the sugar. I immediately stopped when I noticed Brittany's aggravated glare.

"He will," Brittany commented once my clinking stopped. "He tries to front like he doesn't want to settle down, but I think this news will force him to become more family-minded."

"Looks like you have it all figured out." I was being facetious.

"Not really. I'm nervous as hell to tell him. I have to, though, and soon, because he'll be able to tell with me being sick all the time."

"So it looks like you're going to keep it."

"Maybe," she began. "I have about four more weeks to decide."

Talk about overwhelmed? Brittany dropped two really big bombs on me over lunch. We sat in a reflective silence as we finished the meal. There was so much I wanted to tell her, but I knew most of it would fall on deaf ears. "I love you, Brittany," I told her. "I'm always here whenever you need me."

Then we made plans to visit Shari together on Thursday. She was scheduled to be released on Saturday morning, and by then, I'd be on a plane to Texas. I filled her in with updates on Mike and me, and, surprisingly, she didn't have any negative comments to make. After promising to call me as soon as she delivered the news to Warren, I patted her flat belly. We embraced and headed in separate directions.

With less than a week left in the blistering cold Connecticut weather, I was more than anxious to head down south. It was bittersweet, though, because Mike and I had become really close in the last two weeks. The night of the brawl in the club, we decided to just go our separate ways for the evening. I was exhausted from all the commotion and really didn't feel like doing anything else but sleep. We ended up sharing an innocent kiss to seal the night.

On Saturday, Mike and I caught a movie and finally seized the chance to do some catching up.

He attempted to apologize again about the situation that had gone down in college. I let him know that all was forgiven, and we agreed to never bring it up again. Scars never heal unless you let them close.

Mike was living back at home with his parents while he finished his MBA in corporate communications at the Stamford branch of UConn. He also informed me that after the day he saw us at Catalina's, he'd quit. Since Stamford is so small, Mike said running into people from the past was almost a daily occurrence, which he wasn't very comfortable with. Stamford actually isn't that small, but the majority of black and Hispanic people all live within a ten-mile radius. You either live on the East Side, West Side, South End, or the Waterside, or in the Village. Most of the white population of Stamford lives in North Stamford, Springdale, Glenbrook, or downtown.

I'd officially made up my mind to give Mike another chance. That night he was coming over after his final exams to have dinner and maybe watch a movie on cable or something. There was an unspoken mutual agreement that we would consummate our relationship that night. The timing just seemed right. Everything was still so new and exhilarating to both of us. We'd both changed so much; it was like being with a whole new person. Sunday afternoon, when we went to the Maritime Aquarium in Norwalk, we ended up tonguing each other down behind the dolphin tank. The sexual tension had definitely come to its peak.

He came fifteen minutes early, which was fine with me because I could barely wait for him to arrive. I'd prepared grilled chicken and shrimp salads with fresh avocado, plum tomatoes, red onions, grated Parmesan cheese, and homemade honey mustard dressing. Mike walked in looking damn good. His Sugar Daddy complexion looked so smooth as he strode in, leaving a trail of Drakkar Noir behind him.

"You look stunning," he complimented me, although I knew he was stretching the truth just a little.

I'd actually spent quite a bit of time trying to appear like I wasn't trying too hard to look cute. I had on my little white Vicky short set that had SPOILED written across the chest of the tank top in bright red lettering. The shorts were just long enough to barely cover the bottom cusp of my ass. I'd kept it casual, with oversized, white, fuzzy slippers over my freshly manicured feet. I'd applied baby oil gel to my body to create the freshly showered, glistening affect.

"You don't look too shabby yourself," I replied, with a wink. He was dressed plainly in a navy blue sweater, dark jeans, and tan Timbos, but something about his swagger suggested an air of confidence, which was enough to make me moist.

We feasted on the salad I'd prepared like it was the Last Supper. "Where did you learn this recipe?" he asked between chews, exposing half-chewed greens. Even that disgusting little habit of his seemed absolutely adorable at that moment.

"My mother taught me everything I know about

cooking. She can throw down. I can't remember a day when I didn't have a home-cooked meal, unless I was away at camp or something." I devoured a forkful of shrimp and tomatoes. "Papi also taught me a thing or two. He would have to beg Mommy to let him take over for one night. She really gave him a fight, too, but in the end, it was always worth it. Papi would prepare the best and most authentic Cuban dishes ever. That's another thing Mommy hated. She would have to go out and get all Papi's special ingredients." I stopped because I realized I was rambling. "Sorry. I'm going on and on, but just thinking about how I missed Thanksgiving dinner at my parent's house is starting to get to me."

"No prob. I don't mind listening to you ramble. You don't even want me to start talking about my moms. Man, I'd be here all night." He gave a hearty laugh. I followed his lead. Suddenly, we were laughing our heads off for no apparent reason. I think it was the frozen raspberry margaritas I'd mixed up for us starting to take affect.

We left our dishes sitting on the island in my kitchen, which doubled as a dining-room table, with two stools on parallel sides. Lying in the spooning position on the floor, we began watching my favorite movie, *Friday*. It wasn't long before the movie was watching us.

It all began with him palming my right breast with his powerful hands. He just kept his hand there for the longest time, like he'd been waiting a lifetime to touch my full B cups. Then he graduated to slightly tugging my nipples under my shirt.

My tender nipples longed to be touched by a man. I think there's a direct vein from them to my pussy, because with every pull, I felt a direct rush of blood down there. Then his fingers started the journey south, stopping momentarily to tickle and tease my navel. Soon his fingers dived in and began drowning in my warm ocean.

I turned over so that he could lie on top of me. Our eyes froze in an entrancing gaze. He kissed me tenderly, yet with electrifying passion. Mike used the back side of his hand to stroke the side of my face. His hand continued past my neck, over my nipples again, and back inside of me. He then followed that same route with his tongue, which made my back arch in delight. After I exploded three times on his chin, nose, and lips, Mike picked me up and took me into the bedroom. As he carried me in his arms, I carefully wiped my juices from his face with my fingers.

He placed me gently on the satin sheets, which were like ice against my warm skin. He stood at the side of the bed and undressed. In the pitch darkness, I squinted to get a glimpse of Mike's sculptured body as I ridded myself of the cute Vicky suit.

No words were exchanged, but moans and whimpers of ecstasy filled the air. I grasped two handfuls of the sheets and arched my torso upward for deeper penetration. He let out a faint sigh, which let me know he appreciated my erotic gesture. We changed positions, and I ended up facedown, ass up. With one hand on each cheek, he controlled my movements, pulling me in toward him, then pushing me away with equal force in a steady repetition. I decided to add some flavor to his actions by rotating my hips with each of his thrusts. Mike let go of my cheeks and grabbed a fistful of my hair, which made the thrusts shorter, deeper, and more intense.

He finally released my hair, flipped me over on my back, and took his place back on top. I soon tired of the missionary, so I tightened my thighs around his and flipped him over with my legs in a fluid motion, without losing penetration. A look of excitement came over Mike's face. I didn't waste any time. I started grinding and bouncing up and down on him, and he loved it. He cupped my breasts and held on for dear life. Slowing my tempo, I gave him deliberate deep thrusts while bending over to deliver a kiss as he ran his hands through my hair.

I remained on top, giving it to Mike slow and sexy until he reached the height of passion. I had reached mine at least five times by then, so I collapsed beside him on the damp sheets. Usually, I'd jump straight into the shower after lovemaking, but that night we both had been drained and fell asleep, basking in the dampness from our throes of passion.

Brittany

I'd been dreading seeing Shari since the day I'd overheard Dex and Tangie at her house. To look her in the face would be very hard, knowing what I knew. But the time had come to face her again. Nia and I were on our way to visit her before Nia left for Houston for the next two weeks. Nia had convinced me to tell Shari about Dex and Tangie having sex. Knots were churning in my stomach as we stepped into Shari's hospital room. My hands were moist from a cold sweat, and I could feel my legs wobbling as we walked in.

"Hey," we sang together as we entered the room. Surprisingly, Shari looked almost normal again, and her eyes brightened as we approached her.

"Hey, girls," she said as she stretched her arms outward for a group hug. Her embrace was weak, yet filled with so much love and appreciation.

"We miss you so much," Nia commented.

"We can't wait 'til you get out of here," I added ominously, avoiding eye contact with her.

An uncomfortable silence filled the air, and I felt the inevitable approaching all too quickly. Nia's eyes were bugging out of her head, and she nodded her head as a signal that it was time to lay the cards out on the table.

"Sha-Sha, you know I love you, right?" I said. Nia shot me a narrow-eyed, ice-cold stare and mouthed the words "Stop bullshitting." "Shari, I have horrible news to tell you, and I hate to be the bearer of bad news," I said, then paused for dramatic effect. "Remember the other day when I was here and I ran to your house to pick up the pregnancy test?"

"Yeah," Shari said and nodded.

"Shari, while I was there, I overheard something I wish I'd never heard," I said and closed my eyes before continuing.

"She heard Dex and Tangie having sex," said Nia, finishing for me. I was actually relieved that I didn't have to say it. Shari's face remained tranquil. I'd expected her to go exorcist on us. She stared at the wall behind us for a moment and finally spoke.

"Tell me something I don't know," she replied dryly.

"Huh?" Nia and I said in unison as we looked at each other incredulously.

"I already know about their affair. I heard Tangie on the phone with one of her little friends, talking about everything. I was so distraught, leaving the house, and that's how I ended up here. I was on my way over to your house Nia, to cry on your shoulder when I found myself crashing into a tree," Shari said, with a shrug of her good shoulder.

"I'm so sorry I didn't tell you sooner. I just felt so horrible about the whole thing," I said.

"Don't even worry about it, Brittany," said Shari. You have your own worries to deal with. Dex is my problem. I understand."

"I shouldn't have let you take Tangie in, though. It's all my fault," I cried. Guilty tears marched down my cheeks and moistened her sheets. "You're just so damned generous and loving."

"Dex is who he is," replied Shari. "If it wasn't with Tangie, he would have cheated with someone else. I'm just glad that I found out sooner than later, ya know?" She shrugged her shoulder again. There was a solemn look in her eyes, but I guess she had had plenty of time already to take out her anger and sadness. "I just don't want to go back there. I can't face either one of them right now."

"You're more than welcome to crash at my crib while I'm in Houston," Nia offered. "Even longer if you need to." She added, "I have a comfy futon for you."

"I think that's a plan," Shari said seriously. "If I have to go back there, I think I'll shoot someone. But can we change the subject, please? I refuse to waste any more breath on those two. What's going on in your worlds?"

Nia went on and on about how she and Mike were in love all over again. I was glad to see her happy, but their relationship had just started, and she was claiming she loved him already.

"Don't trust him," Shari warned. "Men are all dogs. All of them!" I realized by the way she raised her voice that she was still heated about her situation.

"That's not true," I insisted. "Warren isn't a dog. He's really up front with me about everything."

"That makes him an honest dog then," Shari replied flatly.

"I'll be careful. My eyes are wide open. Plus, he barely has enough time to spend with me because of his schoolwork, never mind trying to have another woman in his life," Nia said, defending Mike.

"He's no good for you, Nia. Did you forget what he did to you?" said Shari. She was becoming very bitter. I wasn't used to that side of her. Dex had really turned her personality sour.

While they were debating, I had Warren on my mind. I began thinking about how the baby would bring us closer together. With Christmas two weeks away, the timing couldn't be any better. I'd tell him as his Christmas gift. That'd be perfect, I fantasized. Keeping it to myself for another two weeks would be too hard because suddenly I was so excited about the baby. I fantasized about our caramel-coated toddler running around in her little Baby Guess clothes, with a sparkling gold bracelet around her chubby little arm. *Her hair will be thick and curly, and I'll part it down the middle and style it in two mini Afro puffs on each side of her head. She'll have her dad's gray eyes and my thick eyelashes.* I could see her so clearly. She and I are going to be best friends. *I'll take her everywhere with me. People will ogle*

over her everywhere we go. I couldn't wait. I thought
I'd name her Alexis. *Alexis. Now that's a diva's name.*

"Brittany, snap out of it," Nia whispered as she
tapped my arm. I'd taken a seat by the window on
the opposite side of the room.

"Oh, sorry. You know I've been out of it lately," I
said.

"Let's go," Nia whispered. "Shari is napping."

I tiptoed over to Shari and kissed her on the forehead before we exited. We traveled back through the
snowy weather and power-walked to Nia's Honda.

"Why was she tripping on Mike like that?" Nia
asked once she started up the car and the heat finally kicked in.

"She's going through some real tough times
right now. It's hard for her to be happy for you
when her life is crumbling. Don't worry 'bout it.
She'll snap out of it. It'll just take some time. You
know deep down she's really happy for you."

"Yeah, I guess." She shrugged her shoulders.
"Wanna grab a pizza from Pappa's?"

"Ummm, sounds perfect. Then take me home.
I'm tired as hell." I gave a deep yawn.

They say that the first trimester and the last
trimester are when you are constantly tired and
lazy. Well *they* are right, because since I'd started my
vacation, I slept until noon, napped from three to
about five, then was in bed by nine. Warren
stopped by at least twice a week in the middle of the
night. Although I'd already be in dreamland by
then, I'd have no problem at all crawling out of bed
to ride his magic stick.

Shari

I was scheduled to get discharged from the hospital at three. I'd finally added Dex's name to my visitors' list, and just as I suspected, he showed up as soon as visiting hours began at ten in the morning. The nurses had told me that he had to be escorted away by security every morning for refusing to leave. Dex argued that the hospital was violating his rights as my husband by allowing me to prohibit his visitation. As far as I was concerned, he'd lost those rights by sticking his dick where it didn't belong.

I was sitting on the chair positioned at the left side of the Craftmatic-style hospital bed closest to the window when he arrived.

"What's going on, Shari?" he barked as he approached me, hands folded across his chest. "Why were you refusing my visits?"

He smelled like the Axe deodorant spray I'd bought him to wear on Thanksgiving. I thought I was ready to confront him and tell him to go to hell, but the mere sound of his voice made me weak. I hadn't realized how much I'd missed my husband. I missed his corny jokes and picking up his dirty socks off the bedroom floor. I missed making love to him. I wondered if he made love to Tangie with the same passion we'd shared. Did he massage her back afterwards, like he did with me, while telling her his dreams, hopes, and fears? I thought I hated him so much, but seeing him again made me feel like running back into his arms.

"I'm not coming home, Dex." I finally summoned up the courage to say those words.

"What?"

"You heard me," I answered, coldly looking past him, not at him. "I'm not coming home."

"What?" he repeated, unfolding his arms and taking a step toward me. "What's up with you? First, you were refusing my visits. Now you're saying that you're not coming home. This is bullshit . . . Shari. You're coming home." He took another step closer and towered over me, so that I had to tilt my head back just to look in his face.

"No, I'm not," I said, with a faint voice.

"Is it because of your face?"

I felt a boiling-hot pang run across my left cheek.

"Bay, you are still the most beautiful woman in the world," he said. "I don't care about those scars. They'll fade in no time."

"Yeah, the physical scarring will fade, but the emotional scarring will take much longer to heal. Much longer."

"Look, I'm not sure what the hell is wrong with

you, but whatever it is, we can get through this. We can go for counseling. Whatever your problem is, we can work it out together. I'm here for you." He knelt down on his knees in front of me and took my hands in his. "What's wrong?" he whispered.

Glaring into his eyes, I began to tremble uncontrollably. Dex grabbed me and hugged me tight as he ran his hands up and down my back. I wanted everything to be back to normal, but I wouldn't allow myself to be blinded by love. I've seen it happen too many times. Women tend to ignore the evidence that is right in front of their faces just to be with the man they love. *Well, not me. Not this time,* I thought.

"I'm not coming home, Dex," I said, that time more forcefully.

"What did I do? Please tell me what I did." He let my hand go and was now standing over me again.

"If you wanna play stupid, then I'll play stupid, too. I don't know. I don't know what you did, but I do know this . . . I'm not coming home. Just leave before I call security and have you escorted out again."

"I'm not moving until you tell me what the fuck is going on!" he barked. Dex had never used that language or tone with me before. I answered by turning my full attention to the episode of *SpongeBob SquarePants* that played on the hospital television.

"Shari!" he screamed. His temper was getting out of control. He scared me so badly that my body jerked and my eyes widened in fear. "I'm not playing games with you anymore. I'm sorry to yell, but I feel like I'm losing my fucking mind." He began pacing back and forth, hitting himself on the forehead with the palms of his hands. "Where are you going then, Shari?"

"Don't worry about it."

"Don't worry about it? Is this a joke? I almost lost my wife on Thanksgiving Day. I have dreamt of the night you'd be lying beside me in bed ever since that day." He found his way back over to me and knelt before me again. With one hand on my knee and the other grasping my hand, he began to cry. Not a boohooing, hiccupping, and stuttering cry, but just silent, masculine tears falling rapidly down his face. With a bewildered look on his face, he asked, "Bay, are you leaving me for someone else?" He squeezed my hand harder in anticipation of the answer.

"I just need some time to figure some things out. Just give me the space I need right now. I promise one day we'll talk about this. I'm just not ready right now."

"Fine. I guess I don't have much of a choice." He paused. "Where are you going to stay?"

"I'm not telling you. I'll call you when I'm ready to talk." I turned to him and looked in his eyes for the first time.

"Don't do this to me, Bay, please," he pleaded.

After what he'd done to me, he had the audacity to be sitting there begging me not to do this to him. What about me? What about my feelings?

"Just leave. Get out, Dexter!" I pointed to the door. I had momentarily begun to feel sorry for his ass. His whole act was very convincing, but I held my ground. Did he think that no matter what he did to me, I was just supposed to forgive and forget? I had to remind him that I was his wife, not his mother.

Dex finally walked out, looking at the ground, with his shoulders slumped. I sat in that chair for another half hour, bawling my eyes out. How could such a small amount of temptation have made him step out on me? I knew he loved me; I felt it when he looked into my eyes. And, Lord knows, I loved that man. As much as I loved him, I could never be capable of imposing so much pain on him. How could he have done it to me?

I finally peeled myself off the comfortable hospital chair, packed my bags, turned in all the discharge paperwork, and called a cab to Nia's.

Nia

Mike and I had planned that he would drive me to LaGuardia Airport at three thirty in the morning in order to catch the six o'clock flight to Houston. With about twelve hours until my departure, I decided to visit Papi and Mommy before I left. Papi assured me there would be no evil half sisters there or beautiful little half nieces and nephews running around. I stopped by the bakery to get Mommy a caramel cheesecake drizzled with chocolate on top. I took I-95, and it was, surprisingly, not a parking lot that day, so I arrived in the Bronx in less than thirty minutes.

Mommy and Papi seemed to have aged since the last time I'd visited them, last Christmas. Papi's thick, jet-black, curly Afro now was sprinkled with gray around the edges of his face. I think he'd added a few inches around his waist, too. Mommy still looked a lot younger than Papi, but I now noticed laugh lines that hadn't been there last year. Mommy's pecan skin was always so smooth. She'd always taught my sisters and me not to use soap on our faces and to sleep with a thick layer of cocoa butter at night. Every morning, especially in the winter, Mommy would inspect our faces before leaving the house.

"Did you put Vaseline on your face this morning?" she'd ask. Vaseline is what Mommy said kept your face soft and moisturized.

"Come here, my little grease monkeys," Papi would sometimes say before he kissed us good-bye. "*Dame muchos besos.*" Krystal and Angel resented Papi calling them grease monkeys, but I thought it was funny. We did look like monkeys.

I guess the Vaseline and cocoa butter regiment really worked, because we all had perfect skin and beautiful complexions.

Papi had kept his promise, and he, Mommy, and I had a wonderful dinner, just the three of us. I never saw a man appreciate his wife like Papi did. His sentences started with, "Honey, can you please," and ended with, "Thank you, sweetheart." After every meal, Papi said, "Thank you, sweetheart. Everything was great." It didn't matter if she had made hot dogs and beans or shrimp scampi and steak.

"How's the business going?" I asked after Papi cleared the dishes from the table.

"Business is doing great. Papi is thinking about expanding to Connecticut so we can take on even more clients. Then he can hire more people and stay his butt home sometimes!" Mommy looked in his direction and cackled.

After we had all graduated and moved out on

our own, Papi had retired from the Postal Service after serving for twenty years. Mommy never worked a day after she married Papi. He would do whatever it took to make ends meet, which included working the midnight shift at Federal Express for eight years.

Once he retired, they decided to open up a cleaning business. Sparkling Cleaning Service started out with two employees: Mommy and Papi. She'd insisted on being by his side throughout the whole process. They started out cleaning up houses out in Scarsdale for ridiculous prices. Although the work was sometimes grueling, their paychecks were fat at the end of the week. Mommy and Papi worked side by side, scrubbing floors and washing windows for three homes.

In the first year they had made enough money to double up on their payments and pay off the mortgage on the house. Exactly twelve months later, Papi made Mommy stay home, and he hired a young Cuban guy to be his cleaning partner. Soon the demand for Sparkling Cleaning Service became overwhelming. Mommy stayed home to answer calls and set appointments for new clients, while Papi and Armando worked their fingers to the bone. In the next six months, Rosa, Marisol, Diana, and Philipe were added to the payroll. Papi stopped doing the actual cleaning and began the marketing and advertising for the business.

That was seven years ago. Now Papi and Mommy own a fleet of yellow Dodge Neons with SPARKLING CLEANING SERVICE painted in orange cursive lettering on the side. With over seventy employees, they were able to secure business with two office buildings and the Westchester Mall. Although Mommy and Papi now owned a condo in Florida and a vacation home in St. Thomas, they refused to move out of the modest three-bedroom house we grew up in.

"I'll never leave the Bronx," Papi sometimes boasted, beating his chest like Tarzan.

"And, as long as you're here, I'll never leave the Bronx, either," Mommy would answer.

"That's great," I remarked about the continued success of their business.

"What about you? How's work going?" Mommy asked me.

I proceeded to tell them about my trip to Houston. They were very excited, and Papi gave me his good-luck cigar box to take with me.

"Thanks, Papi." I hugged him.

"I had this box with me when I applied for the loan to start our business," Papi explained. "With Mommy's and my credit scores, I knew only my lucky box and constant prayer would get us approved."

"Y'all ready for some of this cheesecake?" Mommy asked.

"Yes, please, sweetheart," Papi replied.

"I'll get it, Mommy. You sit down," I told her.

"You ain't got to tell me twice." Mommy waved her hand, sitting back in her chair. "When's the last time you spoke to one of your sisters?" she yelled into the kitchen. I knew it was coming.

"Uh, last Christmas, when Krystal pointed out the fact that she thinks I'm a lesbian in front of the whole family over dinner. Yeah, I think that was the last time." I couldn't hide my sarcasm.

"When are you going to stop holding a grudge against your sisters?" asked Mommy. "It hurts my heart to see y'all not speaking. I carried all of you in my womb. No one got treated any better than the other. Not in this household."

"Never," Papi added for affect.

"Mommy, I have never loved them, and they don't love me, either. That's fine with me. I don't care." I shrugged as I began slicing the cheesecake.

"Oh, Jesus, take me now. My daughters don't love each other!" she screamed, grabbing her heart Fred Sanford style. I didn't realize at first, but she was serious, because tears began tumbling down her smooth cheeks.

"Mommy, I'm sorry," I said. "I love them. I just don't like them much. They've been mean to me my whole life. You don't know half of the stuff that went down behind closed doors." Papi was now standing behind her chair, rubbing her shoulders, giving me a stern look.

"Nia, I never meant to divide this family," said Mommy. "I know everything is all my fault. Your sisters expected me to mourn their father's death. And I did. But as soon as I met Papi, I fell in love all over again. We are soul mates, and I realized that after knowing him less than a week. If I hadn't met Papi, you wouldn't be here, either. And, I'm sorry, but if I had to do it all over again, I'd still marry Papi. This man has given me the best years of my life." She paused to soak up her tears with a napkin. "But I am sorry that I divided the family."

"It's not your fault that they hate me," I replied. "Maybe if they had gotten some type of counseling after their father's death, they could have handled your remarrying a little better."

"They didn't have all those programs back then. Not that we could afford them, anyway," Papi said.

"When are you three gonna grow up? Family is all you have at the end of the day. The sooner you three realize that, the better off you'll be," Mommy whispered. "But I can't force y'all to get along, but you will be civil to each other under my roof."

"I promise I will try to start getting along with them. You're right. We do need to grow up," I agreed.

"Okay, can we eat now?" Papi interjected.

"Sure," Mommy answered. "As long as she's gonna try, I'm happy."

Slowly, we consumed the cheesecake and drank steamy coffee. Papi had an early morning, so he excused himself from the table and went upstairs. I helped Mommy wash the dishes and had to hurry home to pack.

"Take the rest of this cheesecake with you, Nia. You know I love it, but I might as well slice a piece and tape it right here," she said, pointing to her ass.

"Oh, so you want me to be walking around here with a big ole butt like you?" I teased.

"Hey now! You better watch it before I pounce on you with my big ole butt," she yelled as I walked toward her for a hug and kiss good-bye. "Good luck, honey. I'll know you'll do great, though.

You're driven, just like Papi. Just be careful on them planes." She finally let me go.

"All right, Mommy. Bye. Kiss Papi for me."

"Grab that cheesecake!"

Mike and I were on our way to LaGuardia when he stopped at a gas station's pay phone to return an urgent page.

"That was my mom. Please tell me when needing milk became an emergency situation," he said.

We laughed.

The airport was a little over an hour's drive away. I was dreading leaving when Mike and I had just started bonding again.

"I think I'm going to miss you," he said, reading my mind.

"Me, too." I hadn't realized how much Mike had filled a big void in my life until it was time to leave him for two weeks. So many women say how they don't need a man, but I do. Not financially, but physically and emotionally for sure. Getting some lovin' on a regular basis kept a smile on my face. I even found myself singing in the shower from time to time. I now realized how much Shari must have been hurting. Men can be a wonderful thing, but on the other hand, they can really tear you apart.

With only twenty minutes until my plane departed, we embraced half the time and kissed the other. Then I had to quickly boogie to my gate due to the post-9/11 safety precautions.

With only two minutes left, they announced the final boarding of my flight.

"Damn, I'm gonna miss you, girl," Mike said. He squeezed me.

"Me, too." I squeezed back.

"Here," he said, extending a small box toward me. I ripped it open wildly. Inside was a delicate rope chain with a heart locket at the end. "Open the locket after you get on the plane."

"All right." We kissed once again, and then I sprinted to my plane. Once seated and buckled in, I immediately opened the locket. Inside was a picture of Mike and me that we'd taken at a photo booth when we were in college. I clasped the chain around my neck and grasped the locket in my hand.

"I think I'm falling in love," I said aloud.

Brittany

Since finding out about the life growing inside of me, I'd decided to change some of my bad habits. Of course, Absolut had to disappear from my weekly routine. In addition, I tried to consume a lot of fresh fruit and all-natural juices instead of sodas and artificial juice. Instead of my regular cardio and weight-training routine at the gym twice a week, I'd taken up yoga. It's absolutely amazing how relaxing and beneficial yoga is. In class, I'd feel like all my worries were gone, and I felt featherlight when I left. Also, I'd heard yoga keeps the body flexible, and staying fit makes labor and delivery easier.

I'd just finished up my hour-long yoga session at eight and was rushing out when I ran into Vaughn again. I needed to make it home by nine to catch *Girlfriends,* so I hoped he wouldn't talk my ear off.

He was exiting the men's locker room, looking and smelling freshly showered.

"Hey, Brittany." He'd spotted me first.

"Oh, hi, Vaughn." I felt slightly embarrassed, remembering that the last time he saw me was when I was going Laila Ali on Warren's date.

"You take yoga now? You like it?" he asked, noting my floor mat.

"It's cool. Relaxing, ya know?" I knew that he would avoid asking me about the night of the altercation, so I decided to bring it up. "Sorry for the commotion I caused at your show. You men know how to take us there." I let out a nervous laugh. "Thanks for the teddy bear. I keep him on my bed. He matches my new comforters perfectly."

He laughed, too. "You're too old to be acting like that. You know that, right? You're welcome. I meant what I wrote, too. You do deserve better."

"How are you so sure?"

"You are a beautiful person, and I can see through your front."

"What front?" I put my mat down and retrieved a bottle of water from my bag.

"You front like you're too good for people and like you only can have the best of the best. But if that were true, then you wouldn't be with that fool Warren."

"Really? Well, it's a little too late to be choosy. I'm stuck with him. And I'm happy with that."

"It's never too late. Why do you think you're stuck?"

"Because I'm having his baby." I gloated.

"Get out of here!" He nudged my shoulder. I

hated when he did that. "Really?" he asked. "How far along?"

"I'm not sure yet. I have my first doctor's appointment next week, but I think I'm about two months." I was beaming.

"Looks like you're happy about this. What did he say?"

I felt so comfortable sharing with Vaughn. "I didn't tell him yet. I'm waiting for Christmas Day. That'll be his present."

"Wow, he's a lucky man. Doesn't deserve you, but he sure is lucky."

"Oh, whatever. Warren is the most honest guy I've ever dealt with, and I respect him for that. I'm not sure how he'll take the news, though, but I hope he'll be as happy as I am."

"You're going to be a mother. Wow. God bless you." Vaughn kissed my cheek.

"Thanks."

"Can I take you out for a celebration dinner?"

"No, that's okay. I have to catch *Girlfriends*. I don't miss that show for no one."

"Aw, you're dissin' me for a sitcom? Can we reschedule for another time then? I'd love to cook for you sometime."

"You can cook?" I eyed him suspiciously as I put my half-empty bottle of water back in my black tote.

"Of course, I can. Let me know a date, and I'll go all out and prepare a feast for you, since you're eating for two now."

"Okay, then. I'll give you a call. Let me go before I miss my show. Then I'll have to hurt you."

"All right, Miss Brittany. Make sure you call me to set up that date." He paused. "As a matter of fact, give me a call whenever you need someone to talk to . . . about anything at all. I'm there."

He was really trying hard to get close to me. At least I knew he was only interested in friendship, since I was bearing another man's child.

"Definitely," I replied as he reached out for a bear hug.

Shari

Nia left her car for me to get around while she was gone. That was a blessing because that girl had no groceries and didn't leave any toiletries behind for me to use. I took advantage of the opportunity to gather some work clothes and personal items from the house when I figured both Tangie and Dex would be at work. When I pulled up, I noticed that Dex's car was not out front, so I applauded myself for my perfect timing.

When I entered the place I used to call home, the familiar aroma of Dex's homemade biscuits infiltrated my senses. He'd probably made them for that bitch for breakfast. I went straight upstairs and entered what used to be my bedroom. The place where Dex and I had made love so many times. The place where we'd mapped out the rest of our lives together.

When I turned twenty-eight, we would start working on a Dex, Jr. We'd then put this house up for sale and buy a four-bedroom house in North Stamford.

By then Dex would have made senior sales manager for the pharmaceutical company he worked for and would be making close to ninety thousand dollars a year, plus commission. I would stay home and raise Dex, Jr., while at night we would work on Mariah, a little sister for Junior. In my spare time I would start planning my home-based day care. That way our kids could go to day care in our own basement. When Mariah turned six months, she would be sent downstairs with Junior to the day care. Then I would become a full-time clothing designer and would begin designing in the studio that Dex built and decorated for me parallel to his poetry den in the attic. All those plans had been ruined now. Mariah and Dex, Jr., would never even exist.

I took as many things as would fit into my half of the matching luggage Dex had bought for us last year for our second honeymoon to Jamaica. I tried my hardest not to get nostalgic, but it was hard. Every piece of clothing, lingerie, and jewelry had a story behind it. A story of two people in love. It became increasingly harder for me to hold back the tears as I stuffed each article into my bags. Soon tears were falling hard and hot down my face. I was too sad to be angry, so I just cried as I cursed myself for being so trusting. Everything was my entire fault.

I tossed the suitcases down the stairs, knowing full well that I wouldn't be able to carry them down. I skipped down the stairs, with every intention of heading straight back to the car and back to my new home. Something called me, lured me to the back of the house. It was like I heard someone whispering my name repeatedly. I don't remember taking steps. It was like I floated toward Tangie's room and opened the door.

Inside, I found the last piece of the puzzle, which I needed to gain some closure on this situation. Tangie had boldly left her journal on her pillow, with a pen stuck between the pages to mark where she'd last left off. Instinct led me to make myself comfortable on the queen-sized bed my mom had bought Dex and me as a housewarming gift, and I read from beginning to end.

She'd evidently started her entries the day she moved in here. I was described as "cool, but a complete control freak." Dex was "blazin' and built, but was pussy-whipped and a cornball." Then there was page after page of incessant rambling about her exes and gossip about her hoochie mama friends. I finally reached November twenty-seventh, Thanksgiving Day. This was the day after the love affair began. Dex must have snuck out of bed in the middle of the night to fuck her.

November 27, 2003

Happy Thanksgiving!

I finally got some!! Shit, it has been a long time. I knew that motherfucker wanted me from the first time he laid eyes on me. I know he supposedly belongs to someone else, but I couldn't resist him. He arrived at about three in the morning. I'd just gotten in from Violet's. I took a quick shower and hopped in the bed, butt-ass naked.

Couple of minutes went by, and he was here. I

opened the door for him and got right back under the covers. He climbed right in the bed, next to me, like he just knew I would give him some. I think we both knew the deal. That shit was the bomb, too. You would have thought the nigga just got out of jail the way he was tearing my back out!!

I called Sherita the next morning, and she was all trippin' on me and shit. Talkin' 'bout I am foul for doing that, and I should be ashamed to do that to another woman. My philosophy is this: if you can't keep yo' man happy, he'll find happiness elsewhere. As far as I'm concerned, he ain't her man, anyway, if he's climbing up in my bed at night, right?

November 30, 2003

Fuck!! Brittany almost busted us out! I had just climbed on top and was getting right into the groove of things. Then we heard her screaming and banging on the door. Thank God I had locked it. I thought she was going to kick the damn thing in! He was SHOOK. You should have seen his face. I had to suck his dick for like ten minutes after she finally left just to get him hard again.

Brittany gets on my fucking nerves, thinking she's somebody's mama. She's lucky I didn't open that door and kick her ass for being all up in business that doesn't concern her.

December 1, 2003

I am starting to feel a tiny little bit guilty. I really thought this was going to be a once or twice thing, but he just can't get enough of me. I don't mind, either. It's strictly a sex thing, though, and he told me that, *too. He says he really cares about his woman and would never leave her for anyone. I don't want him like that, anyway. But, damn, the sex is off the hook!*

Connecticut is boring as hell! Every time I wanna go out, I gotta hop on the Metro North and go to the City. This weekend, this chick I met at the mall is supposed to be taking me out to a club called Speed in Manhattan. She said it has like five different floors and there are more than enough niggas to choose from. Okay?!

December 10, 2003

I think I'm a nymphomaniac. We've sexed every day since she's been gone. I hope I'm not falling for him, but I fantasize about him all the time. And the sex is different every time. Every damn time! Yesterday he started calling me his peach because he said my pussy feels like a peach when you keep it for too long and it gets real soft and mushy.

You know what I can't understand? How he can say he loves her so much but yet fuck the shit out of me every chance he gets? That ain't love. When I get a real boyfriend, I hope he doesn't love me like that. If that's love, I don't want it.

December 11, 2003

I gotta get away for a minute. This situation is getting out of hand. I'm going to Philadelphia to visit my friend Sierra for a minute. Sierra is my girl!! I can't wait to see her. As soon as I get back, I'll let you know all about the Philly niggas.

See ya!!

Smooches . . .

I'd had enough. That was the last entry, anyway. I carefully placed the diary back on her pillow with shaky hands. As far as I was concerned, Dex could go straight to hell. I would never take him back after this betrayal. It's one thing to succumb to temptation once, then realize you've made a mistake. But to keep doing what you know is wrong is just unforgivable. I slammed the door behind me and ran toward the front of the house. My head felt light, and I was beginning to feel dizzy. I had to get out of there before I passed out. My breath had become short, and I was struggling for every breath as I whisked the door open with all the strength I could muster.

On the other side stood Dex—the last person I wanted to see at that moment. He had his hand outstretched, as if he was about to stick his key in the door. I screamed and jumped back about five feet. I landed on my ass because I was just completely flummoxed at that moment. He attempted to assist me in standing back up.

"Don't touch me, muthafucker!" I slapped his hand away.

"What the hell is your problem?" he said, ignoring my command and snatching me to my feet with ease.

"You! You are my fucking problem," I screamed as I shoved him away. "Don't you dare touch me, you bastard!"

He barely budged.

"Move!" I shouted.

"Are you losing your mind, Shari? What the hell is your issue?"

I scurried around him and made it back to the doorway. I ran out the door, screaming every obscenity that I could think of and jumped into Nia's Honda.

"Shari, talk to me, please," he begged through the glass of the car door.

"Fuck you," I replied, sticking up my middle finger before revving up the engine. "Get out of my way before I run your stupid ass over."

I reversed out of my old driveway and sped down the street. No sooner had I turned the corner than Dex's Explorer was on my tail. *Don't make this any uglier than it already is,* I thought. At that point I didn't care if he knew where I was staying. I had no intention of going back to him, so I drove right back to my new temporary home. I'd stopped racing through the streets and took my sweet time getting there, too. Dex followed every step of the way.

I calmly parked and exited the Honda. Dex stepped out of his car and followed me to the door. I let him follow, and once I stepped inside, I slammed the door in his face.

"Shari, open this door!" Bang. Bang. Bang. Bang. I ignored him. He stood there banging for ten minutes. He sounded like a maniac, screaming my name over and over again.

Finally, after I couldn't take his noise anymore, I approached the door. "Dexter, if you don't leave right this second, I'm calling the police. Don't test me."

The banging stopped, and I heard his footsteps.

I peeked out the window to make sure he'd really retreated. He climbed into his Explorer and sped away.

No sooner had I seen Dex turn the corner then my cell phone began humming and vibrating in my purse. He was text-messaging me. Call me when you are ready to be an adult about this.

I returned with, Fuck you, asshole!

Nia

Sixty-eight degrees in December and I was loving every minute of it. Houston was starting to make a great impression on me. My room at the Hilton Americas–Houston Hotel wasn't the grandiose suite I'd imagined, but it was clean, spacious, and actually quite comfortable. The queen-sized bed had a coral spread and bed skirt that matched the floor-length, airy coral curtains. Above the headboard was a mirror that stretched the entire length of the wall. The desk, located to the immediate right of the entrance, had a high-gloss mahogany finish. The beige walls and carpeting added to the earthy feel of the room.

Instead of resting or getting prepared for the next day, I decided I would enjoy my first night in Houston. I changed out of my loose jeans and jean jacket ensemble into a tight pair of boot-cut jeans from Express and a sheer grape peasant blouse. I'd gotten my mid-back-length, curly mane straight-

ened for this business trip, and that night I decided
to part it down the middle and wear two ponytails,
like I did back in the day when I was dubbed Pocahontas. A style, by the way, that Brittany would
never let me get away with back home. But I figured
I was halfway across the country, so I wanted to be
a little adventurous. For final touches, I threw on
some silver hoops, my new locket, and a silver
charm bracelet. After fishing my purple clutch out
of my luggage, I slipped in my lip gloss, hotel key
card, cash, ID, and a pack of gum, then headed
down the dimly lit elevator to the hotel bar.

At the near-filled bar, I took a seat next to a petite
honey-colored woman. She wore the face of a
green-eyed cat tattooed on the back of her right
shoulder. Have you ever met a person and immediately thought they were insane because the second
you learned their name, they started telling you
their whole life story? Well, Tara was one of those.

In a half hour's time, over a raspberry margarita,
I learned that she'd just broken up with her
boyfriend of two years because he'd slept with her
best friend. I learned she was what she called
"Blasian." Her mother was Filipino, and her father
was African-American. Her father was in the mili-
tary and served two years in the Philippines. Her
real name was Kitara, but her ex had nicknamed
her Kitty (hence the tattoo), so now she just wanted
to go by Tara.

Another hour passed, and after finishing another
raspberry margarita, we were blabbing like we'd
known each other forever, and she didn't seem

insane anymore. Kitara turned out to be a great drinking partner. Although she was doing most of the talking, I was content with laughing and enjoying her stories.

It turned out that about six months before, she had agreed to have a threesome with her best friend and boyfriend as a birthday gift to him. Well, after that night, unbeknownst to Tara, her boyfriend and friend continued sleeping with each other. Kitara also indulged in lesbian trysts with her trifling friend while her boyfriend was at work. Kitara had just caught them that morning and was staying at the hotel until she decided what her next move would be.

"I'm thinking about moving to New Yawk," she confided in me, with a slight southern drawl. "I always wanted to live there, ever since I was knee-high to a grasshopper. I need to get out of Houston. If I don't, I just know I'll end up reconciling with Chaz. He always makes me so weak. But, girl, he's been carrying on like this for two years. I just never thought he'd sleep with my best friend."

"New York's all right. I like to visit, but I don't think I could ever live there."

"You've been to New Yawk?" Her eyes widened. Her childlike amazement surprised me. You would have thought I was talking about visiting the Taj Mahal.

"Zillions of times. I live less than half an hour away, well, from the Bronx, but Manhattan is only about forty-five minutes away."

"My dream is to be a personal trainer to the stars. Did I tell you I'm a personal trainer?"

"No, but that sounds like an exciting job, though. Here." I went into my clutch to get a business card but then realized that I'd switched purses and left my wallet in my room. "Oops, I thought I had some b-cards with me. If you want, follow me to my room, and I'll give you one. And, if you actually decide to make that move to New York, call me, and I can be your first new client. Lord knows, I could use some toning."

"Please. You know you got it going on already, but, hey, who am I to pass up business? I'm right behind you."

We settled our bill at the bar and headed toward the elevators. As she pressed the UP button, I noticed three Chinese-looking symbols tattooed on her inner wrist.

"Damn, that one must have hurt," I said as I grabbed her hand to get a closer look.

"Like hell, but I don't mind a little pain, though."

"How many tattoos do you have?" I was done inspecting her hand, so I let it go.

"Four. And six piercings."

Then I was the one with the childlike excitement. Well, maybe not excitement, but curiosity. I had always wanted to get my nipple pierced, but just the thought of the pain it would cause gave me a headache.

"Where?" I wondered as the elevator dinged and we entered.

"I usually keep them a secret, but I'll tell you. Tattoos or piercings?"

"Piercings."

"One. Two. Three. Four. Five and six," she whispered as she pointed to each earlobe, each breast, and her vagina, and stuck out her tongue on six.

"One day I'll be brave enough to get my navel pierced. Didn't the nipple piercing hurt?"

"Like I said, I don't mind a little pain." She winked. It almost felt like she was flirting with me.

We reached my door, I slid the card, and Kitara followed me inside. I gave her my business card, and she gave me her room number.

"Oh, you're right above me," I said.

"Yup. How long are you in town?"

"Two weeks."

"Well, we definitely should hook up again before you leave. Call me."

"Sounds great. I will."

"It was nice meeting you, Nia. Thanks for listening to me tonight. Sometimes it just feels good to vent."

"Any time. I know the feeling."

"Good night." Kitara reached out for a hug. Although her overly friendly act caught me off guard, I extended my arms to return the gesture. She held on a little longer than I felt comfortable with, but I didn't push her away. I felt sorry for her; she'd just had her heart broken and was seeking solace in a mere stranger.

"Night-night," I said. She released her grip, and I watched her five-foot-two, curvaceous frame walk through the door.

In the privacy of my room, I scrubbed the make-up off my face, threw on Mike's UConn T-shirt, and decided to give my baby a call before going to sleep. I got no answer, but I left him a message telling him how much I loved him and how I couldn't wait to speak to him the next day. I wanted to tell him about Kitara and how I thought she had a crush on me.

Brittany

Warren and I had just finished up our Christmas Eve meal, and *A Christmas Story* had just ended. I'd done a little decorating to enhance the Christmas spirit. In the corner, on an end table, I'd decorated a three-foot tree with those mini decorations from CVS. Red and green garland hung from each doorway, along with mistletoe. I'd even gone as far as to spray Christmas tree–scented air freshener in every room.

Warren showed up an hour late, but that was okay because I had a lot of last-minute loose ends to tie up. I'd bought the cutest little bib, which had the words IF YOU THINK I'M CUTE, YOU SHOULD SEE MY DADDY stitched in yellow letters across the front. The plan was to wrap it up as his gift, with the baby's first sonogram behind it. I put it in a small box with metallic silver wrapping and a huge silver bow.

"Honey, I want you to open my gift now," I said as I swayed over to him.

"I didn't bring your gift. I thought we would exchange on Christmas Day," Warren replied.

"That's okay. I still want you to open mine tonight." I handed him the silver package.

He slowly unwrapped our future, and my heart began beating rapidly. I twisted my sweaty hands together in anticipation. Then he froze. My heart pounded, and my hands became cold. He lifted the bib to expose our child's first photo.

"What the fuck is this?" Warren yelled as he flung the box across the room. The contents scattered.

"Our child. Why'd you throw it like that?" I went to retrieve our future.

"Brittany, you know what? I knew I should have never messed with you. Women like you are always trying to get a good brotha trapped. You ain't trappin' me."

"Wait a minute," I protested. "I'm confused. You never insisted that we use protection. You can't just blame me." I didn't lose my temper right away, because I'd expected him to be a little taken aback by the news.

"You wasn't on no birth control?" He was now pacing around the sofa, where I was seated, throwing his hands in the air.

"No," I replied sheepishly.

"You stupider than I thought then. How could you have been so irresponsible?" Warren was right up in my face by then. I could feel his spit hit my face as he yelled.

"Hey, don't call me stupid. Okay, I made a mistake, but the damage is done. Are you going to take care of your responsibilities?" I stepped back a foot to get away from his intimidating stance.

"What responsibility?" He folded his arms.

"Me and the baby. We should definitely get married."

He began laughing so hard that he had to hold his stomach. "Marry you? Yeah, right. You can't turn a ho into a housewife." He continued chuckling.

When he called me a ho, I swear I felt the baby quake in my belly. Immediately, my knees began shaking. "Ho? Who you calling a ho?" I'd had enough, so I stepped back in his face.

"Yo, Brittany, get out of my face," Warren warned, trying to walk away from me.

"I'm not going to get out of your face. I am pregnant with your child, and you're standing there calling me a ho?" I blocked him from walking away and then used my index finger to push his forehead back.

"Bitch, don't you ever touch me again. Furthermore, the shit ain't mine, anyway, so I don't even know why you're telling me about it. You thought I would be happy about this? Sheeit!"

"Bitch? I got yo' bitch," I screamed as I ran into my kitchen and grabbed the nearest butcher knife and charged at him.

He dodged me. Then he grabbed my arm and

gripped my wrist so hard that I had no choice but to release the knife. It fell to the ground with a thud.

"I'll kill your ass in here. You better calm down!" He was still holding my arm. I couldn't calm down. I was hysterical, screaming and swinging my arms and legs around.

"Let me go!" I yelped.

He let me go, and as soon as I turned around, I spat right in his face. He raised his hand to his face in slow motion to remove the spit. I was frozen like a deer in headlights. I knew I had gone too far.

He gave me a backhanded slap, and I fell to the floor. "You're a crazy ho," he shouted. "If I ever see you again, you better pretend you don't know me. Even if that shit is mine, I don't want it, so you better kill it. I'll never raise a child with a whore." He stood over me, his chest heaving, daring me to get up from the floor. Then he stepped over me, got his coat from the closet, and opened the door to leave. "Lose my number, bitch." He slammed the door so hard, the mistletoe and garland fell off the door and onto the floor.

I crawled over to the bookcase where I kept my cordless telephone, still dizzy from the pimp slap. I wanted to call Shari but quickly dismissed that idea because I knew she had her own drama to deal with. And what could Nia do for me from Texas? I found myself dialing numbers imprinted in my mind's eye.

"Vaughn?" I said.

"Oh hey, Brittany. What's up, girl?" he answered jubilantly.

"I need someone to talk to. Can you come over?"

I whispered, still a little light-headed. My face was stinging like a wet-ass whooping. I just couldn't be alone right then.

"I'll be there in half an hour. Is everything okay?"

"Not really. Just come. I don't wanna be alone right now."

"Say no more. I'm on my way."

Shari

There's nothing worse than being alone on the holidays. That morning, FedEx delivered a package from Dex. I hesitated to open it, knowing that inside I'd find something that would probably make me even more upset. As I stared at the featherweight box for the millionth time that morning, the phone rang. On the caller ID, I could see it was Nia calling again from her hotel room. She called at least times a day, but I never answered. I needed some time alone, but this time when the phone rang, I realized I needed my friend.

"Hello," I answered.

"Merry Christmas, girl!" she yelled into the phone, sounding like a radio announcer giving away a cash prize.

"Christmas is tomorrow." My voice sounded as dry as sandpaper.

"I know, but tomorrow is a busy day for me. I have to return the rental car, do all my packing, and get ready for my flight. When I get back in town, I'm going straight to Mike's house. So Merry Christmas," she babbled.

"Merry Christmas." There was a slight pause. I knew she felt uncomfortable asking, but it was inevitable.

"What's up with your situation with Dex?"

"He's been over here a couple of times, begging me to open the door so we could talk. I haven't given him the time of day, though. He even sent a package over here. I guess it's supposed to be my Christmas gift."

"You didn't open it yet?" Nia sounded surprised.

"No."

"Well, open it then," she urged.

"Okay. Hold on. I'll go get it." I was sitting on her stool. The package was already sitting right in front of me on the counter, but I didn't want to look silly. "All right. I got it. I'm opening it right now." I was glad that Nia had called and given me the courage to open the box. "Oh, my God." I began to weep.

"What?" she screamed.

"He is so sweet." I continued to weep. Dex had made a collage of us. Pictures from our first date, our wedding, and almost every place we'd gone together since then were framed. "Oh, there's a card, too." I ripped it open.

"Read it out loud," Nia insisted.

Whenever you get through whatever is troubling you, I'll be here. I wish I could be there for you to help you with it, but I respect that some things you have to do

*alone. Waiting patiently, Your Husband. P.S. Please
come home. I love you.* I had to close my eyes
tightly to prevent more tears from escaping.

"Whoa. So what are you going to do?" asked Nia.

"Nothing. I'm gonna stay here until I find my
own place. I'll never go back to him."

"Sha-Sha, you don't even have hard-core evidence yet."

"Yes, I do. I found Tangie's diary the other day."
I put the card and collage back into the box and
threw it on the floor beside me.

"No, you didn't."

"Yes, I did. She was saying how good the sex is
and how everything has just gotten better since I've
been gone. . . ."

"No way," she interrupted.

"Yes, girl, and he calls her his peach because of
how she feels inside and tastes and everything. So
Dex can take this collage and stick it up his ass." I
kicked the package across the floor.

"His peach! Damn, that's deep. I think they are
getting a little too close."

"You're telling me." I paused to retrieve the box
and throw it into the burning fireplace. "I'm burning that shit as we speak."

"Burn it, girl!" she cheered.

"Sometimes I miss him so much, it hurts, but
every time I think of what he has done, I hate him
more and more. It's obvious that he doesn't give a
fuck, because he continues to do it."

"Maybe if you'd gone home, he wouldn't still be

doing it. He's probably really vulnerable right now, and Tangie is all he has."

"Well, she can have his ass. Let's change the subject. Talking about them is making my stomach hurt. How's your trip?"

"Your girl is on point. I landed fifteen accounts. FIFTEEN!" she emphasized. "Capri is going to be so jealous when she finds out that she'll have to cut a tax-free check for fifteen thousand dollars to yours truly. Now *that's* a Christmas bonus!" Nia sounded so excited.

"Fifteen? Nia, that is great. How did you manage that down in Hickville?"

"That's just it. Houston isn't Hickville at all. There are black people all over the place. They are so many black-owned restaurants and businesses that it was easy to get fifteen accounts. If I had another week, I think I could double that number."

"That's great. I'm really proud of you. I guess this means Brittany and I will be having some really nice gifts this year."

"You know it. I really wanna throw a New Year's party, though. It will be the party of all parties."

"I think that's just what I need right now to get my mind off that fool and that ho."

"Great. You can help me plan it. Brittany, too. I have to call her. How's she doing, anyway? I've called her a couple of times and just got her machine."

"I dunno. This is the first time I answered this phone in two weeks. I'm sure she's doing fine, though. You know her. She's a survivor."

"All right then. It's settled. Let's meet at Catalina's

for lunch on Monday to delegate the party assignments. I'll e-mail Brittany tonight to invite her."

Usually Dex and I would be putting the finishing touches on our gifts and finally putting them all under the tree. By now we would have gone to Rockefeller Center to see the colossal Christmas tree. We would have already held hands as we ice-skated around the tree, already would have seen *The Nutcracker* on Broadway. Some years we would visit my mother in Boston and would see *Black Nativity*.

The fireplace's blaze was now reduced to speckles of bright orange ash, like the ends of cigarettes. Times like these, I wished I'd had kids to keep me occupied. I'd be doing so much decorating, baking, and last-minute shopping that I wouldn't even have time to sit around feeling sorry for myself. With no solution, no way out, and no one to share Christmas with, I decided to lean on the one shoulder I knew was always free—my mother's.

Without packing a bag or as much as a toothbrush, I found myself revving up the Honda and starting the four-hour ride to Boston.

I pulled out my cell phone and dialed my mother's phone number from I-95.

"Hey, Ma. It's Shari," I said.

"I know my only child's voice." Ma's voice was instantly soothing.

"I'm on my way up there. Okay?"

"I haven't heard from you in a while. Is everything all right?"

"Ma, I'll talk to you when I get there," I told her. I could feel a thick lump forming in my throat, so I wanted to cut the conversation short.

"All right. Is Dex coming, too?" Her voice brightened at the mention of his name.

"Just me," I answered somberly.

"Oh."

We shared an uncomfortable, yet knowing, silence.

"I'll see you in a couple hours," I said, then hung up.

Ma and I have a great relationship. She's only sixteen years older than me, so there's always been this sisterly bond between us. Growing up, it was always just me and her. My father disappeared from my life before I was even born. If Ma had boyfriends while I was still living at home, I never knew. But now she lives with her boyfriend, who is five years her junior and eleven years my senior. At first, it was a little weird for me to accept, but as long as he makes her happy, I'm happy.

Ma loved Dex from the first day she met him, which surprised me because although we got along great, Ma had never approved of any of my boyfriends. She always thought I set my standards too low, which, in retrospect, might be true, judging from my terrible track record.

"There's something about him, Sha-Sha. It's the way he looks at you from across the room. The way he anticipates your every need. Shoot, before you can even take the last sip of your juice, he's refilling your glass. You better appreciate that man." If she'd only known then what I knew now.

I made it to Boston in five hours, an hour longer than normal. I had to pull over three times into the emergency lane because Jagged Edge's "Let's Get Married," Maxwell's "Fortunate," and Mary's "Not Gon' Cry" triggered a downpour of salty water from my eyes.

"You look like shit on toast," Ma said as she pulled me through the door, inspecting my face like a dermatologist.

The house was immaculately cluttered, as usual, and overly decorated in red, silver, and greens. My mother's house was always filled with a million doo-dads, but they all had a specific place and meaning.

I was wearing the navy blue sweat suit that I'd had on for the past two days. My honey blond hair had about one inch of jet-black new growth. I couldn't even remember the last time I'd relaxed my hair, so the beadie-beads had formed in my kitchen. I hadn't noticed, but the second thing out of Ma's mouth was, "Girl, you ain't nothing but skin 'n' bones. Come here." She spun me around by my left arm. Her genuine look of disgust actually made me laugh for the first time in weeks.

"I don't look that bad," I said between chuckles.

"Only a man can do this to a woman." Shaking her head from side to side, clucking her tongue, my mother pointed at me from head to toe, lingering at my feet, which were ashy and adorned with flip-flops—in the dead of December. "Sit down. Tell me what's going on." She pulled out a chair to her black lacquer dining table. "You want some cocoa?" She knew me too well.

"Yes, please, with three marshmallows," I whined.

"Four."

"Oh yeah, four." Every time I asked for three, I always ended up asking for one more because it was not sweet enough.

"All right. Begin," she demanded, delivering my drink and taking the seat parallel to mine. I relayed everything from Genesis to Revelations about my source of despair.

"That's not like Dex. You sure?" Ma sat back in her chair, appearing skeptical.

"Positive." I nodded my head.

"What're you going to do?"

"Get a divorce," I said, without hesitation.

"So you're just gonna give up on your marriage because that man is human and made a mistake? Be sensible."

"If he cheats once, he'll cheat again!" I howled.

"That's not always true. Now I've been around a little longer than you. And I'm a pretty good judge of character. If"—she paused to emphasize—"*if* he has cheated on you, I know he's sorry. He could never love anyone other than you. It was a mistake, Sha. The only thing that should end a marriage is, number one, if he is going upside your head every time he gets upset, number two, if he cheats and fathers a child with another woman, and number three, if he falls in love with another woman. *Then* you should divorce his ass." She pounded the table with her right fist.

I absorbed the wisdom, knowing better than to interrupt Ma's lecture.

"And why on God's green earth do you still have that little girl living in your house?" Ma asked. She was getting more riled up by the minute.

"I don't have the strength to fight anymore. If he wants her, he can have her. Ma, I've been fighting all my life. I give up. Every man I've ever been with, we end up fighting in the end. Fighting over another woman, fighting for his attention, fighting for us to stay together, fighting for him to leave me alone, fighting to keep the possessions he'd given me, or just plain ol' fist fighting, just because. Plus, she's out of town right now. I think she's in Philly."

"LaShari Marie Brown, of all the men you've been with, Dex is the only one actually *worth* fighting for. The first thing you have to do is confront Tangie. I don't understand why you haven't done that yet. I don't care if you think she is away. And what do you mean *think?* You need to be calling and stopping by there every day until you know that she is back, and then confront her. Secondly, although there's only about a week left of her stay, tell Brittany her sister needs to go stay with her, which is where she should have stayed in the first damn place.

"Then you need to get your man back. Now I know I can't make you, but it don't get no better than Dex, and you know it. It will take time for you to trust him again, but as much as that man has done for you, he deserves a second chance."

"I know, Ma. It just hurts so bad. I don't think I'll

ever get through this. Forget our past. If he loves me so much, how could he have done something that would jeopardize our marriage?"

"I don't know, baby. Things just happen sometime. I can't even begin to explain it."

Ma put my empty mug into the sink. "Now this is an order. Go wash your funky butt, put a thick slab of shea butter on those ashy feet, then go to your room and get some sleep. I'll bring up some extra clothes and a new toothbrush."

"Yes, ma'am." I obeyed.

I took a two-hour nap, my first sound sleep in weeks, and awoke to the sweet aroma of corn bread baking in the oven. Ma had prepared her Christmas Eve dinner, and Omar, her boyfriend, had come home by then. Ever the nonconformist, Ma hadn't prepared the traditional meal of poultry, stuffing, and all the fixings. She'd made gumbo, crab cakes, and dirty rice. Nevertheless, we enjoyed the meal, while Omar kept us in tears with his hilarious stories. After dinner, Ma dyed my roots for me and gave me seventy dollars to get my hair relaxed in two weeks.

Leaving that next morning, I felt like a new woman. Still unsure of what to do about Dex and Tangie, but feeling like I'd made the first steps in the right direction. Ma's words had not gone in one ear and out the other. Her voice echoed in my head the entire ride home. "Dex is the only one actually *worth* fighting for," I repeated.

Nia

It was Christmas Eve morning. I was wearing black Capri pants with a three-quarter-length black shirt. My sandals were black, with a tan cork heel that perfectly complimented my oversized straw hat, the tan buttons on my shirt, and the tan sweater I had tied preppy style around my neck in case it got chilly. Kitara was wearing a cute, little, too-short cherry T-shirt dress by Polo, with matching cherry Polo sneakers. Her lips were painted apple red, and her hair was tied back with a red scrunchie. We were kindred souls: we knew how to coordinate.

"Where are you taking me today?" I asked all touristlike over breakfast. Over the past two weeks, Tara and I had gone to Bayou Place, Space Center Houston, and Toyota Center to see R. Kelly, and we had eaten out at the best restaurants almost every night.

"I thought maybe you could come with me to my old apartment while I grab a couple things. I don't want to run into Chaz or Alana, but if I do, I want you there to have my back," said Kitara.

"Sure. Let's go early, so then I can treat you to dinner at Massa's Seafood Grill before we go back to my room and pack."

"Bet. We can go straight from here. Then, after dinner, I want to hit up this new club around the corner if that's okay with you."

"Hell, yeah. Send me off with a bang!" We high-fived.

Tara lived in South Houston, about twenty minutes from the hotel. The outside of her apartment complex was lined with skyscraping palm trees. The massive complex was composed of eight beige five-story buildings with espresso-colored roofs. Each unit had it's own spacious balcony. With four buildings on either side of the driveway, we pulled up to the third building on our right.

"Shit. Her car is here," Kitara said as she lightly slammed her head against the steering wheel.

"So what? Let's go." I touched her wrist. "She won't try anything funny with two of us here," I assured her.

"Wanna have a little fun with me?" Kitara gave me a sly grin.

"What's on your mind?" I wondered.

"Okay. For the sake of maintaining my dignity, and so she can run back and tell Chaz, I want you to pretend you're my girlfriend."

"Huh? But she knows you're not a lesbian. That won't work."

"Yes, it will. She knows I'm bisexual. I told you,

me and her used to get it on all the time without Chaz. She'll be so jealous!" Kitara clasped her hands together just thinking of the revenge.

"All right. Fine. Let's have some fun. I'll just follow your lead."

As soon as we exited Kitara's azure Yukon Denali, she grabbed my hand and led me up the cement outer staircase to her apartment door. Right before we stepped in, she forcefully clutched my hand with anticipation.

The one-bedroom apartment was decorated in dark shades of gray and black. I came to the conclusion that the apartment belonged to Chaz, and she had moved in with him. The bachelor pad was decked out with black leather couches and countless African artifacts. Over the black- and silver-lined fireplace was a larger-than-life black-and-white-print of Malcolm X.

We passed through the nondescript kitchen and into her old bedroom, where her presence was apparent. The bedroom was banana and peach. On the nightstand, a picture of her and lover boy was still on display. The king-sized bed was covered with a barrage of banana and peach pillows on crisp white sheets. More noticeably, her ex–best friend was lying comfortably across the bed, napping. We were only in the room for about three seconds before she woke up.

"Hey, Kitty. Where you been?" Alana's voice sounded surprisingly apologetic.

"Wouldn't you like to know?" Kitara replied,

rolling her eyes. "Alana, this is my girlfriend Nia. Nia, this is Alana. I've told you about her, right?"

"I've heard a lot about you. Nice to finally meet you," I said as I extended my hand.

Alana was the complete opposite of Kitara. Kitara stood no more than five-two, whereas when Alana stood up from the bed, she was about five-nine without shoes. Alana was voluptuous. Kitara's figure was tight and toned like Halle. Alana's ink black skin looked like she'd been properly schooled in black skin care. Her hair was cut in one of those short pixie cuts. She was delightfully beautiful; she reminded me of that girl who played DMX's girlfriend, Kisha, in the movie *Belly*. Although I'm not gay, I could see why both Kitara and Chaz couldn't resist her.

"How long have you known her?" Alana asked Kitara, ignoring my extended hand.

"Long enough," Kitara replied as she turned her attention back to me. "Come on, baby. This won't take long. Let's start in the closet." She grabbed my hand and led me to her walk-in closet, where she began feverishly stuffing her belongings into bags.

Alana entered the closet, passing me and going straight for Kitara. "How dare you bring this bitch in here!" she screamed.

"Excuse me?" said Kitatra. "This is *my* apartment. which I used to live in with *my* boyfriend. I should be asking you what the hell you're doing here, but I won't, 'cause I don't even give a fuck anymore."

"Well, obviously Chaz doesn't mind me being here, now does he?" said Alana.

Kitara's face turned ruby red, and she looked like she wanted to say something but couldn't find the right words. The rage disappeared from her face, and she said, "Well, I'm happy for you two. Be blessed. And I hope you're happy for me, too, 'cause I'm in love, and I'm happy for once in my life."

Kitara handed me a bag, and she put an over-stuffed Louis Vuitton book bag on her back. "Come on, honey. Let's go," she said. She walked past Alana and grabbed my hand again as we walked out of the large closet. She stopped by the pinewood dresser to snatch her jewelry box and a few perfume bottles and stuffed them into the book bag hanging off her shoulder.

Once we loaded the truck with her belongings, Kitara began to cry. "I feel like this chapter of my life has finally ended. I'll be calling you as soon as I get to New York. I'm staying one more week here in Houston just to tie up some loose ends; then I'm out."

"My door is always open. You have my numbers." This time I gave her an extra long hug. "Fuck 'em, girl. They deserve each other."

"Yeah, fuck 'em."

Kitara and I had gotten in from the club that night at four in the morning. We'd drank so much that we had to leave her car at the club and walk ten minutes back to the hotel. We'd enjoyed three Long Island Iced Teas each. Then, after dancing off our buzz, we'd started doing Jell-O shots and shots of Woo-Woo. After wobbling all the way to the hotel, we both knew it was time for a hot shower and some aspirin. It seemed like I had just closed my eyes when the phone rang.

"Hey, girl. I can't sleep, and I hate that you're leaving on Christmas day," said Kitara. Her slight southern drawl was so comforting on Christmas morning. She truly felt like one of the crew back home.

"Tara, I'm so tired." I yawned. I rolled over to see what time it actually was, and the red digits read 5:00 a.m. "Why are you calling me so darned early, anyway? We just got in an hour ago. I'm going back to sleep for a couple hours. You're crazy."

"Sorry, Nia, but the people in the next room are getting their early-morning freak on, and I can't sleep. Can I come sleep with you?"

"You have two minutes to get down here, Tara. Any longer than that and I'll be back asleep, and I refuse to be awakened again by you."

"I'm on my way." CLICK.

Moments later, Kitara was knocking on the door. She was wearing a short, silk mango robe with a matching negligee underneath. Her size 6 feet were bare, exposing her French-manicured toes.

"I don't believe you walked down here like that," I commented as I turned back around to crawl into bed, with my head spinning.

"Please. No one is up this early," she said, climbing in the bed.

I was lying on my side, and she got in the bed, right behind me, so that my butt was wedged into the front side of her vagina. Then Tara put her arm around me. *Why is this woman spooning with me?*

I thought. But the lingering alcohol allowed me to relax and surprisingly enjoy the cuddle.

I thought I was dreaming when I felt my clitoris shudder in an orgasmic spasm. It woke me up out of my pissy drunk slumber. I started to moan and clenched the sheets beside me with both my hands. When I opened my eyes, I realized it wasn't a dream, but Tara's head was positioned between my legs, giving me oral pleasure.

My arms felt as heavy as lead when I tried to reach out and push her away, but it felt so glorious, I couldn't stop her. Her spongy tongue explored me inside and out while I stared at the rotating ceiling, unable to focus my vision.

I'm not sure how long Tara was licking and sucking on me, but once she stopped, I longed for her to continue.

"I'm sorry," she said, coming back up to face level.

I was in a different, confused, titillated, exhilarated world. My chest was heaving, and I was short of breath. Tara wiped the sweat off my forehead before she kissed it. "I just couldn't resist you," she whispered.

"Uh . . ." I swallowed hard. My throat was as dry as a towel. "I'm not gay, Tara."

"I know. I'm sorry. It's the liquor. I get so freaking horny when I drink. Please forgive me, Nia. I should have never gone there with you. I hope we can still be friends."

"We'll talk about it when I get up," I said, struggling to keep my eyelids open.

Brittany

Vaughn made it in less than ten minutes. I had regained my composure by then. I'd undressed and slipped on my short peach silk robe. That robe always made me feel comfortable. When I answered the door, Vaughn angrily pushed me out of the way and let himself in.

"Who did that to you?" he demanded, his hands on his hips. I hadn't realized at that point that I had a bruise covering half of the right side of my face.

"Huh?" I wondered how he knew. He grabbed my arm and dragged me over to the oval mirror hanging over the dining-room table.

"That," he yelled, pointing in the mirror. "Who did *that* to you?" The rage in his eyes scared me a little.

"Damn. I didn't know it was that bad. I—"

"Who did it?" he interrupted.

"Warren," I said as I looked at the floor, scraping the carpet with my toe.

"What happened, Brittany?"

We walked over to the sofa. I sat Indian style to his left side. He had one arm over the back of the sofa, and the other he used to hold my hand while I replayed the story for him. By the time I had dished the dirt, I was crying my heart out. I really hadn't had time to think about the reality of raising a child alone, or the possibility of having an abortion. I think I was crying the most because Warren was right about me. I was a whore.

"Calm down. Can I get you anything?" His voice oozed with sympathy as he rubbed my hand. I was crying so hard, I could barely get my words out at that point.

I sniffled a couple of times before I answered. "Can you make me some tea? Whenever I don't f-feel good, m-my b-best friend makes me ch-ch-chamomile t-tea." I broke down again.

"Sure thing. Why don't you lie down. I'll bring it to you as soon as it's done."

"All right." I nodded, then got up and trudged into my bedroom. I couldn't stop crying no matter how hard I tried. I collapsed on my ottoman, then suddenly felt dinner coming up. I charged into the bathroom and threw up all over the floor. Weakened, I sat outside the bathroom door, with my back against the wall.

"Aww. Poor thing," Vaughn said as he walked by with my tea. He placed it on my nightstand, then walked over to help me up. He carried me "over the threshold" style to my bed and tucked me in.

"Lie down next to me," I said. I patted the bed, then reached for my tea and began sipping.

"You sure?" he questioned.

"Yeah, I wanna talk some more," I pleaded, with bloodshot eyes.

"Okay then. Lemme just clean up this mess you made in the bathroom."

Vaughn went to the kitchen and returned with the Pine Sol and the sponge from the kitchen sink. I was too torn up to even feel embarrassed that he had to clean up my vomit. Better him than me.

Once he was done cleaning, he removed his shoes, then finally lay beside me. "What's up?" he asked.

I propped my pillows up against the headboard so that I could lean on them while I sat up to drink my tea. I took a sip, then began. "I don't know who my baby's father is," I said, with no emotion. "As much as I wanted to convince myself that Warren was the father, I shouldn't have tried to force the responsibility on him until I was sure. He was right about that, too. I had unprotected sex with four guys in less than two weeks." I didn't feel ashamed to tell Vaughn this. It felt redeeming to tell the truth.

"Really? Did we have sex within those two weeks?"

"Yeah."

"So there is a twenty-five percent chance that I am the father?"

"I wouldn't say that high of a chance. We only did it once. Warren and I did it *several* times."

"What about the other guys?"

"One-night stands, just like you were."

He began lecturing me. "I think you should also get screened for STDs. In this day and age, it is so hard to believe people still have unprotected sex."

"You could've put on a condom that night. Don't blame it all on me. There was nothing stopping you."

"Very true, but I did pull out. I guess I was just too excited to think about the consequences." Vaughn stared at the ceiling in a reflective silence.

"I've been checked out. Don't worry. My obstetrician checked me for everything on my first prenatal-care visit. STDs can be fatal to an unborn child. Don't worry. I came up clean."

"God watches over children and fools."

"I guess so, huh?" I sighed. "You think I'm some kind of whore, don't you?" I asked, scared to look into his eyes. He reached over with one hand and turned my face toward his.

"It's not my place to judge you, Brittany." Vaughn stared into my misty eyes. "You're okay in my eyes. Everyone makes poor judgments, but as long as you learn from them, then I think some mistakes are worth making."

"Although I am learning the hard way, I will think twice before having unprotected sex again." I paused. "That's if any man will ever want me again after I have the baby."

"And why wouldn't they?" Vaughn looked shocked.

"I'll probably get all fat and sloppy. I'll be a single mom, so I'll look stressed out all the time. And, with the baby, I won't have time to date at all."

"That's not true. You're in great shape now, so I'm sure you'll bounce right back. And, you'll adjust to being a single mom, and your friends will help out a lot, too."

"I guess." I pouted. "I'm gonna go take a quick shower. Be right back." I rose from the bed.

When I returned fifteen minutes later, Vaughn was knocked out on my bed. I decided against waking him. I was so grateful to have had his company that night, and I didn't want to make him sleep on my sofa. I lay beside him, carefully trying not to wake him. As soon as my head hit the pillow, I must have fallen asleep, because I don't remember thinking about anything after getting back into bed.

Christmas morning I awakened to the smell of breakfast. Seconds after I sat up and cleared the sleep from my eyes with my hand, Vaughn appeared, holding a tray full of food.

"Merry Christmas," he sang as he placed the tray in my lap. He'd prepared sausage, pancakes, scrambled cheese eggs, and cinnamon rolls. He'd even sliced some fresh mango for me.

"Merry Christmas," I grumbled. "This looks delicious."

"Well, dig in. Do you mind if I join you?"

"Of course not." He grabbed another tray of food and sat beside me on my bed.

"How you feeling?" he asked.

"Just a little nauseous, but I think I'll be okay after I eat." I paused to put a forkful of eggs in my mouth. "Face still hurts a little." I rubbed my warm cheek.

"You look great."

"Shut up. I probably look like a mess right now. I haven't even washed my face yet." I nudged him on the shoulder for lying but still being a sweetheart.

"Seriously. My mother always told me never to fall for those women with heavily painted faces because when you wake up in the morning beside her, she might not look as beautiful as she did the night before. A truly beautiful woman is as beautiful first thing in the morning as she is decked out for an evening on the town."

"If you say so. Thank you." Breakfast was delicious. I shoveled it all down and couldn't believe I wanted seconds. "Is there any more left over?" I asked my personal chef.

"No, but I'll make some more," he said, with a southern twang, as he exited to the kitchen. "It ain't nothin' but a thang."

I got out of bed to brush my teeth. I should have known better. The toothbrush always did it to me. I barfed the wonderful breakfast into the toilet and cursed myself for being so careless. I tried again, this time ensuring I took great care not to poke the toothbrush too far into my mouth and provoke another regurgitation.

"Is everything all right in there?" Vaughn yelled from the kitchen.

"Um, yeah. I'm okay," I yelled, with the toothbrush sticking out my mouth.

After cleaning my mess, I joined him in the kitchen. I sat at the counter and watched him cook.

"What are your plans for today?" I asked. "I feel

awful that you are stuck here with me." I was completely sincere.

"Nothing. I sent my Mom and her fiancé to Paris for Christmas, and other than them, there's no one else left for me to spend Christmas with."

"Paris? Wow. I've never been to Paris."

"Oh, it's beautiful. I try to go at least once a year."

"How can you afford that working as a bank teller?" I knew that was a rude question, but I just had to know.

"I'm not a bank teller," he said, a mischievous grin playing around his lips.

"Vaughn, I saw you with my own two eyes. You deposited money into my bank account for me and everything. That night at dinner, we talked about how it is such a waste of your intelligence to be working as a teller. What the hell are you talking about?"

"You *assumed* that I was a bank teller. I never told you that."

"Okay. You were sitting behind the counter, taking and giving money to people at a bank, but you're not a bank teller."

"You seem to be feeling a lot better, Inspector Gadget."

"Don't change the subject. But, yes, after my morning barf, I usually feel a little better. Now spill the beans, Vaughn."

He chuckled before he answered. "I am now officially the president and CEO of the fifteen branches of First National Bank located here, in the tristate area. When we met, I was simply filling in for a teller that had a family emergency, until her coverage got there."

Vaughn fumbled with the knife as he began slicing a mango. "If you had come a week earlier, you would have seen me over at the loan processor's area and assumed I was a loan officer." He finished with another chuckle as he placed my loaded plate before me. "That day someone had quit, just up and walked out after getting into it with a colleague. Hey, I gotta do what I gotta do to ensure the customer service in my branches don't fall apart."

"Are you lying?" I asked, with a suspicious eye. He retrieved his wallet and pulled out a business card. "Vice President, First National Bank, Tristate Division," I read aloud.

"My assistant has ordered my new cards, but they won't be ready until after the new year, but I assure you that I am now the president."

"Get out of here." I laughed as I chewed on a slice of mango. "So what's the story behind your raggedy car?"

"No story. I just don't want women to like me for what I have. If I wanted to be real whack, I would've explained the day we met that I was merely filling in for someone and given you my business card. But I want women to like me for who I am. I have a couple of other cars, but I mainly use my trusty, dusty Taurus. It gets me around just fine."

"What kind of cars do you have?"

"Dang, Brittany, you nosy girl!" he teased. "I have a BMW 745i and a Mercedes 600, and when I go out with the fellas, we roll in my Cadillac Escalade, sittin' on twenty-fours."

"Oh, so you're a baller, huh?"

"A little somethin' somethin'"

"You don't seem like it, though. You're so cool and down to earth."

"I would never let money change me. It can go just as easy as it comes. I am grateful for every time I'm able to save a dollar. You should see my closet. The only really expensive things are my suits and shoes for work. Other than that, I am just a jeans and sneakers type of guy. I do have a huge collection of Jordans, though. They're my weakness." He sat across from me, sipping on a cup of coffee.

Inside, I regretted treating him so badly in the past. I was wishing then that I had given him a chance rather than just a booty call. He was everything I ever wanted in a man. He probably made about half a million a year. He was an absolute sweetheart, and for the first time since I'd met him, I could admit he was also very handsome. I was just so caught up with Warren, I couldn't see it. He was not my usual Shaka Zulu type, but the man was handsome, nonetheless. I couldn't believe I'd passed him up for Warren's trifling ass.

"How old are you? You look awfully young to have so much power," I said.

"Thirty-three—youngest president in the company's history," he boasted, displaying all his teeth.

"You don't look a day over twenty-five. How is that possible with such a stressful and demanding job?"

"The truth is that once you reach a certain height on the corporate ladder, everyone below you does most of the work. My main responsibility is to delegate the right assignments to the right people and follow up to make sure they get the job done."

"Damn, that sounds easy."

"I wouldn't say it is easy, but it's not as hard as people think." He paused to take away my now-emptied plate. "I don't want to talk about work anymore. It's Christmas! If you don't already have plans, then I'd love to spend today with you."

"I'm not going to be much fun. I'm still feeling bad about last night, but I would love it if you kept me company today. I really don't want to be alone."

"Your wish is my command."

"I really don't know what I want to do," I admitted, shrugging my shoulders.

"How 'bout we catch a matinee?" Vaughn suggested. "You know the best movies come out on Christmas Day."

"Sounds great, but I don't think we'll make the matinee. You're not going to believe this, but I am tired already. I need to take a nap." I yawned. I had only been up less than two hours, but I couldn't keep my eyes open another moment.

"No problem, sweetie. You go take a nap. I'll clean this kitchen and watch the idiot box until you get up."

Shari

"Dex, I know you're fucking Tangie," I slurred. I had just finished celebrating my last night alone at Nia's by polishing off a pint of Tanqueray mixed with pink grapefruit juice. Tired of playing games and beating around the bush, I decided to call Dex and let him know the jig was up.

"Bay, what are you talking about? Have you been drinking?" The man knew me like the back of his hand.

"Don't cloud the issue. I know. That's all I wanted you to know. I know. Now you can stop all your fucking, lying, and sneaking around. I hope you're happy." I hung up in his face.

He'd evidently dialed me back using the speed-dial key with NIA written on it, because that phone rang as soon as I'd hung it up.

"Hello?" I screamed.

"Shari, is this what this whole thing is about? Your insecurities running wild again?"

"My insecurities? Don't insult my intelligence." I collapsed on the floor and lay flat on my back, staring at the ceiling. The room began spinning.

"Bay, are you there?"

"I'm still here," I whimpered.

"I have not and never will sleep with Tangie."

"You're lying. Don't you lie. It just makes the situation worse."

"I'm not lying," Dex bellowed.

"Admit it!" I screamed at the top of my lungs.

"I will never admit to something that I didn't do," he said innocently. "I hate when you get like this." He sounded like he was losing patience with me.

"*You're* making me like this." I closed my eyes to keep the room from spinning, but it made me feel even more dizzy, so I opened them again.

"You're doing it to yourself."

"Dexter Brown, I know the truth. I heard it from Tangie's mouth."

"Well, then she must have been lying to you."

"Not to me. She was on the phone with one of her little friends, telling them how great a lover you are."

"She must have been trying to impress her friend then."

"Oh yeah? Then why did she write the same thing in her journal? Is she trying to impress the paper?"

"Just stop it. Shari, you're drunk and delirious. That accident must have your mind all messed up."

"Don't tell me to stop. How do you explain the

Monday after the accident, when Brittany overheard you two fucking in her room?" I couldn't stop yelling.

"It wasn't me," he pleaded.

"Your fucking car was in the driveway!" I pushed the END button again.

He was taking me for a fool, with that weak-ass line from Shaggy. It wasn't gonna work on me. He could have at least apologized, and then maybe I'd have been able to begin forgiving him.

The phone rang repeatedly, in a series of six rings each. I just let it ring as I rose from the floor and assumed the fetal position on the futon. I blasted the volume on the television so that it was almost loud enough to drown out the piercing rings from the phone. After about ten series, I picked up without a hello. He didn't deserve any pleasantries at that moment.

"Shari, that Monday I'd let Tangie borrow my car while I was at work. She had to register for her classes and go shopping for her dorm room."

I hung up the phone again, refusing to entertain any excuses he was trying to offer.

Arguing with Dex had eventually killed my buzz, so I decided to take a couple shots of Jose Cuervo tequila. Usually, after gulping down any liquor straight, I gag and have to chase it with juice or soda. Not that night. The tequila massaged my throat and created a warm, tingling sensation. I guzzled two shots, but the next three that followed had less of a tingly effect, so I put the bottle away. It was no longer giving me the satisfaction I yearned for.

In a befuddled stupor, I took a shower and dove onto Nia's bed. My eyes fluttered, and the next thing I knew, Dex was standing over me, decked out in his gray Sean Jean sweat suit, looking scrumptious.

"How'd you get in here?" I asked, a little startled. He held up a shiny key. I rolled over slowly, sat up on the edge of the bed, and spread my legs so that he was then standing between my thighs. My face was parallel to his six-pack. I couldn't resist lifting his shirt and licking his navel, and then my tongue jaunted over his abdomen as he tenderly stroked the nape of my neck.

Dex placed his hands under my armpits and lifted me to my feet. With his index and middle fingers, he lifted my chin up so that our eyes met.

"Is this charade over?" he asked.

"No," I garbled, apparently still tipsy. "But just make love to me, anyway."

Dex carried me into the spare bedroom and placed me on my stomach. He grabbed the baby oil off the dresser and began massaging my neck, back, and then butt. Slowly, he stuck his middle finger inside of me and told me to turn over. I did—all the while keeping Dex's finger inside me. Pushing down on my pelvis—right above the hairline, but below my navel—Dex curved the fingers of his free hand upward in a "come here" motion so that his hand on the outside and his fingers on the inside met at my spongy G-spot. My body went into convulsions. Then I felt his fleshy tongue flicker across my opening. As he buried his face in my pussy, my mind raced back to our first date. Our first kiss. The first time he made me climb the walls in ecstasy. Our first night in our home, "christening" every room.

"Slow down, Bay. Take your time," he said. I obeyed and he stretched his arm to attentively caress my breasts.

Our honeymoon cruise to the Bahamas. "Ooooo, Dex. You feel so good." I squirmed in pleasure.

When Dex surprised me on Valentine's Day with an all-day spa treatment for two. We ate caviar—yuck—and drank cheap champagne all day while being pampered from head to toe.

Now this? He'd violated our vows . . . violated my trust . . . my body . . . our household. "Stop, Dex. Just stop!" I wailed. "Stop it. Just get off me!" I kicked my legs and attempted to push his head from between my legs. But when I reached down, I grasped nothing but air. My eyes opened, and my drunk ass woke up. I was sitting in an empty tub. With the bright lights blaring in my eyes, I had to shut them quickly and find my way to the switch to turn out the light.

"Damn, girl. You need to get it together," I told myself before struggling to the kitchen to get a glass of water. My mouth was parched.

I ended up crying myself to sleep that night thinking about Dexter Brown. For a brief moment, I wished I was home, lying on my husband's chest.

Brittany

Having Vaughn in my life had been an unexpected blessing. I was so sick and fatigued all the time, and he was really being a great friend and was understanding about my pregnancy. I began talking to him about any and everything. Sometimes I'd fall asleep on the phone after talking for hours on end about nothing at all. I actually even let him read some of my poetry. He thought I was talented and insisted I try to get published. But I didn't do it for the recognition; I did it for the therapy.

One snowy morning I was on my way to the grocery store, and I suddenly felt the urge to puke. I couldn't hold it, so I started puking right there in my car, which caused me to swerve and start sliding all over the road. Luckily, I stopped right before slamming head-on into a parked car. I was a little shaken up but didn't have a scratch on me. Once Vaughn heard that story, he insisted on being my chauffeur until I was no longer unpredictably ill.

He was also on vacation, so no matter how big or small the errand was, if he was around, he'd take me, and sometimes he'd just do it for me.

Vaughn had just driven me to Catalina's to meet with the girls and promised to be on call if I needed him to come scoop me up. I assured him that I'd catch a ride with Nia or Shari, but he said he'd remain available for the next couple hours, anyway.

My appetite had started to increase a little, but nothing big. But when I felt hunger coming on, I had to eat, and eat quickly, or I'd get nauseous. Since feeling nauseous was beginning to really piss me off, I quickly located my friends, sat down, and called the waiter over immediately.

"We're ready to order," I told him, not even greeting Nia and Shari. I ordered us all the barbecue chicken lunch special, without giving them a chance to order their preferences. No one complained, though.

"Damn, Brittany. Are you hungry or something?" Nia teased.

"You know it," I said. They hadn't been there long, because the apple juice that they'd ordered for me was still ice-cold. "Y'all better come give me a hug. I haven't seen y'all in like two weeks." They both rose and hugged me simultaneously.

Shari no longer looked sad; I guess she'd started her healing process. Nia, on the other hand, looked like she was getting dicked down on a regular basis, the way she was glowing. We discussed in great detail Mike and Nia's developments, her new friend Kitara, my and Vaughn's friendship, and my pregnancy. Then Nia gave us our New Year's Eve party assignments before getting into the serious stuff: Dex and Tangie.

"Girl, what are you going to do?" I asked Shari.

"I'm gonna start looking for an apartment after the New Year and start with the divorce proceedings as soon as possible."

"Are you sure that's what you want to do?" I asked.

"Positive. I finally confronted him about sleeping with Tangie, and he won't even admit it," replied Shari.

"You confronted Dex? Don't you think it's time to confront Tangie?" I asked. Nia'd been away, and I had been sick as a dog lately. Shari was too busy grieving over her failed marriage. We all had seemed to forget that Tangie was still living up in Shari's house, sleeping with her husband like she owned the place.

"I would, but I don't think she is there right now. In her diary she said she'd be in Philly for the next couple weeks," said Shari.

"Well, we can check," I said.

"I don't know, guys," replied Shari. "I'm not trying to walk in on something I am not prepared to deal with."

"So you're just gonna let her chill up in your house and sleep with your man like that?" Nia asked. "If you don't want to go, that's fine, but Brittany and I are going to confront that bitch. Sorry, Brittany." Nia looked at me.

"Don't apologize," I said. "She's my sister, but if she's sleeping with my best friend's man, I can think of a lot more derogatory names for her my damn self."

Shari barely touched her lunch; I finished mine and ate a little of Nia's, too.

"Let's go, Nia," I ordered, reaching into my purse and throwing a fifty on the table to cover lunch and the tip.

Without warning, a medieval whisper bellowed from the depths of Shari's soul. "I'm coming, too. That's my muthafucking house." She gathered her purse and began putting her scarf and coat on in haste. Nia and I looked at each other and couldn't help but bust out laughing. Shari looked like she was ready for war.

We all hopped in the Honda. Dex's car was not in the driveway, and I noticed that Shari looked visibly relieved. We entered through the front door. There was a stale odor in the house. It hadn't had a thorough cleaning in a while. Joe Budden's "Pump It Up" was blaring from the direction of Tangie's room.

"That's my song," said Nia, trying to lighten the mood by bopping her head and pumping her fist in the air Black Panther style. Shari beelined for the room, ignoring Nia's attempt to make her laugh. We followed the leader.

When Shari reached the door, she froze and suddenly looked scared to face her destiny. I took the initiative and knocked for her. Then she snapped out of her trance.

"This is my house. I don't need to knock." She turned the knob and walked inside of the tiny room. We followed the leader.

Tangie was sitting on the bed, painting her toe-
nails. When we came in, she reached over to the
nightstand to turn the music down. Guilt was en-
graved all over her face. Shari stood in front of her,
while Nia and I stood side by side behind her, like
Beyoncé and the rest of Destiny's Child.

"Hey?" Tangie greeted us nervously, her eyes
darting around the room.

"How long did you think I would let this go on in
my own home?" Shari spoke up.

"What?" said Tangie, looking confused.

"Don't play dumb," I growled.

"You're fucking my husband. That's what," Shari
said, standing with both hands on her hips.

"Shari, I would never do that to you. You gave me
a place to stay when my own sister turned me away,"
Tangie said, then shot me an accusing glare.

"Don't sit there and lie. We already know. We
have even heard you," said Shari.

"Heard me doing what?" asked Tangie.

"Having sex," Nia chimed in. We were triple-
teaming Tangie, and she was growing more nervous by the second. She was tapping her foot a mile
a minute on the bed.

"Okay? Just because you overheard me getting
my freak on doesn't mean that I was having sex with
Dex," said Tangie. "There are other men in this
world, believe it or not." She rolled her eyes at
Shari. I couldn't believe she was sitting there, lying
and insulting Shari on top of it.

"That's my whole point. Of all the men in the

world, why did you choose my husband to have sex with?" Shari asked, remaining collected.

She was clearly more hurt than upset. All the while I felt my temperature starting to rage out of control. I may have had a lot of sex in my day, but I would never knowingly sleep with another woman's man. I began tapping my foot on the rug.

"So if you're not having sex with Dex, then who are you having sex with?" Nia wanted to know.

"That's none of your business," Tangie stated just as plain as day. That remark caused me to explode because now she was being just rude. I jumped on top of her and started choking the shit out of her.

"Brittany, stop! She's turning blue," Shari yelled. Tangie was flailing her legs wildly and trying to slap me with her bony little arms. Nia pushed me off the girl, but I went right back for her. This time I just punched her repeatedly in the face. I was moving so fast, she didn't have the opportunity to attempt to hit me back. Nia grabbed me under my arms and wrestled me out of the room.

"You fucking bitch!" Tangie yelled after me. I ignored her. My fists had done enough talking already.

"I'm straight, Nia. I'm straight," I assured her as I straightened out my clothes and hair. "I won't touch her again."

We were right outside the door, so Tangie and Shari were still in clear view. Tangie was soaking up blood from her nose with a napkin. Shari was just standing there, with her arms folded across her chest. Then she spoke.

"Get the fuck outta my house."

Nia

Mike and I were lying in my bed late one freezing-cold night when the phone rang. We had just finished making the most incredible love. He started stirring his forefinger around in my flesh.

"Don't start nothing you can't finish," I warned him.

"All I need is about ten more minutes, and I'll tear you up again." He winked. I'd started writhing with pleasure while he climbed back on top. He started caressing my breasts with his free hand while twirling his tongue around in my ear. That's when the phone interrupted my ecstasy.

"Answer it," he whispered.

"No," I whined.

"Answer it," he urged. I felt him get rock hard on my leg. The phone was only an arm's reach away, so without totally disturbing my nirvana, I answered.

"Hello." My breath was heavy.

"Nia. It's Dex."

"You know Shari isn't taking your calls, and, plus, she ain't here. Good-bye." Mike's tongue had traveled down my body and had landed inside me. My legs began quivering. Although Mike held his own in the bedroom, I couldn't resist thinking about Kitara while he was down there.

I hadn't gotten a chance to see her the next morning. When I woke up, she was gone and had checked out of the hotel. When I was completely sober, the reality of the night before sunk in like a dagger into flesh. My initial rage quickly subsided when I realized how damn good the experience had felt. I wanted to talk to her to let her know that as long as it never happened again, she and I could still be friends. She'd crossed the line big time. There wasn't that much good head in the world that could make me change my sexual preference.

"NO. NO. Wait. Don't hang up!" Dex yelled into the phone. "Where is she?"

"Wh-what?" I stuttered, trying to mask my moans. "Don't worry about her whereabouts."

"I didn't call to speak to Shari, anyway. I called to speak to you. I'm desperate, Nia. Can we talk?"

"Hold on a s-sec." I placed the phone under the pillow. I was reaching my climax and just had to let out a scream, while squeezing Mike's head with my thighs and hands. Mike rose, with a mischievous, cocky grin, and kissed my moist forehead.

"Dex sounds pitiful. He needs to talk to me," I said between pants.

"No problem. I have some things to do, anyway. I'll just take a quick shower and be out." He kissed my hand as he exited the bed and went into the bathroom. I retrieved the phone from under the pillow.

"What's up, Dex?" I said.

"I'm so sorry to call so late, but I'm losing my mind."

"Am I suppose to feel sorry for you?" I was stern.

After a heavy sigh, he continued. "I am innocent, Nia. I swear on all that is holy, I have not cheated on my wife."

"You don't have to lie to me. We have too much proof."

"Has anyone physically seen, with their own eyes, me and Tangie having sex?"

"No," I admitted.

"Okay then. So how can she give up on our marriage over assumptions?"

"Look, Dex, you know I've always liked you, but if you're trying to get me to side with you over my best friend, I won't do it."

"No, I'm not trying to get you to side with me. Just help me. Please?" I think he had begun to cry, but I wasn't sure.

"There is nothing I can do. Her mind is made up."

"I need to prove myself."

"We know for a fact that Tangie is sleeping with someone. Since you claim it's not you, then somehow find out who that person is. It may solve the problem."

"How can I do that?"

"Dex, I don't know."

Mike had emerged from the bathroom and started piddling around the room, getting dressed.

"Like I said, you gotta play detective. Find out who Tangie is sleeping with, and that should be the missing piece to the puzzle."

Mike dressed in a flash, kissed my forehead, and left, leaving behind his manly scent.

"I love Shari more than anything in this world. You know that, too. If she divorces me, it will be the biggest mistake of her life. Please don't let her ruin the potential of having a near-perfect existence with me. Help me, Nia."

"I hate to admit it, but I was having a hard time believing you were cheating. I'm not saying that I believe you. But I'll think of something. You are innocent until proven guilty. Give me a couple of days, and I'll call you when I have a plan together."

"Nia, you're not making a mistake." Just then I heard a female voice in the background.

"Dex, who the hell is that?" Just when I had started to believe him.

"That's Tangie."

"Have you lost your everlasting mind? Shari kicked her out for sleeping with you. And you've let her back in? And, you expect me to believe you are innocent!" I couldn't believe he'd had me fooled.

I angrily charged out of the bed, wrapping the comforter around me.

"It's not like that. Tangie showed up at the door, looking like 'who done it and ran,' with nowhere to go. I couldn't turn her away. She's a young girl. She doesn't deserve to be sleeping out in the cold when she hasn't done anything."

"Unbelievable, Dexter!" I said as I hopped around on the nippy floor.

"Fuck! Nia listen to me. I'm just a good man with a good heart. She didn't deserve to get kicked out over a big misunderstanding. And Brittany should be ashamed of herself for fighting her own flesh and blood."

"If all you claim is true, then I understand. If you are trying to have your cake and eat it, too, then I swear, Dex, I'll kill you myself."

I found my slippers and put them on before walking to the kitchen to get a glass of water.

"I'd kill myself before I'd cheat on Shari. Are you still going to help me?"

"I'll call you in a couple of days." I hung up before he could do any more pleading.

Brittany

Vaughn had just arrived to take me to his house for an evening of watching movies and pigging out. He'd ordered another feast from Kotubiku to be delivered. I couldn't wait to get there and grub. When he arrived, of course, I still wasn't ready. I was not letting this pregnancy make me any less diva-licious, so I still took my time to make sure I was gorgeous every time I left the house.

"Hey, your phone is ringing," he yelled as he tapped on the bathroom door.

"You can answer it. It's probably just Shari."

When I emerged from the bathroom, looking like a queen, I ran into the living room area because I heard Vaughn screaming obscenities.

"I'll let you talk to her this time, but I'm warning you, you better respect her." He handed me the phone. I was bewildered by his anger.

"Hello?" I answered.

"Hey, it's Warren. Uh, look, I was wondering if we

could meet and talk about your, uh, our situation."
He sounded weakened.

"Not in a million years. The baby ain't yours, anyways. I just thought you might have appreciated the
privilege of being my baby's father." I paused.
"Warren?"

"Yeah?"

"Do me a favor, baby?" I asked sweetly.

"Anything you want," he replied, sounding desperate.

"Lose my number, asshole!" I hung up feeling
liberated. Vaughn gave me a high five.

"You go, girl!"

"That felt great," I admitted. "Let's bounce."

"Yeah, we gotta hurry. I already ordered the
food. It should be there any minute."

"Did you get California rolls?"

"And you know it."

"Hooray!" I cheered as I skipped through the
door, clapping my hands.

We arrived at his gates, and the delivery guy
pulled up right behind us. We were right on time.
We drove up his super long driveway and pulled
into the four-car garage.

"Let yourself in," he instructed as he handed me
the key. "I'm gonna pay the delivery guy, and I'll be
right in, okay?"

"Okay." I entered his mini palace, gasping at the
interior. His place was huge. The foyer was the size
of my bedroom and living room put together. The
floor was black-and white-marble. On the right side
was a huge walk-in closet, which I entered to hang

my coat. The hangers were made of solid polished oak. There were only two coats hanging there, a leather bomber and a Phat Farm jacket. Vaughn came through the door only moments later.

"Get it while it's hot," he said. He was speed walking into the dining room, trying to juggle five bags of food. I followed him into his lavish dining room.

"I never eat in here," he said. The dining room and kitchen were separated by an island. Those two rooms were bigger than my entire condo. The table was meticulous. Every setting was adorned with a large gold-trimmed plate, with a matching bread plate atop it. Forks and knives with golden handles were positioned to the right of each plate. Red wineglasses with golden stems were placed perfectly between the knives and forks. There were crisp white linen napkins on top of the bread plates.

"Let's not eat in here now, either. I think I might break something." I laughed. "How 'bout we just spread out on the floor in the living room and watch a movie," I suggested.

"I'm so glad you said that. I wanted to suggest it myself, but I would never ask a lady to sit on the floor to eat. Plus, Gisella would kill me if I touched this table."

"Who's Gisella?"

"My cleaning lady. You don't think I take care of this house by myself, do you?" He laughed as I followed him into the immaculate living area.

"You have a cleaning lady?"

"Yeah, I turned the basement into a three-bedroom apartment for her and her two kids.

They have their own entrance, bathroom, and kitchen. I never even see or hear her kids. A couple of times a week, I might run into Gisella doing some cleaning, though. I'll be right back. I gotta get some plates and something to drink."

He returned in less than a minute with plates, apple juice for me, and a Heineken for himself. We opened up all the containers, and I went straight for the California rolls. Vaughn then put on the *Paid in Full* DVD, sat back down, and popped a couple rolls in his mouth at once.

"I don't want to be rude, but I gotta ask," I said.

"Here you go." Vaughn sighed.

"What?" I whined.

"You are so nosy, girl. What's up, though?" He smiled.

"You cannot afford all this," I said, pointing all around.

"How do you know what I can afford or not?"

"You are living like a millionaire, and I know you make a lot of money, but this house, a live-in maid, and all those cars?"

"When I was two, my father got killed by a police officer in a routine traffic stop. He was reaching for his seat belt to get out of the car, as the officer instructed. Before he could even unclasp his belt, the officer lit him up with eleven bullets. So my mother sued the state for wrongful death, and when I turned twenty-one, I got my portion of the settlement."

"Which was?"

"Dang, I never met anyone so bold. No one has ever asked me that before."

"I'm sorry," I said apologetically. I knew I was being too nosy.

"Na, I don't mind. I got a couple million for it. As long as you invest it right, your money can work for you. So over the years it has grown way beyond the initial amount."

My plate was now overflowing with lobster, shrimp, and lo mein. "Why do you work then?" I asked between chews.

"I love to work. If I didn't have a job, I'd be out there with all my knucklehead friends, spending all my money on bullshit and trying to impress women."

"I respect that." My voice sounded garbled through a mouthful of food.

"Now are you done gettin' all up in my business?" he teased. "I'm missing the movie."

"I'm done."

As we ate, I became spellbound by the true story of the infamous Harlem drug lords. By the time the movie ended, I could barely keep my eyes open.

"I'm tired," I said and yawned.

"Already? It's only nine thirty."

"I know, but this baby is wearing me out."

"All right. Let me just clean up this mess and put the food away. Then I'll show you to one of the guest rooms."

I nodded off a couple of times before he returned to escort me upstairs.

"You have a beautiful home," I told him wearily.

"Thanks. This is your room." He opened the door and turned on the light. The room was stunning and stark white. The walls were bare and clean. The room had a very sterile feel to it. The colossal white canopy bed devoured the fluffy white pillows, and a goose down comforter looked so inviting that I jumped into it like a pile of leaves.

"I love this room. It looks so clean," I squealed as I squeezed a pillow between my thighs.

"Oh, I forgot to bring your nightgown. I figured you might get sleepy and want to stay, so I bought you a nightgown. I'll be right back." I felt like a princess for a day, lying in that extremely comfortable king-sized bed. He returned with the gown and a pack of saltines.

"Why did you bring me crackers?"

"Well, I was doing some research on morning sickness. And it said that if you eat a couple saltines first thing in the morning, even before you get out of bed, it will help dissolve the acid in your stomach, and you won't feel nauseous."

"That was thoughtful." I almost cried. That was the sweetest thing a man had ever done for me. "Cute nightgown," I said sarcastically.

"You don't like it?" He looked a little embarrassed as he held it out for me to take.

"Well, I'm not somebody's grandmother." It was a pink and white, ankle-length plaid flannel gown. "But it's cute. Thanks. You are too sweet."

"The bathroom is over in the corner. I guess I'll see you in the morning, okay?"

"No, wait for me. I want to model this thing for you."

I folded my clothes and left them on the white

chaise in the bathroom. I came out parading and dancing around in my muumuu.

"Dang, that is a little old ladyish," he admitted.

"Don't worry about it. I am a mother now. I can't be trying to look sexy all the time." I crawled back on top of the bed, next to where he was seated, and lay down next to him.

"Put your feet up." He patted his lap to show me where. He didn't have to tell me twice. He massaged my tired feet so well, it was almost orgasmic.

"I got another question," I said.

"Here you go." He sighed.

"Now this one may offend you, but I don't mean it in a bad way—"

"Just spit it out, Miss Nosy," he interrupted.

"Are you gay?"

"Hell, no! Why do you ask?"

"'Cause you just seem too good to be true."

"My mother just raised me right. That's all."

"I'm glad that I have a friend like you in my life," I told Vaughn.

"Me, too. You make me laugh," he agreed.

I must've fallen asleep while he was rubbing my feet, because that was the last thing I remembered before waking up twice to pee. I realized the next morning that for the first time in my life, I had slept over at a man's house and he hadn't even attempted to have sex with me.

Nia

"I promise I'll make it by eleven at the latest," Mike said. "I know how much hard work you put into this party."

"Promise?" I pouted.

"I promise. But I gotta do a little shopping for tomorrow, so I'll talk to you later, aight?" Mike laid a sloppy kiss on my lips and sped through the door. He had received an invite to a New Year's Eve bash held by one of the execs over at UBS Warburg, a prestigious investment bank located here in Stamford. He said that it was a great opportunity for him to network and get his name out there. As long as he made it to my party in time to bring in the New Year, I was all smiles. I would never hold him back from a career move. I admired his drive.

I was sorta relieved that he left early, because I had some serious decorating to do, and I had to call the two caterers and make sure everything was ready for delivery by six o'clock the next day. I'd hired two caterers because I wanted a variety of foods, since everyone came from varied backgrounds. One caterer specialized in island delicacies and was scheduled to bring curry goat and chicken, stewed peas, oxtails, plantains, and rice and peas. The other caterer was straight up soul food, so they were bringing the baked macaroni and cheese, collard greens, corn bread, dirty rice, pork shoulder, fried catfish, and candied yams. Finally, I arranged for some appetizers to be delivered from the Food Stop around the corner, and especially for Papi, I planned to prepare *ropa vieja, frijoles negros,* and *tostones.*

The drink menu consisted of piña coladas; a special punch I make with fruit punch, ginger ale, and sorbet; an assorted variety of hard liquors to choose from; and, of course, a couple of bottles of Moët to bring in the New Year with.

For decorations, I decided on a black and silver theme. I found metallic silver strips used for making bows, but I curled them into spirals with the edge of a pair of scissors and tacked them about a foot apart into the ceiling so that they hung about a foot over my head. Every other spiral held a metallic black star at its end. I'd purchased a silver paint pen and wrote "Happy New Year 2004" on each star. I strategically sprinkled black and silver confetti on the serving tables and floor. Also, I put handfuls of the confetti in plastic baggies so that at the end of the countdown, we could all throw it into the air.

The biggest decision of the night would be what

to wear, and I had to get it done the night before,
or I'd rush and end up throwing any ole thing on.
It sounds ridiculous, but I bought about ten different outfits to decide from. Nine of them I would
return the next week, of course. I wanted to surprise everyone and not be my usually conservative
self. I spread the outfits across my bed, along with a
few choice things from my wardrobe, for mix-and-
match purposes.

An hour later I was torn between two finalists.
The shimmery mint green minidress that had a
thin strap on just one shoulder and hung delicately.
And the black mini with the split all the way down
past my navel, like J.Lo's famous Grammy dress. I
left them both draped across the rocking chair in
the corner of my bedroom. It was only nine, but I
had a hectic day ahead of me, so I turned in early.
I heard Shari come in about an hour later, but I
didn't feel like getting up and talking all night.
When she peeked into my room, I pretended to
be asleep.

Brittany

It was seven o' clock on New Year's Eve. Vaughn was starting to lie heavy on my heart, but Warren was still heavy on my mind. The alleged father of my unborn child still had me missing him, even though he'd put his hands on me. I'd been looking at his number on my caller ID for too long, so I decided to give him one last chance before giving up on him.

"Hello," a deeply southern-accented, gruff voice answered. "Hello?" he repeated.

I cleared my throat. "Sorry. Hi. Is Warren there?"

"This is Warren."

"Um . . . this is Brittany." It obviously wasn't *my* Warren on the line.

"Brittany?" he questioned. "Oh, sweetie pie, you must be looking for Warren Junior. He's not here right now, though. Gone to a party or something. I think."

"Oh, okay. I didn't realize he lived with you."

"Well, gumdrop, I can't get around too good anymore these days. Just had my seventy-second birthday not too long ago. My knees done gone out, my back is weak, and I can't even wash my own ass too good no more." A thunderous laugh echoed from inside of him.

I shared a short giggle just not to seem rude. "Okay. Well, can you tell him that I called, please?"

"Okay, Tamara."

"Sir? My name is Brittany," I corrected him politely.

"Oh, I'm so sorry, baby. Warren has got so many women coming in and out of here, I just can't even keep up anymore. Excuse my mistake."

"Oh really?" I was now thankful for his talkativeness. "I didn't realize that."

Sensing my tone, the old man knew he'd said too much.

"I'm so sorry, little girl. That's just how he is. Ain't never gonna change, either. Gets it from me, though. No matter how many times I warn him, he won't change. He'll just have to learn the hard way like me. I been married four times and ain't got shit to show for it but a whole bunch of ungrateful damned kids. All them women I done romanced and spent up all my money on and none of 'em around now to help my old ass out." He let out an indignant grunt, then simmered down a bit. "But see, honey, me and Warren is different."

"How so?" I had settled in on my love seat, with a pillow propped between my legs. I even muted the TV 'cause I didn't want to miss a word.

"See me," he began. "See, I love women. I could

never resist a beautiful woman. I didn't have a lot of women because I had no respect for them. It was because I had no self-control. I just had no self-control. All a woman had to do was bat her pretty little eyelashes, and I was sold . . . Hold on, honey." He went into a small coughing fit and then continued where he'd left off.

"I made my women feel like queens. But my boy, he just ain't got no respect for women. I be hearing the way he talk to his woman. I don't see how he even gets none acting the way he act. These women be spending they money on him. He don't even have to wine and dine 'em.

"I remember when he was thirteen and his Momma left us, because she was tired of my shit. He cursed me out . . . told me he hopes he never turns out to be a sorry excuse for a man like I was. But look at him now. He was right. He ain't like me. He's ten times worse! All these damn sons running around here. They gonna grow up just like his sorry ass."

"Sons? I didn't know Warren had kids," I replied. I felt all the air escape from my lungs and wanted to throw up just from the mention of Warren having other kids.

I guess I'd made a joke, because the old man couldn't stop laughing. He ended up with another coughing fit.

"Girl, he gots four sons that he know of and already another one on the way."

"Oh my goodness. I don't believe it." My head felt a little light, and I could feel a stress headache coming on. I started to tell the old man that instead of five, he was about to have six grandchildren. I started to tell him about the way Warren treated me. But then I figured why bother? At that moment I decided I didn't need his pity, nor anyone else's. And, I definitely didn't want to be known as one of Warren Bank's baby's mommas.

From the long pause, I could tell that the old man's wisdom had kicked in. "You ain't pregnant, is you, honey?"

I had to clear the ball out of my throat so he couldn't here the trembling of my voice. "No, no, sir, I'm not," I lied.

"Good, girl. I guess you're one of the smart ones then."

"Yeah, I guess so. Thanks. There goes my other line."

"All right. I'll tell him you called."

"Don't bother, sir."

"Yup, you sure is a smart one. Take care of yourself."

"You, too." I smiled to myself.

On the other line was Nia, pressuring me to be on time to the party. I didn't even waste my energy telling her what I'd just discovered about Warren. I was relieved to have put closure to that relationship.

As soon as I got off with her, I called Vaughn.

"Vaughn, Nia just called. She wants us there by eight o'clock sharp. You have to hurry up. I don't wanna miss anything." I was so excited to get there but still wasn't sure on the outfit de jour.

"Calm down. I'm two minutes away. I was coming

early, anyway, to help you out, 'cause I know you ain't even dressed yet."

"Great. What car are you driving?"

"The Escalade, Brittany. Get your head out of the gutter."

"Whatever. Just get here," I rushed, embarrassed that I thought it important to know which one of his cars we'd be rolling in for the night. "I'll leave the door unlocked."

Vaughn had become a very close and dear friend in a short period of time. I didn't know what to feel for him, but I was definitely feeling something. When I'd asked him to escort me to the party, he was thrilled. I figured he'd have better things to do, but he said he would be honored to join me. Almost two minutes later, to the second, he arrived.

"Brittany, I'm here," he called to me. "Come here for a sec."

"You're gonna make us late," I yelled from my bedroom.

"Just get out here," he yelled back from the living room.

I was still wearing my peach silk robe, while deciding what to wear. As I entered the room, he handed me a single white rose, along with a gift-wrapped box.

"Thank you so much, but what is all this for?" I asked.

"Open it. I hope you like it. It took me an hour to pick it out."

He'd bought me the most beautiful dress in the world.

"Don't think I haven't noticed those extra pounds your're starting to put on. I figured that most of your old sexy outfits don't fit quite like you'd like them to anymore, so I bought you something one size bigger."

"You don't even know what size I am. I'll try it on, though."

I hated to admit it, but the size 8 dress fit perfectly. It was a white, Marilyn Monroe–type dress that looked perfect with my diamond accessories and silver, strappy sandals.

"You look like an angel," he commented after I appeared almost thirty minutes later. His mouth was open in awe.

"You don't look too bad yourself." He was wearing a traditional black tuxedo, which made me realize just how fine he was. "Close your mouth and let's go." I laughed.

We locked arms and headed out. It only seemed appropriate. Outside, he had a white stretch Mercedes limo waiting for us.

"Oh my gosh!" I squealed.

"Surprise!" he beamed.

"This almost feels like a real date," I chided.

"Let's go before Nia has our heads for being late." He held my hand as I entered the limo.

The ride was short, and for that, I was thankful. I was starting to feel a little sad because after all my years of searching for a man like this, when I finally found him, I happened to be pregnant with another man's child. Even without all his money,

Vaughn was a great guy, so I was grateful to at least have him as a friend.

We arrived at five minutes after eight, and Nia was pleased. She looked ravishing in her sexy black dress and stiletto-heeled, ankle-high boots. There was a group of beautiful sistas there, with fine-ass men that I didn't recognize, but I was sure that eventually Nia would introduce everyone.

"Who are they?" I whispered in her ear as we hugged.

"That's my family." She was smiling brightly.

"Seriously?" I was able to distinguish Mommy, Krystal, and Angel by their ages. I had never heard Nia utter a kind word about her sisters, but them being there was a good sign of change in their relationships.

"Where's Shari?" I asked.

"Oh. she went to get a facial at Noelle's, and then she had to stop by Lord & Taylor to pick out some accessories to match her dress. She should be back any minute. I told that cow to be back by eight, but she's on CP time."

"Okay. Great. You know a party ain't a party without all three of us."

"Hey, Vaughn!" Nia greeted him with a wave of her hand. "Y'all help yourselves to anything in sight. The appetizers are over there." She pointed to the black-and silver-speckled table with lobster tails, shrimp cocktail, pigs in a blanket, sliced fruit and veggies, and mozzarella sticks.

"Girlfriend, you did a fabulous job decorating!"

I yelled as she sashayed to the other side of the room.

"Thanks!" she answered, not even looking back.

"Have a seat, and I'll make us some sampler plates," Vaughn offered.

"Okay. Can I have some punch, too?" I said.

"Sure. I'll be right back." He left me sitting on Nia's sofa, next to the CD player. I wasn't feeling the Macy Gray CD Nia had playing, so I took it upon myself to put on a classic Mary joint. Nia was so far into hostess mode that she didn't even notice the switch.

Vaughn returned with two overflowing plates in one hand and a champagne glass filled with punch. We scarfed down the goodies like two buddies watching a football game, while we tuned into the festivities going on in the city for the holiday.

Shari

When it seems like it's all over, all you can do is sit back and reminisce about all the good times that you will never share together again. The realization of entering 2004 as a single woman was not something I was prepared for. There were so many good memories with Dex and me. In retrospect, the negative ones were so very small that when I looked back, I just had to chuckle.

While the apricot-almond mask soaked into my pores for an hour, I couldn't help thinking about the day I met Dexter Brown. He'd seemed so unhappy with his current situation, and I had just gotten out of that mess with Chris and the death of his unborn child. We were both an emotional mess that winter.

Having spent over a month with Nia after being evicted, I'd finally found a cozy little apartment near Cove Beach. Against everyone's advice, I accepted the apartment and decided to move in on

January first. It also happened to be in the midst of the biggest snowstorm New England had had in ten years.

I was driving two miles an hour down a slushy, yet ice-laden, hill on my way to pick up the U-Haul truck when I noticed a small red sports car stuck in a pile of snow on the side of the road. The wheels were just a spinning and going nowhere fast. The Good Samaritan in me couldn't resist helping out someone in need. I gingerly tapped my brakes and glided on over to the car. Just as I stepped out, the furious man exited his car, too. Slamming his car door behind him, he met me halfway.

"Hello, Miss. Would you happen to have a cell phone?" The man looked frustrated.

Even through the thick blanket of snow, I could appreciate his handsome features, perfectly trimmed goatee, and passionate eyes.

Before I could answer him a tall, bony, light, and bright woman with long, wavy hair flowing from under her chocolate mink hat started running toward us. She had an ankle-length mink coat to match the hat, immaculately applied make-up, shimmering green eyes, and some fuck-'em-girl black stilettos.

Suddenly, I felt like a peasant standing there next to those two. His attire matched hers; he was all decked out in a black tux with gray accents.

I was wearing black, knee-high, patent-leather snow boots with a pair of bleach-spotted baggy jeans that sloppily flowed over the edges of the boots. My puffy coat was yield sign yellow, and I, too, had a hat to match my coat. Mine was just a stretched-out, linty wool one.

"Dammit, Dexter!" she screamed. "How many times have I told you to charge your fucking phone before we leave the house?"

I reached into my purse to hand my phone to the irritated stranger.

"It's like dealing with a fucking child," she said. She glared at him as she snatched the phone from me and began walking back toward the car to make her call.

"Whoa. She is mad at you," I teased as I rubbed my icy hands together.

"She's always mad at me." He rolled his eyes and was able to crack a smile at my tease. "Her company's New Year's Eve party was cancelled last night because of the snow, so instead they are giving a brunch celebration today. I don't want to go, any damn way!"

"So, why are you going then?"

"Hey, sometimes you gotta do what you gotta do to keep peace in the relationship."

"That's pretty sweet of you, although it doesn't seem that she is concerned with keeping any peace." I noticed her emerging from the car again. "Here she comes now. Let me shut my mouth."

Once she made it over to us, her demeanor softened a bit from minutes earlier. "Thank you so much. What is your name, honey?" she said as she handed the phone back to me.

"Shari," I replied.

"Shari, this is Dexter and I'm Vivian," the woman

said as she pointed at his chest and then at her own. "We are late to a speech I am supposed to be giving, and I needed to call and let them know I'd be a little late." Then her snarl returned as she turned to Dexter. "I'm surprised you can even hold your own dick while you piss." She took the opportunity to insult him once again before spinning around and heading back to the car.

"I guess I owe you one, Shari," he said.

I sympathized with him; he looked so embarrassed.

"I could use one today, too. It's a shame you already have plans," I said. "I'm moving into the Park View Terrace near Cove Beach today. But I should be all right. I have my girls."

"Today *is* a bad day, but give me your number, and I promise we'll make it up to you."

His mention of "we" made my insides burn. He thought of that monster as his other half. With a forced smile, I grudgingly gave him the cell phone number.

"So, what are you guys going to do now?" I was trying my best to prolong our conversation.

"I didn't want to ruin my tux, but it looks like I'll be digging us out of this slush."

"You need help?" I felt desperate as soon as the words left my mouth. "I'm dressed for the occasion." I attempted to make a little joke out of my desperateness.

"I can't have that. You've done enough. I'll handle it from here. Then she'll be pissed that I'll be dirty in front of her coworkers, but like I said, she's always pissed." A sincere look of regret clouded his eyes. "Look, I'm sorry I can't help you out today, but I promise I'll call you." At that point, he was yelling and waving good-bye as he ran toward his car to retrieve his shovel.

I got back in my car and realized it was for the best that he was pussy-whipped because the last thing I needed was to be caught up in another man. After I picked up Brittany and Nia, we packed, loaded, and unloaded as much crap as we could before we decided it was time for a break.

Almost an hour after the girls left, there was a knock at the door. I couldn't believe it when I saw Dexter on the other side of the door.

"How did you know where I live?" I yelled through the closed door.

"You told me, remember? All I had to do was follow the U-Haul truck, and I figured the only door with no welcome mat on the whole floor must be a new neighbor."

"What happened to your plans?" I cracked the door open slightly and noticed he was holding a bucket of KFC and a two-liter Pepsi. I was in full flirt mode now, putting one hand on my hip and tilting my head to the side.

"I can tell you all about it over dinner if you'll let me in."

"Only because I'm starving." I let down my guard and opened up my door—and my heart.

Dexter initiated the conversation that started our relationship. He said that while at the party with Vivian, she was phony, rude, and snotty as usual.

His subconscious mind kept telling him, *Man, you need a girl that'll be willing to help you shovel out the car in the middle of a snowstorm.*

And so with that one act of kindness, which came as second nature to me, I snagged the perfect man.

The perfect man that's worth fighting for. At that moment, all my sadness was erased, and I knew it was time to get my husband back. I would forgive him, and we would move on. Remembering that day and how Vivian had taken him for granted made me appreciate him more than ever.

Nia

Mommy and Papi had brought Krystal and Angel to the party as a surprise. Whoa. Big surprise. Before even saying hi, though, Krystal made amends.

"Look, Nia, I know we have a shady history, but we're blood, and we are too old to be acting the way we do. I speak for Angel, too, when I say I'm sorry. Now let's start this new year out on the good foot."

All three sisters, created in the same womb, embraced in a triangle of love. We all emerged with wet faces, and Mommy and Papi started cracking up. So did we. I had felt silly for being so childish all those years. In an instant, our relationships were restored. All because Krystal was woman enough to say what needed to be said years ago. I could've put up a fight, but seeing the strained relationship between Brittany and Tangie, it suddenly didn't make so much sense to carry on this sibling rivalry.

"This is Ahmad Wilkins," said Mommy. "Ahmad, this is my youngest daughter, Nia."

Ahmad extended his massive hand. I couldn't believe Mommy had gone against my wishes and was trying to hook me up.

"Nice to meet you, Ahmad. Help yourself. The appetizers are over there," I said as I pointed to the table. "Mommy, no, you didn't!" I whined as soon as he was out of earshot.

"Yes, I did," she replied.

I heaved a sigh of resignation.

"Fine, ain't he?" she boasted. Brotha was fine, too.

"Mommy, I'm already dating someone else."

"Well, you ain't tell nobody! Where is he, then?"

"He'll be here around eleven. Now you better explain that to Ahmad, 'cause my name is Bennett and I ain't in it." We laughed as I skipped away.

My party had turned out to be a great success. Everywhere I turned, people were laughing, smiling, and having a great time. Even Brittany was blushing like a teenager on a first date. Damn, even in pregnancy that girl outdid me. She told me that Vaughn had bought her the new duds. She looked like total class and sophistication that night. Soon after getting Brittany and Vaughn settled, I went to play catch-up with my sisters.

"So, how's life been?" I asked whichever was willing to start babbling. Why did I do that? They both started sputtering about their children's every development.

"Stanley is sitting up . . . Naomi says "ba-ba" . . . Eric almost broke his neck jumping off the top bunk . . . Whitney got into her first fight in school . . . ."

After three stories each, I reminded myself never to

open up that can of worms again. I badly yearned to get to know my nieces and nephews. But I didn't need a play-by-play of their daily encounters. I guess being a mother, you take every opportunity to boast about your kids' talents and accomplishments. My mind was on Mike and his pending arrival. I wondered how handsome he would look in his Ralph Lauren tux. I decided to keep him a secret until he showed up. Finally, I had someone to show off, someone I could be proud of, someone I could introduce to Papi. I had no reason to feel insecure anymore. I had Mike.

Krystal and Angel were still updating me, while passing me numerous pictures of their offspring, when the phone rang. Saved by the bell, I excused myself and bolted to the phone. I squeezed past Brittany and Vaughn, cutting up the rug to Sean Paul's "Gimme the Light" remix with Busta Rhymes. By the time I reached the phone, it had stopped ringing. I hoped it wasn't Mike trying to call, so I dialed star sixty-nine. A delicate, but gruff, female voice answered.

"I must have the wrong number. Sorry," I apologized. I momentarily wondered who that was but was quickly whisked away from my thoughts by Papi. He began winding his hips like a professional reggae dancer and held my hands tight as he swung my arms back and forth.

Everyone circled around us, chanting, "Go, Papi. It's your birthday. We're gonna party like it's your birthday. Go. Go. Go. Go, Papi!"

I couldn't contain my laughter as I attempted to dance with my father. When the song ended, he hugged me close and whispered in my ear how happy I'd made Mommy tonight by reconciling with my sisters. I answered him with a big, wet kiss on the cheek. Once he finally released me, Brittany was beckoning for me to come hither.

"Yes, muh dear? What can I do for you?" I said. I enjoyed being the hostess.

"Where is Shari?" asked Brittany. I sat next to her to relieve some of the pressure my stilettos were causing.

"I don't even know. She should have been here by now. It's almost ten. Mike should be here soon, too."

"Call her then. I can't wait to see her."

I dialed Shari's number.

"Talk to me," Shari answered.

"Get your behind to my party. I have a surprise coming for you at ten thirty."

"What is it? You know I love surprises," said Shari.

"It's a s-u-r-p-r-i-s-e," I repeated.

"Look, I'm on my way. Just gotta make one more stop."

"All right, but I'm telling you now that Brittany's asking for you, and if you're not here to bring in the New Year with us, then it's on."

"What-eva. I'm on my way."

We hung up, and I felt an awkward sense of relief. She hadn't sounded that happy in months. I wondered what had caused this sudden rush of happiness. Either way, I was elated for her. Maybe she'd met someone, but for the sake of all my hard work, I hoped she hadn't.

Brittany

I was starting to feel the sandman tapping my shoulder. Vaughn and I were partners, and we had just served up a pot of whoop-ass on Angel and her husband in Spades.

"I'm getting sleepy," I told Vaughn, who was putting the cards away after the losers left the table.

"Again? It's New Year's Eve. You've got to stay awake."

"No. It's okay. I really just need a power nap. Just ten minutes."

"If you insist, party pooper."

I advised Nia, who was preoccupied with filling glasses and making plates, that I would be taking a nap in her bed and if I wasn't out in fifteen minutes to come wake me up. As I headed down the long, narrow hallway, I noticed Vaughn two steps behind me.

"Boy, you'd better leave me alone if you know what's good for you," I warned.

"I just gotta talk to you real quick. Just give me two minutes." He looked like a Sunday school student nervous about reciting a speech in front of the congregation.

After removing my silver stilettos, I carefully arranged my dress so as not to wrinkle it too much from lying down and propped a couple pillows behind me.

"So what's up?" I asked Vaughn.

"You," Vaughn replied coyly, suddenly seeming much more confident. He sat on the bed, beside me, so close that I could smell the tangerine Altoid he'd eaten while we played Spades. It was making me slightly nauseous.

"Are you flirting with me, Mr. Vaughn?" I batted my eyelashes. A comfortable laugh was shared between us; then, in an instant, the air became dense. Ignoring my question, he began the speech I'm sure he'd practiced a million times.

"Brittany, my first impression of you was that you were nothing more than a gold-digging ho. And I played my part in your little scheme by treating you to expensive meals and being at your beck and call when ol' boy stood you up. I shouldn't have played your game, but damn, girl, you are just so beautiful."

He reached into the inside pocket of his tux and pulled out a petite box adorned with a metallic pink ribbon.

"Vaughn, are you trying to propose to me?" I felt my heart pound through my chest and microscopic beads of sweat gather on my neck.

"No. Actually, I'm not."

Then I was really confused. A tiny box and a long speech. If he wasn't trying to propose, then what was he doing?

"Then what are you saying, Vaughn?" I was getting a little annoyed and felt stupid about jumping to a false conclusion.

"I'm saying that I want to have your back. I don't want you to do this alone. This ring represents how much I care about you. This ring represents our friendship. This ring represents that I've fallen in love with you, Brittany. We'll see what happens with us, but for now I just want you to know that I am here if you want me to be. Whenever and for whatever."

Vaughn opened the box, and inside was a pink princess-cut diamond that looked at least three carats, in a platinum setting and a thick platinum band.

"Brittany, this is a promise ring. I promise that I will take good care of you and be the best man you ever had as long as you promise to do the same for me. I promise you that if you want to make this work that I will make you an honest woman before the baby is born. I promise I will love that child as my own. I want to offer you this ring, along with all the promises that come with it, if you can, in turn, promise me that you want this friendship to blossom into something beautiful."

"I promise." My tired eyes began producing tears, which never made it down my cheeks, because Vaughn wiped each one away as soon as they surfaced.

"No more tears, baby. No more tears." He freed

the ring from the box and delicately slid it on the ring finger of my left hand.

"Vaughn, I—"

"Shhh," he instructed. "Take your nap. I'll be back in twenty minutes to wake you up. We'll have plenty of time to talk later."

"Okay," I obeyed.

"Hey," Vaughn said, stopping at the doorway and turning around to face me again.

"Hey," I answered, not knowing what else to say in my state of shock.

"Or . . . We ain't got to take it there. We can just be friends," he offered.

"No, I definitely think we can take it there," I replied to his silhouette standing in the doorway.

Vaughn smiled again, then closed the door softly behind him. After staring at the rock on my hand for as long as I could, my eyes finally gave in to the sandman, and I floated into dreamland.

Shari

I'd pulled into my driveway at approximately ten fifteen. Dex's car wasn't out front, but instinct told me to check inside, anyway. Upon opening the door, I realized that someone was home; I was just hoping it wasn't Tangie, or even worse, Tangie and Dex together. I could see soft lighting peeking under the door of Tangie's room. I raced up the stairs to tell my husband that I'd forgiven him and wanted to work things out. But when I reached the bathroom, I could tell that he had recently showered and shaved. Like always, he had not rinsed the sink out, and there was jet-black stubble all over the place. Traces of his aftershave still floated in the air.

Feeling betrayed, I moped down the stairs. How could he have plans on New Year's Eve when I could barely make it to my best friend's bash without him? Tears were on autopilot as I reached the final stair. Had he gone out to party, or could it be possible that he was behind Tangie's door, celebrating with her? I tried to dismiss the latter, knowing that my husband loved and respected me more than that. But then again, she had been his lover for over a month, so who better than to celebrate with—right?

Suddenly, a layer of sweat covered my entire body, and I felt deranged. Stoically, I turned right back around and took the steps two at a time. *Fuck this*, I thought. Careful not to alert Dex and Tangie downstairs, I tiptoed into the walk-in closet and uncovered the old shoe box hidden under several of Dex's folded sweaters. We'd kept a gun in that box for years but never had a use for it—that is, until now. I tore the cover off of the box, checked the chamber to make sure it was loaded, and made sure the safety lock was off, just like Dex had showed me the day we brought it home.

Ha, I thought. *I got something for you motherfuckers!* I was going to have the last laugh this time. I wasn't going to crawl under a rock and die because my husband was cheating on me; I was going to get mine. Creeping down the stairs like a thief in my own home, I held the gun low by my side, careful to keep my finger off the trigger. My clothes were stuck to me from the immense amount of sweat my body was producing.

Slowly, I approached Tangie's door, keeping my eye on the spotlight that shown under it. Suddenly, I wasn't as hard-core as I thought I was. My knees became Jell-O, and my arms and hands started shaking without my permission. I wanted to be strong. I tried to resist the fear that was now swallowing me whole.

I stood in front of Tangie's door for almost ten minutes, contemplating my next action. I could hear faint sounds of fellatio. The familiar slurps, pants, and gagging were slightly muffled by the music playing in the background. I was losing my will, so I gripped the gun tighter, trying to rummage up the same anger I'd felt only minutes before. The image behind the door would remain permanently in my brain, and I wasn't sure if I could ever forgive and forget after having a full visual, so I hesitated to open the door. Was I going to commit murder? Wouldn't a real woman admit defeat and move on? My judgment was impaired, and fear turned into confusion. Who did I think I was? I'd never fired a gun before. Could I really kill a human being? The fact that my body was shaking like a vibrating cell phone and I was crying like a baby answered all my questions for me. I admitted defeat, tucked the gun in my purse, and ran out of the house, feeling just like a damn fool.

I don't know which route I took or how long it took me to get there, but it seemed like an instantaneous arrival at Nia's. With a household full of people, I felt ashamed to enter looking like who did it and forgot to finish. My eyes were scarlet, and I couldn't have stopped shaking if I'd wanted to. I'd lost the best thing that had ever happened to me. There was nothing more to live for.

I walked into the party, with my shoulders slouched

and my face to the floor. Immediately, both Brittany and Nia were at my side.

"What happened, girl?" Brittany wondered. I couldn't even look them in the face. The carpet was my shield.

"It's over. It's really over," I cried.

"What happened?" Nia asked. I had only stepped one foot through the door and refused to go any farther. Then I felt a strong grip on my right shoulder.

"Are you okay?" The voice didn't belong to either of my friends or even to the female species. The voice belonged to my husband.

Finally, I looked up.

"Surprise!" Nia yelled.

"Happy New Year, Bay!" Dex yelled. I fell into his arms like a child returned to its parents on ransom. My screams echoed throughout Nia's apartment, and someone turned the music down to see what was going on. About ten people ran over to see what the commotion was about. I screamed and pounded my fists on Dex's chest. I had made a mistake. But had it been a mistake all along?

"Did something happen to you?" Dex asked. The concern in his eyes and the tenderness of his words reaffirmed for me that it had indeed been a mistake all along.

"If you're here, then who's at the house with Tangie?" I asked. Of course, he had no idea what I was talking about.

"Huh?" they all replied.

I felt so confused, but I managed to give a brief

outline of what I'd heard at the house and how once again, I'd thought it was Dex. Immediately, Brittany grabbed my hand as Nia grabbed hers, and we jetted like Charlie's Angels. There was a barrage of noise behind us. It was Papi and Vaughn following us out. We hopped in the Honda and made it to Maplewood Drive in no time. Another car pulled up right behind us.

"I can't believe he was really telling the truth," Brittany squealed half of the ride there. Nia told us how badly she had felt for him late one night when he'd called her. She'd invited him to the party so we could finally talk things through.

"Call me young and naïve, but there was such sincerity in his words, Shari," Nia explained, speaking of the conversation she'd had with Dex. "I knew if I told you ahead of time that he'd be here, you'd be against it. And Dex agreed that if you weren't open to him being there so you could talk things through, then he'd quietly leave."

"I feel like such a fool," I said.

"I'm so sorry I filled your head with all that bullshit. I was just trying to look out for you," said Brittany.

"I would've done the same for you," I assured Brittany.

We all took a deep breath before entering the house to uncover the truth. All I needed was to know that Dex hadn't rushed over from getting head and beat me to Nia's house to make it look like he'd been there all the while. I wanted to erase any room for doubt.

Without knocking, I opened Tangie's door. Inside was a whole 'nother scenario that none of us were prepared for.

"Miiiikke!" Nia screamed. "What the fuck are *you* doing here?" Tangie and Mike pulled the covers over their fornicating bodies and sat there frozen in their web of deceit.

Nia ran crying out of the room.

"You mean to tell me you knew my marriage was about to be over, and you couldn't be a man and say something, or at least stop fucking her in my house!" I screamed at Mike.

Mike ignored me, sat up, and started pulling on his pants, which were beside the bed. Tangie wrapped the covers around her body like a towel and stood up, looking ashamed.

"And you! You little bitch! You could've said something, too!" I said, pointing to Tangie.

"Leave her out of it," Mike said sharply.

"I didn't know, Shari. I promise I didn't know why you and Dex were beefing!" said Tangie.

"But you knew you were fucking Nia's man, though, and that was okay?" Brittany asked in a surprisingly calm voice.

Of course, no one had an answer for that.

"If Nia wasn't so fucking goody-goody in bed, I wouldn't have had to go nowhere else!" Mike screamed toward the door, loud enough for Nia to hear from the other room. He was now fully dressed and looking for his shoes.

Nia came flying back into the room. "I cannot

believe I let you back in my life. I trusted you!" she sobbed. "Twice!"

Ever the gentleman, Dex started toward Nia. "Don't let this poor excuse for a man let you think any less of yourself. You've cried enough over him. Let's go," he said, lightly grabbing her arm and leading her out of the room.

I heard the words and, in an instant, knew that there was about to be some serious problems.

"Fuck you, nigga. You think you better than me?" Mike spat belligerently, rolling up on Dex.

Dex let go of Nia's arm and turned around, with a snarl on his face. Then he punched Mike in the face so hard that blood splattered across the room. Mike fell on the floor but quickly sprang back to his feet and lunged towards Dex. Dex met him halfway; he was not backing down.

"Stop, you two!" I pleaded. But they weren't listening to a damn thing I was saying.

Everyone ran back into the room to see what was going on. I had to run toward the door to get out of the way because they were tearing that room apart. Vaughn tried to get in there and break them up, but they were like wild animals and totally disregarded him.

Dex had him; he punched Mike in the stomach and knocked the wind out of him and then pushed him on the floor. They began wrestling around, knocking over the nightstand and breaking the lamp into big, jagged pieces. Mike was underneath Dex. Dex had one hand around his throat and with the other was repeatedly punching him in the face. Vaughn attempted again to break up the fight, and this time was successful. Although Dex put up quite a fight, Vaughn was finally able to lift him off of Mike.

I rushed over to hug Dex and was checking his face for any bruises or open cuts when suddenly his chest jerked forward.

"Bay, are you okay?" I asked, puzzled.

"Shit," Dex said, collapsing forward onto his knees, reaching for his back.

Mike had lodged a thick piece of the porcelain lamp into Dex's back.

"Vaughn, he's hurt. Oh my God! Call 911!" I cried.

Mike was standing there, shaking in fear, like he couldn't believe what he'd just done.

Dex was now writhing in pain. Papi and Vaughn tackled Mike to the floor and held him there. My husband was in tears; all the women in the house were in tears, except me. I was lost somewhere between the nightmarish reality and the verge of insanity.

"Everybody get the fuck out of my way!" I yelled, but no one listened. *Okay, don't listen*, I thought. "Papi and Vaughn, get the hell out of the way!"

"What do you think you're going to do?" Vaughn asked. "We're going to hold his ass right here until the police get here."

Mike was struggling like a fish out of water to get loose, but they were relentless in detaining him.

"Brittany, did you call 911?" Vaughn yelled toward the door.

I fished the gun out of my purse, looked down at

Dex's blood spreading across the floor, and cocked the hammer.

"Move! Get out of the way. I don't want to hurt anyone but Mike, so I suggest y'all move. Now!" I screamed, demanding everyone's attention.

Papi and Vaughn got off Mike and both stepped toward me.

"Put the gun down, Shari," Papi pleaded. "There's been enough mess here tonight."

"Shari, you're not thinking straight right now. Dex will be okay. Just put the gun down," said Vaughn.

They cautiously stepped around the shards of broken lamp.

"Shari, please calm down. He's not worth it," Nia called from the door.

"Everybody shut the fuck up," I screamed through painful sobs. "And you two need to tend to my husband. Never mind this fool," I directed Papi and Vaughn. "I have something for him."

"Please don't shoot me. I-I'm sorry," Mike begged pitifully as he backed up against the wall.

I planted my feet on the carpet, wiped the tears away from my blurry eyes with my shoulders, and took a deep breath before pulling the trigger.

"Noooo, Shari!" Dex yelled as he sprang toward me.

"Nooooo, Dex!" I screamed back.

But it was too late; the bullet had fired. Mike stood against the wall, with his hands clasped over his heart, his mouth wide open. Dex had fallen straight on his back, with his arms spread out on both sides. His chest was flooding with blood.

Confused, I looked at Mike. He looked back at me, lowering his hands to his side in amazement. I looked back down at Dex; he wasn't moving. Mike was okay; I'd shot my husband.

"No!" I screamed, throwing the gun. I rushed over to the bed, where Dex lay, and shoved him. "Get up. Get up! Bay, I love you. Get up!"

Vaughn quickly grabbed me and pulled me out of the room. It wasn't easy, though, because I was going off!

"Don't worry about it. We'll tell the police it was an accident. Just relax. He'll be okay. He's still breathing," Vaughn tried to assure me as he planted me on the couch. I looked up to see everyone staring down at me, with pity on their faces. I immediately turned away from the accusing eyes and buried my face into the couch's cushion and screamed until my lungs felt tight.

When the ambulance arrived, Dex was still breathing, but barely. I wasn't allowed to accompany him on the ambulance ride. I was put in cuffs and locked in the back of a police car, although everyone had told the police it was all an accident. Watching the ambulance become smaller and smaller through cloudy vision, I wondered how I had ever let my insecurities ruin my life.

Turn the page for the alternate ending to
TAKE ME THERE.

* * *

Slowly, I approached Tangie's door, keeping my eye on the spotlight that shown under it. Suddenly, I wasn't as hard-core as I thought I was. My knees became Jell-O, and my arms and hands started shaking without my permission. I wanted to be strong. I tried to resist the fear that was now swallowing me whole.

For almost ten minutes, I stood in front of Tangie's door, contemplating my next action. I could hear faint sounds of fellatio. The familiar slurps, pants, and gagging were slightly muffled by the music playing in the background. I was losing my will, so I gripped the gun tighter, trying to rummage up the same anger I'd felt only minutes before. The image behind the door would remain permanently in my brain, and I wasn't sure if I could ever forgive and forget after having a full visual, so I hesitated to open the door. Was I going to commit murder? Wouldn't a real woman admit defeat and move on? My judgment was impaired, and fear turned into confusion. Who did I think I was? I'd never fired a gun before. Could I really kill a human being? The fact that my body was shaking like a vibrating cell phone and I was crying like a baby answered all my questions for me. I admitted defeat, tucked the gun in my purse, and ran out of the house, feeling just like a damn fool.

I made it to my car, put my hand on the door

handle, and from somewhere, the anger rushed right back into my body.

"I am ending this today. Right now," I said to myself. "No more!"

I opened the car door and threw the gun inside. I didn't want to kill anybody, but I did want answers.

Back in front of Tangie's door, I made sure I had some control of myself before I turned the knob.

Tangie stopped going down and turned her head toward the door when she heard it open.

"Oh shit," she said, jumping up and stumbling against the dresser.

"Oh . . . my . . . goodness!" I yelled. "You son of a bitch!"

Mike's eyes widened, and his little dick immediately went limp.

I felt a strong mixture of emotions. Guilt because I'd put my husband through hell and didn't trust him. Joy because he actually was being true to me. Betrayal because Mike had hurt Nia enough already. And disgust that Tangie would go there with him.

"Shari, I'm sorry," Tangie said not looking in my eyes.

"Yeah, you are sorry," I said. "And I'm sorry that I opened up my house to someone like you."

"I know you're going to run and tell Nia, 'cause that's how you females are," Mike said, finally deciding to tuck himself in and zip his pants.

"Don't worry about what I'm going to do," I said.

"But you, you can get the fuck outta my house before I call the police and have you escorted out."

"I'll go, too," Tangie offered.

"You know what, Tangie? You can stay," I said. "I'll let your sister handle you, because I'm not even mad at you. I just feel sorry for you."

"I'm out," Mike said, heading toward the door.

"And don't you *dare* show your face at Nia's party tonight. I swear, I'll kill you myself if you do," I warned.

"Yeah, whatever," he mumbled, pushing past me.

Tangie and I were alone, caught in an uncomfortable silence. *So where the hell is Dex?*

"I know you're going to lecture me, so go ahead. Get it over with," Tangie said.

I recalled the days of being a stupid twenty-year-old and doing scandalous things. Sometimes it was all part of growing up and learning.

"Have you seen Dex tonight?" I asked her.

"Nope," she answered. "So you're not going to let me have it?"

"Nope. As a matter of fact, do you have anything fly to wear? I want you to come with me to Nia's party."

"Uh, yeah, I think so. You sure don't look like you're going to no party."

"My outfit is in the car. Can you be ready in ten minutes?"

"Sure," she said, her face lighting up.

Maybe if we had included her more in our lives,

she wouldn't have had the time, space, or desire to cheat with Mike, I reasoned.

Tangie emerged in an emerald green halter-topped dress, with matching shoes and an Alicia Keys type of hat almost covering half of her face.

"You look great," I complimented her, trying to give her the positive reinforcement that she probably never received growing up.

"Thanks. I can't wait to see your outfit later."

The ride to Nia's house was silent until I parked and we were about to get out.

"I'll tell Brittany about tonight, okay? Promise. I want her to hear it from me," Tangie said.

"Okay. That sounds good."

"That's if she doesn't tackle me as soon as she sees me."

"Maybe you should just walk up to her and give her a hug. Tell her everything's okay and you'll explain everything tomorrow. Tell her you love her, too," I suggested. Brittany had a hard exterior, but inside, she was all soft and pink like everyone else.

"I'll definitely do it. Tonight is about fun, and I don't want to ruin anyone's night. If she's not feeling me, I'll just leave. There are plenty of spots popping tonight."

We walked up to the door, and I used my key to get in. The ambiance was amazing; Nia had really done her thing. The aroma was an inviting balance of food, perfume, and cologne.

"Mmmm," Tangie sang. "I'm going to make a plate, then find my big sis."

She pranced off, leaving me in the foyer alone. With my clothes in hand, I decided to sneak off to the bathroom to get dressed before anyone saw me looking a hot mess. Inside, I reflected on the past month and felt like choking myself for being such a fool. But where was my husband?

I was fully dressed and applying my make-up when there was a knock at the door.

"Just a minute," I called.

"Shari, let me in. I gotta pee!" Brittany said in a frantic tone.

I opened the door and was floored by Brittany's beauty.

"You look great, girl!" I told her.

"You don't look too shabby yourself," she said, pulling up her dress and squatting on the seat. There was no shame in her game.

I was wearing a spaghetti-strapped, powder pink, floor-length dress, with a plethora of accessories to match.

"Damn," I complained. "I can never get this eyeliner to act right."

Brittany flushed the toilet, bumped me out of the way so she could wash her hands, and snatched the eyeliner out of my hands.

"This is what happens when you send a little girl to do a grown woman's job," Brittany quipped.

The funny thing about Brittany is that she always had something witty to say. Most people would think she was a jokester, but she was dead serious most of the time, which made her comments all the more funny to me.

"All right. Now close your eyes," she instructed.

"Wait a minute!" I gasped. "What is that thing hangin' off your finger?" I grabbed her hand and took a closer look at the sparkling bauble on her finger.

"Oh this," she said nonchalantly. "Just a li'l sum-sum."

"What?" I yelled.

"Girl, Vaughn proposed to me. Well, kinda."

"And what did you say?" I was steadily examining the huge diamond.

Brittany looked a little sheepish. "I said yes." Then her eyes began to water slightly. "I really love him, Shari. No one has ever treated me as nice as he does. I mean, he knows the real me. He knows how I slept around. He knows I can have an attitude problem sometimes."

"*Sometimes?*" I joked.

"Fuck you!" she yelled before busting out laughing. "But he loves me, anyway."

"I am so happy for you, Brittany."

We embraced, and I didn't want to let go. I was happy she'd found her match. She deserved better than the men she always fell for.

Then there was another knock at the door. It was Nia.

"What y'all doing in there?" called Nia.

I opened the door. "Did you know about this?" I said, holding out Brittany's hand.

"I helped pick it out!" Nia admitted. "So what did you say?" she asked Brittany.

"What you think I said?" replied Brittany.

Nia screeched, and we gathered in a group hug.

"All right. That's enough," Brittany said, breaking up the love. "This girl needs some serious help with her make-up, so we're going to be at least another five minutes in here."

Nia closed the toilet cover and took a seat. I was standing with my eyes closed, letting Brittany work her magic, pondering whether to tell her about Mike and Tangie, but I didn't want to ruin her night. *Damn him!*

"Mike called," Nia whispered.

My eyes sprang open, and Brittany damn near slapped me.

"Hold still! What's wrong with you? You almost messed up my work!" she yelled.

"He said he needs some time away from me to sort some things out," Nia said.

"What a crock of shit!" Brittany said, all the while applying my make-up with a steady hand.

"Is that all he said?" I asked.

"He said he met someone else and that he still cares about me, so he'd rather end it before he hurts me again. Blah, blah, blah. And, if we were really meant to be together, then we'll be together again."

"Are you okay, Mama?" Brittany asked Nia.

"Not really. I'm kinda glad my mother brought Ahmad here tonight, though. At least I can keep myself preoccupied. But how could Mike do this on New Year's? That's kinda dirty," said Nia.

"Ahmad is fine, too," Brittany added.

I knew Nia was falling apart inside, but with her whole family there, it was no time to feel the hurt. She'd probably cry herself a river tomorrow, but I hoped that Ahmad would be the perfect distraction from her mess.

"I don't know. I guess I always expected something to go wrong, anyway. I'll be all right. I worked too hard to make this party a success. I *will* have fun tonight," Nia declared.

I kept my mouth shut tight. There was no way I'd tell her right then what the real deal was. But I would tell her soon. He'd broken up with her, and she seemed all right with it. The fact that the other person was sitting right out in her living room, eating her food, would've taken her over the edge. Why the hell did I invite Tangie, anyway? What was I thinking?

"All right. You are done. And, damn, I did a good job!" said Brittany.

"Yeah, you look beautiful," said Nia as she looked at me dreamily.

I turned around and had to concur. I looked great! We all did.

"We are on fire tonight, girls. Let's get outta this bathroom!" Brittany directed.

We exited the bathroom one by one, looking like we were about to hit the runway.

"Surprise!" Nia said once we reached the living room.

My husband turned around, with a plate full of food in his hand, giving me a goofy, but sexy, grin. When our eyes locked, I knew everything was going to be all right. He put his plate on the counter, ran over to me, and spun me around in the air.

"Hey, Dex!" Brittany yelled. "I didn't spend all that time making her beautiful just for you to come bum-rush her like that!"

We ignored Brittany and kissed like we hadn't seen each other in years. Then I started crying and was thankful for waterproof eyeliner. Dex was crying, too.

"I don't have any answers for you, but I can tell you with every fiber of my being that I was not unfaithful to you, Shari," he said.

He was still holding me very close.

"Shhh. I know. *Now* I know," I whispered. "And we can talk about that later. You're *not* going to believe it."

"Bay, I love you so much. Can you come back home tonight?" Dex said.

"Of course, I will," I answered. "We need the house to ourselves tonight, so I'll send Tangie home with her sister. Better yet, Tangie will just have to stay with Brittany until school starts. I don't care how soon it is."

"Absolutely," he said, rubbing his hands across my cheeks like he was admiring a newborn baby. "You ain't getting off that easy, though. You owe me."

"I know. I know. I'm so sorry. I'll make it up to you tonight," I said, suggestively rubbing my finger down his tie. "But can you make me a plate, though, Bay? I'm starving."

"That sounds good, and, of course, I'll fix you a plate, but I need a little more than that. I want to start couples' counseling. I know a good doctor. He's a brother, too."

"Counseling?" I whined. "We don't need counseling."

"You owe me, remember?"

"Okay. Okay. Anything for you, Bay."

Dex winked at me. "All right, I'ma go make you a plate. You're looking so good tonight. I can't wait to get you home."

I'd never heard sweeter words.

"I can't wait to get home, too."

Acknowledgements

Thank you, Jesus!

My family—you're the greatest. Mom, although I was bashful about you reading my sex scenes, thanks for encouraging me to write when I thought I had nothing that anyone would want to read. Thanks for the unwavering support through this process and with everything else I've ever wanted to do since birth. Nana, you are a remarkable woman. Thanks for taking care of Mya and me when I needed you. Day Day and Jazz, you guys are too young to read this, but hopefully, one day you'll read it and be proud of your big sis. I sure am proud of you and the gorgeous women you're turning into with every passing day.

Shauntane Scott, my bestest friend! Thanks for brainstorming with me when both of us were supposed to be working and had no business talking on the phone that long. And for telling me when my ideas were whack! (and when they were good).

Natasha McEwan, your input was invaluable. Oh yeah, and thanks for introducing me to African American fiction. If you had never handed me that Eric Jerome Dickey book seven years ago, I probably would've never had the urge to write. *(I don't like the way!)*

Maxine Thompson, thanks for doing a beautiful job editing my book and for being patient and honest with me when I kept coming up with off-the-wall ideas.

CHERYL FAYE!! I love you. You are my first "author" friend. Thank you for reading my book and doing the first-round edits when you had your own books to write and promote. You are unbelievable. I knew if you liked it, then I could make it! (Y'all check out her book *Be Careful What you Wish For,* published by Strebor Books.)

Mya, you are my constant source of inspiration. When I feel like life can't get any worse, I look into your eyes and instantly remember what I was put on this earth for. You make every day better. Mommy loves you, baby. I do it all for you.

Thank you to everyone that purchased this book. I hope you enjoy it, and don't forget to go to my Web site, www.kairadenee.com, and vote for your favorite ending. Whichever ending gets the most votes, I will use to begin the sequel.

For more information, please visit:
www.kairadenee.com

Thank you for your support!